LUCIFER'S CURSE

THE DEVIL'S DEAL

ELIZA RAINE

Editors: Dayna Hart

Cover: Ana Cruz

For those who struggle to believe.
Never give up.

ONE

NOX

"Is there anything else I can get for you?" The girl pouted, then slowly slid the strap of her low-cut top down her shoulder. With an exaggerated sway of her curvy hips, she moved around my desk toward me.

"What else do you have?" I asked her, flicking my eyes from her full cleavage to the sandwich trolley she had wheeled into my office.

Her tongue darted out of her mouth, licking at her lips in an overtly obvious gesture. "Whatever you want, handsome." She smiled, dipping her manicured fingers into her top and flashing me the soft skin of her breast, the dark pink of a nipple visible briefly.

She was wasting her time.

. . .

Fallen angels were powerful, and I was the most powerful of them all. But that amounted to nothing in the face of a god. And I had been cursed, by the most feared god of them all. As one of my punishments, Exanimus had taken away my ability to physically respond to arousal. He had been kind enough to leave my desire fully intact though, and the longer I went unable to feel any release, the more it built.

It was fucking torture.

I watched the lustful woman inching closer to me. I had brought my curse upon myself. And now I had no choice but to bear it.

TWO

BETH

"Oh god, oh god, oh god, I'm so sorry."

I dropped to my knees, my cheeks burning so hot I half expected them to actually burst into flames as I crouched, gathering up the papers that had fallen from my hands.

That would teach me not to knock.

I couldn't help peeping up from the papers, to look over at my boss's desk. The woman in his office had long blonde hair falling down her back and wasn't even trying to hide the fact that her spaghetti strap top was pulled down, or that she was definitely not wearing a bra. Dragging my eyes from her breasts as she lazily began to wriggle her top back up, I focused on my boss, Mr. Nox.

The look on his face was almost gleeful, a predatory hunger in his bright blue eyes that made me squirm.

"Can I help you?" His deep voice had an Irish lilt, and my cheeks defied science and somehow got even hotter.

"I'm sorry, sir. I didn't know you were in today." My words were a whisper, like I'd interrupted him in a meeting or something, not cavorting with a half-naked lady in his damned office.

"Well, here I am." He gestured to the woman, who was slipping the straps back up her bare arms. She kept her gaze on Mr. Nox, not looking at me once. "I'm a little busy just now. You can leave the papers there if you like."

"On the floor?"

"Unless you would like to bring them here?" The gleam in his eyes was wicked, the quirk of his full lips pure sin. I shook my head, dropped the reports I had gathered up, and backed out of the room as fast as my flats could carry me.

"Thank you, Beth," his voice carried after me as the frosted glass door swung shut.

"Shit!" I muttered fiercely, moving fast to the elevator. Could that have been any more embarrassing? As I chided myself for not knocking, a small voice of indignation broke through my shame. *If anyone had acted inappropriately, it had been him.* I mean, doors have locks for a reason. If he wanted to take women's clothes off in his office, he should use them.

The image of his chiseled cheeks, thick, dark hair, and bright, hungry blue eyes filled my mind.

He knew my name. The realization hit me as the elevator pinged and the doors slid silently open. Mr. Nox, of LMS Financial Services, knew my name. How? He was the millionaire owner of the entire company, and I was a lowly analyst.

Oh god, why did I agree to cover for Anna? She was the one who usually took reports up to the top floor. Her lunch date had run over, though, and in a moment of happiness for her one good date this month, I'd offered to cover for her. Now I wished I hadn't.

I sought out Anna's desk as soon as I got back down to floor nine, the floor I *belonged on* in the towering London skyscraper that housed LMS Financial Services. She wasn't there. I hightailed it back to my own desk and pulled out my cell, quickly writing a text.

Anna, I went into his office without knocking and he had a girl in there! You owe me. What if he sacks me?

A reply beeped onto the screen a moment later.

Hahaha, OOPS! He won't sack you. Did you see him naked?

I shook my head and locked the phone, putting it back in my desk drawer. What if I had seen him naked? I'd only seen him in a suit before, but... My imagination immediately did what was needed to envisage Mr. Nox minus his perfectly tailored suit. Tanned skin taut over defined abs, strong broad shoulders, the V of his waist leading down, down, down...

Oh god. Imagining my boss naked was massively inappropriate. *Get it together, Beth,* I told myself, shaking my head again in the hopes that if I did it hard enough the image would go away.

It didn't.

I tried to concentrate on the two high-profile market reports I had to get finished for the rest of the afternoon. Whenever the elevator pinged, I looked up sharply, dreading the approach of my boss. But mercifully, I didn't see Mr. Nox.

Nor did I see the girl who'd been in his office. I sort of envied her confidence. I mean, I liked sex well enough, but I couldn't imagine having the guts to get it on with my boyfriend in an office building, with the door unlocked.

At the thought of my boyfriend, Alex, I groaned. An uncomfortable feeling settled in my stomach; that feeling I got when I really didn't want to deal with something, but couldn't avoid it. I knew where the conversation we had to have that night would end up. But I couldn't put it off.

My cell vibrated inside the drawer, and I pulled it out, grateful for the distraction.

Beth, I'm not going to be able to get back to the office today, please could you take the flash reports up before you leave? I'll owe you big time.

"Anna!" I exclaimed her name aloud, earning me a glare from Rupert on the desk opposite me.

My face began to heat just thinking about going back upstairs and seeing that gorgeous face again. *He knew my name.* The fact flashed into my head, and I closed my eyes with a deep breath.

I was a professional. I'd worked for Mr. Nox for two years, and I was going places. Eventually. I was not going to screw that up now. I could take a damn report upstairs.

When I approached Mr. Nox's office for the second time, I made a point of knocking on the glass as loudly as was possible without hurting my knuckles. When there was no response, I called out. "Mr. Nox? I have the flash reports."

Still no response. I looked down nervously at the bundle of papers in my hand. Why the hell couldn't he use email like the rest of the world?

I knocked again, adding another call. "Hello? Can I come in?"

When I was positive there was nobody in the room beyond, I pushed the door open cautiously, and peeked around the edge.

There was nobody there. With a sigh of relief, I strode into the room, heading toward the desk. It was a huge mahogany thing, a little out of place in the ultra-modern corner office. Two of the walls were floor to ceiling glass, giving me an incredible view of dusk falling over the London City skyline. I took a moment to stare, the impressive vista breathtaking, before laying the report on the perfectly tidy desk. Papers were stacked neatly, a Mont Blanc pen stood straight in a fancy pen stand, and a letter opener in the shape of a tiny dagger lay in the center of the polished wood.

Did they have sex on this desk after I left? A strange feeling stirred in my gut, dangerously *south* of my gut, as I remembered Mr. Nox's hungry face again. What would it be like to be with a man like that?

I tutted aloud, chiding myself again for the direction of my thoughts. I had to stop thinking about him.

As I turned to leave the room, I caught sight of something on the floor, just behind the desk. Hair. Gold hair.

I froze, my pulse quickening.

A feeling of something being very, very wrong washed over me as I took a hesitant step closer.

Bile rose in my throat as I reached the end of the desk, and the body, sprawled on the floor behind it, came onto view.

It was the girl who had been here before. And she was dead.

THREE

BETH

"Tell me, have you seen the victim before?"

The policewoman's voice faded into nothing as the door of the office swung open and Mr. Nox strode in. My head snapped up from where I'd been sitting on the plush carpet with my head between my knees, taking deep breaths as the police questioned me. My stomach lurched.

I hadn't considered myself weak or squeamish before, but seeing a young girl with her head bashed in had knocked me for a loop. The sight of all the blood, the shock of the discovery and the fear that my own boss was a murderer had sent me dizzy and made me feel sick.

The two uniformed policemen and three white-suited medical people paused too, to look up at the famous businessman.

"Mr. Nox," said the policewoman who had had been speaking to me. "I'm Inspector Singh. Do you know this woman?"

She gestured bluntly to the body, and I stopped myself from following her movement and looking again.

"Yes. She is called Sarah Thornton. She delivers sandwiches to this building at lunchtimes. I believe her employers are called Susie's Sandwiches. I'll check."

A fresh wave of bile rose in my throat as I processed his words. I'd not seen her face when she'd been staring at Mr. Nox earlier, and now with her head caved in on one side it was even harder to recognize her. But he was right. She was the office sandwich girl.

"When did you last see her?" Inspector Singh asked Mr. Nox.

His eyes flicked down to me, then back to the Inspector. "Does Miss Abbott need to be here any longer? She looks quite unwell."

Inspector Singh looked down at me. "No, probably not. I think we've asked you everything we need for now." She handed me a business card. "If you think of anything else, please call me. Give my officer on the door your address and phone number on your way out."

"I have her address and phone number," cut in Mr. Nox. His piercing gaze settled on me, and my heart hammered in my chest. Was he making a point? Or worse, a threat?

"Fine," the Inspector said. "You may go, Miss Abbott." I pushed myself slowly to my feet. "Thank you for your help and I'm sorry you had to be involved in something so unpleasant," she added more gently. I gave her a weak smile.

"Will you be okay getting home, Miss Abbott?" Mr.

Nox's Irish accent made his words soft, but I avoided making eye contact with him again and shook my head quickly.

"I'll be fine," I mumbled, and pushed my way through the glass door, quite ready to be a million miles from the smell of blood. And possibly a murderer.

It took me fifty minutes to get home, and most of those to stop shaking. I didn't know for sure that Mr. Nox had killed the girl. He hadn't looked like he was about to beat her over the head when I'd seen them together earlier that day.

When I thought logically about it, whilst rammed between four other commuters heading west on the London Underground, it made even less sense that he had killed her. Why would a man that rich do the dirty work himself, in his own office? That wasn't smart. And his words were unlikely to have been a threat, in front of all those police.

When I reached Wimbledon station, I was grateful to get off the packed train and into the cool air. The walk to my apartment helped settle my nerves, the distance I had put between myself and that poor girl helping immeasurably. When I reached my front door though, my stomach sank again. I still had to talk to Alex.

∼

"Are you even listening to me?" Alex glanced up at me, tearing his eyes from the TV screen where his computer avatar was running around in a war zone, shouts and gunfire trickling from the cheap TVs tinny speakers.

"Course I am, babe."

"Then what did I just say?" He wouldn't be able to answer me. Alex wasn't a bad guy, but he wasn't a particularly good guy either. He was downright lazy. I had known that when I agreed to let him move in with me when he was booted out of his bedsit, but I hadn't realized that he would refuse to get a job and pay no rent at all.

"Something about your boss," Alex said, and mashed at the keys on his PlayStation controller.

"I found a body in his damn office!"

Alex looked at me again, his eyes wide. "A body? Like, a dead body?"

"Yes. And I knew her, sort of. She brought sandwiches to the office every day."

Alex's eyes flickered with interest before settling back on the TV screen. "How'd she die?"

"Someone killed her." I didn't want to say out loud that she'd clearly been hit over the head with something heavy. More than once. It made me feel sick again.

"Shit," Alex said, hitting more keys on the controller.

"Is that all you've got? I found a dead body, and even that won't get you to stop playing video games?"

"Sorry, babe. Do you need a hug?"

"Alex, I need more than a damn hug." The tone of my voice must have changed because Alex turned fully on the couch to look at me. I took a breath. I didn't want to ask him the question I had to. I already knew what the answer would be. Trepidation made my chest tight. "Did you take money from my purse this morning?"

Alex shrugged. "I took a twenty, yeah." My stomach clenched.

"Why, Alex? We agreed that if you wanted money, you'd ask me."

Alex tossed the controller onto the cushion beside him and stood up. He was wearing gray sweatpants and a tight blue t-shirt, and his red-brown hair was too long, curling around his ears. He was gorgeous, and that, combined with a great sense of humor, had been enough to hook me. I'd been stupid.

"Jesus Christ, you sound like my mother, not my girlfriend."

"If you didn't act like a child, then I wouldn't need to sound like your mother."

"You knew my circumstances when we started all this," he said, his voice hard.

"I knew you were broke, yes. I didn't know you'd help yourself to my money!" I folded my arms and took another deep breath. I knew where this was going, and it was to a place I didn't want to be.

"It's not my fault you've got debt. Why should I pay for your mistakes?"

His words cut through my resolve to stay calm, fury billowing through my gut. "Are you serious? I let you live here for free. You don't even have a job! I am busting my ass every day and paying for everything!"

"God, you're so uptight. Just relax, will you?"

"I've already told you, Alex, you can't just sit around all day, refusing to get work and stealing from me!"

"Fuck this," Alex muttered, and scooped up his hoodie from the back of the couch. "I'm going out for a bit, so you can calm down."

"Alex, I want you to move out." A tear escaped my left eye, hot as it tracked down my cheek.

"No, no, babe. You're just mad right now." His demeanor changed instantly, and he dropped the hoodie and moved around the couch toward me, big brown eyes pleading.

"I've been mad for months, Alex. And I told you that if you took money from my purse again, you couldn't live here anymore. I meant it."

Alex halted. "Give me another chance."

"No."

"But I love you."

"Then why didn't you ask me for the money?"

"You're overreacting, it's just a twenty—"

I cut him off, raising my voice again. "That's not the point! This is about you doing something I asked you not to! I told you how important it was to me!" Alex's expression hardened as I continued. "I told you that if you did it again we were over, and you promised. You promised me." My voice broke on the last sentence.

"You're so fucking righteous." The tone of his voice surprised me. Alex never spoke harshly. "Well, you know what? I don't want to be here anyway. It's boring. You're boring."

"Leave. Get your stuff and leave."

"I intend to." His usually warm expression was cold, and there was a cruel bite to his voice that I'd never heard before. "And when I'm gone, you can get back to working in your shitty boring office, and hanging out with your shitty boring seventy-five-year-old best friend, and being the single-most shitty boring woman I've ever met. And for the record? You're shitty and boring in bed too."

Silent tears rolled down my face as fury filled me.

I'd had no idea he would be nasty. None. He'd never been nasty in the three years we had been together.

Every part of me wanted to retaliate, to call him names, to demand back all the unpaid rent. But what good would it do? I had been brought up with strict rules, and I knew that stooping to his level stripped me of the moral high ground. My poor mom would be ashamed if I let out the tirade of cursing and shouting that was gathering inside my head like a freight train.

"Leave. Now," I said instead.

"Oh, fuck off, Beth, you don't need to tell me again. I'm getting my stuff, and then I'm out of here." He turned and stamped up the stairs.

Anger was crashing through me in waves, and the compulsion to follow him and throw something at his asshole head was so strong I almost acted on it.

With a snarl, I turned to the door. I had to leave, or the anger would escape.

FOUR

BETH

Alex hadn't been exaggerating when he'd said my best friend was seventy-five, but he'd been wrong in calling her shitty and boring. I marched across the grass common area toward the retirement home, swiping at my cheeks hard. Living in London was expensive, and the only reason I was still here was because I had been left an apartment by my mother's sister. I'd never met her, as my mom had moved to America when she was young, and never returned to England after she met my dad and had me. But the sisters had kept in touch, and my Aunt Penny had never had a family of her own. She died of a heart attack just two months before my parents went missing, and I ended up inheriting her home, fully paid for. It had been a refuge five years ago when I had been forced to accept the loss of my parents. A place I could try and start again.

With Alex gone, I would be making yet another new start, alone. He may have been lazy, and apparently more of an ass than I had realized, but at least he had been good company, for the most part. I screwed my face up, trying to pull myself together. I'd known for ages it wasn't going anywhere. He didn't love me. It was time to move on.

The depressing feeling that even a jerk who took advantage of me was better than nothing crept into my mind. A tidal wave of self-doubt rose up inside me, teetering on the brink of crashing down, until the sight of the front entrance of Lavender Oaks Retirement Home snatched at my focus.

My two-story apartment was in a small block with three other identical apartments, and that block was one of six. But the other five blocks had been sold off and turned into a private retirement home. It meant I couldn't make any noise after 9pm, and I regularly had nutty old folk knocking on my door or wandering around the grounds with barely any clothes on, but that kind of added to the appeal for me. My upbringing had been strict and formal, and there was something undeniably liberating about watching the old folks decide they'd been well-behaved for long enough.

And Francis was my absolute favorite of the badly-behaved biddies.

"Honey, whatever is the matter?" Her booming voice rang from her La-Z-Boy as I walked into the large recreation room of Lavender Oaks.

"I told Alex to leave," I told her, throwing myself into an ancient and tattered armchair beside her. She set her knitting down in her overly large lap and tilted her head to one side. Her dark skin was wrinkled in all the places that gave testament to a life filled with fun; smile lines surrounding her eyes and mouth.

"Thank the Lord for that."

"Really?" I looked at her, surprised.

"He was no good for you, honey." A fellow American, she had a distinct southern drawl that set my flaming temper a little calmer.

"Maybe not, no. He wasn't very nice when I told him to go. I had to leave, before I lost my temper."

"Asshole." The orderlies were always telling the old folk off for swearing, Francis particularly, and they had asked me to do the same. But in this case, I felt the situation warranted it, so I said nothing. "What did he do to finally make you give him the boot?"

"He took money from my purse," I told her.

"What did he spend it on?"

"It could have been diamonds or drugs for all I care," I said angrily. "It wasn't his to take."

"I love drugs," she said. "And diamonds, too, for that matter." I gave her a look, and she patted my knee. "Sorry, honey. He's a lazy-ass layabout who takes advantage of you."

"Exactly," I said. "Well, anyway, I saw his true colors when he realized I was serious about him leaving. He said I was boring."

Francis frowned at me. "I don't like him much, but honey, that ain't the worst insult I've ever heard. In fact, I've been called a hell of a lot ruder than that."

I didn't doubt it.

I lowered my voice and carried on before she could loudly list the rude things she'd been called and get us both in trouble. "He said I was boring in bed."

"He said what?" she exploded. There was only one other resident in the lounge, and she started so hard in surprise at Francis' outburst that she knocked over her jigsaw puzzle. "Asshole. Ain't no good reason ever for going after a woman's sexual prowess. That's an underhand thing to say."

The other old lady scowled in our direction.

"What if he's right?" I whispered. "I guess I am pretty dull. That may have carried over into the bedroom." The self-doubt tidal wave was back, crashing against the weak barrier of my confidence.

"Honey, ain't nobody in this whole damn world who's bad in bed. If the sex is bad, you're with the wrong person. It's that simple."

"I didn't think the sex was bad, though," I mumbled.

My cheeks were heating at the topic of conversation, but I had nobody else I could talk to about this sort of thing. Francis had a no-judgment attitude to everything, unlike most of my other friends. And my long-lost parents.

"Did he make you come?"

"Francis!" I hissed, real heat burning in my face now.

"You're a prude, honey, but that means nothing. You just need to spend time with the right man."

I shifted in my chair uncomfortably, crossing and uncrossing my legs to avoid looking at her. "If you'd been brought up by my mother, you'd be a prude too," I muttered. I'd had to learn how babies were made from the teasing of school-friends and stolen library books.

"Ain't nothing wrong with doing what your body tells you to do," Francis said firmly, leaning forward and patting my knee again.

"Right," I nodded. In an effort to move on before she got back to asking about orgasms, I spoke quickly. "Well, I'm less upset than I thought I would be," I said. "Mostly angry. So, I think I must have known deep down that this breakup was coming."

"If I knew it was coming, then so did you. You've had nothing good to say about him for the last six months."

"Oh. Why didn't you say anything?"

Francis' dark eyes softened as she stared at me. "Honey, I can understand why you wouldn't want to live alone. I had no place telling you to kick him out. But I'm glad you have."

"I'll be fine living alone," I said with a bravado I didn't really feel. When I had first come to London and met Francis, I was still coming to terms with losing my parents, and the long nights by myself had been the hardest. She'd seen me at my weakest in those times.

But that was five years ago. The saying about time being a healer was true. I could manage. I had to manage.

"I know you will. And besides, I'm just here, over the grass." She beamed at me and I squeezed her hand.

"Want to play cribbage?" I asked her.

"Always."

She'd taught me many card games over the last few years, but I knew cribbage was her favorite. It was quick and competitive, and it gave her plenty of chances to swear at me.

While we played, I told her about my awful discovery in the office. I left out the bit about walking in on the girl with Mr. Nox, unwilling to steer the conversation to sex again.

"You've had quite a day, honey." I nodded and turned over the card in the middle of the table. "Now, of all the damn cards you could turn over-" Francis' fledgling tirade was cut off by a shriek ringing through the quiet lounge. I dropped my cards in surprise, whipping my head around to see where the noise was coming from.

A tiny, wizened old lady was standing in the doorway, and she was holding up a shaking arm. Pointed at me.

"You! You consort with the devil!"

"Erm, what?"

"I can see him around you, your aura is black!" She tottered toward our card table, and Francis sighed.

"Tabitha is new, and a teensy bit mental," she whispered loudly.

"Hello, Tabitha," I said, nervously as she reached us. She was still pointing at me with a wobbly hand, and her eyes were wide.

"You are part of him," she croaked.

"Honey, this young lady ain't got nothing to do with the devil," said Francis slowly. "She's called Beth, and she's my friend."

Tabitha's eyes didn't leave mine as Francis spoke though. "You will save him. You will release him. You consort with the devil!" She wailed the last sentence, and Francis heaved herself up from her chair, shaking her head.

"Come on now, Tabitha. Let's find Sally the orderly."

I blinked after them as Francis led her back through the entrance. If there was anyone in London likely to be consorting with devils, it certainly wasn't me.

I said goodnight to Francis an hour later and made my way across the grass to my apartment. It had been a while since I had slept alone, and having to do it the day I had found a dead body wasn't ideal.

But Alex had been better than nothing for too long, and I refused to feel so pathetic any longer. I gathered my resolve, trying to strengthen it.

He had to go. I didn't love him. I hadn't loved him for a long time. I felt sad not to see him again, but not devastated, and when I remembered his cruel, unnecessary words, the sadness morphed to anger. It was definitely time to learn to live alone.

When I turned the key in my front door and pushed it open, I had hoped to see Alex's key on the little table in the hallway. Maybe a note apologizing for being a dick. Or my twenty pounds back.

There was nothing.

I sighed. That meant I would have to get my key back from him or change the locks. With money I didn't have.

I froze when I walked into the living room.

Alex had definitely gone. And so had my TV.

My jaw dropped slightly as I moved to the kitchen. The microwave was missing.

"He wouldn't..." Disbelief froze the words on my lips as I worked my way around the rest of my apartment. Anything worth more than fifty pounds had gone. He'd even taken my hairdryer.

Thank god, he hadn't taken the half bottle of white wine left in the fridge. I poured most of it into a glass and sat down hard on the couch.

Other than the appliances, there was little of value in the apartment. Thankfully, I'd left my laptop at work, and Mom's jewelry and my other precious belongings were in storage. But what the hell was I going to do with no appliances?

Although my debt hadn't grown in the last year, it hadn't shrunk either. I couldn't get credit to replace all my stuff. I would have to call the police. The thought of the police made me think of that awful office, of the blood and the body.

I took another swig of wine. How had I not known what a total and utter jerk Alex could be? I'd lived with him, for heaven's sake, and I'd had no idea what an asshole he was.

What a truly shitty Monday.

FIVE

BETH

As I approached my office building the next day, apprehension built inside me, making the bagel I'd eaten that morning churn in my stomach. LMS's building was one of the more impressive buildings in the City. It was bang in the middle of the financial district and shaped like a giant, square microphone, plated with gleaming reflective glass. It had been nicknamed the walkie-talkie building. When it was first built, it gleamed so bright that the reflected rays of the sun melted part of a car, and they had to add a film of netting to dull the shine.

Tourists could visit the building too, and an expansive and luscious 'skygarden' housed at the top drew them in daily. I'd never been up there. It cost thirty pounds a ticket, and as far as I knew, staff got no concession. Thirty pounds was two weeks' food budget. I couldn't blow it on visiting a rooftop garden.

City salaries were good, though, even at my junior

level, and if it weren't for the debt I'd amassed trying to find my parents, I would have been living well.

My apartment was paid for, and my only other large expense was my London train pass. I smiled at the security guard as I badged through the shiny security gates, then threw a jealous glance at the fancy coffee vendor just inside the main doors. I had my own instant coffee in my desk drawer. Grocery-store budget brand. It tasted a bit like old biscuits and didn't smell much better, but it was cheap and contained caffeine, so I made do.

As the elevator rose, I realized that the woman who had got in at the same time as me seemed to be giving me too many sideways glances. My apprehension grew. What if everyone knew what had happened in Mr. Nox's office already? What if they asked me questions? I didn't want to relive a single second of yesterday's awful discovery.

There was a note on my desk when I reached it.

Please see Mr. Nox as soon as you get in.

I felt sick.

"Beth! Oh my god, I can't believe it!" Anna half squealed as she leapt up from her chair a few desks away and tottered over to me on her scarlet skyscraper heels. Dressing well was mandatory when you worked in a London office. What my colleagues may suspect, but didn't know for sure, was that all my nice clothes were bought second-hand on eBay.

Everyone swiveled on their chairs as she reached me, and I inwardly cursed the open layout of the office.

"Yeah. Crazy, right?" I mumbled awkwardly.

"That's an understatement! A murder, in our office! I mean, who'd have thought?" She dropped her voice, but she was still easily loud enough for everyone to hear. "Was there a lot of blood?"

I gripped the note in my fist and waved it at her. "I've got to go," I said, and dropped my purse onto my chair before bolting for the elevator.

Today was going to be a long day.

Inspector Singh was standing in the polished elevator hall and her dark eyes widened, then narrowed, as she saw me step out.

"Miss Abbott, I was just coming to find you."

My heart skipped a beat. "Really? Why?"

"Please, come through." When we reached Mr. Nox's office I faltered, totally unwilling to enter the room.

"Can we do this someplace else?" The inspector cocked her head at me, then nodded. We made our way to another office a few doors down, a large conference room with an oblong table dominating the space, and about fifteen chairs. I picked one at random and sat down in it, my heart pounding. I was sure I was just wanted for follow up questions, but being interviewed by the police was not something I was exactly comfortable with.

No sooner than my ass had hit the leather, the door swung open again, and my heart did another somersault as Mr. Nox walked in.

"I would like for my staff to have representation," he said smoothly. I scanned him quickly, taking in his dark navy suit, perfectly trimmed stubble, and achingly hand-some face.

Why the hell was he here? To make sure I didn't say anything? His bright eyes met mine, and I looked away fast.

"Fine, if that's alright with you, Miss Abbott?" said Inspector Singh.

I nodded mutely. I sure as hell wasn't going to argue with him.

My overly intimidating boss pulled out a chair three down from mine. Inspector Singh stayed standing. "Miss Abbott-"

I cut her off. "Beth, please." Her formality was only heightening my nerves.

"Beth, did you know Sarah Thornton?" A graphic image of the girls caved-in head filled my mind and I swallowed hard against the nausea.

"No. I mean, I saw her in the office sometimes at lunch, but I'd never spoken to her."

"Okay. Did your boyfriend ever mention her name?"

"What? Alex? Why would Alex mention her?" Confusion gripped me, tighter even than my nerves. The inspector gave me a slightly pitying look.

"Alex Smith knew Sarah." I stared at her, waiting for more. "We have reason to believe he... spent time with her yesterday."

The sick feeling returned in full force. "I don't under-stand what you're saying."

Inspector Singh let out a long sigh. I could feel Mr. Nox's gaze boring into me. "Beth, Alex and Sarah have been in a sexual relationship for at least three months, according to her housemate. He saw her yesterday morning, and we are reasonably sure he was purchasing cannabis from her."

"He took a twenty from my purse," I whispered. "All that time I was at work, he was screwing someone else?"

"I'm afraid it looks that way. Can you just confirm, for the record, that you knew nothing of this?"

"Are you freaking serious? Of course I didn't know! I thought he was playing video games all day!" I instantly regretting shouting and laid my sweating palms flat on the glass table and closed my eyes. "I'm sorry. I'm sorry for being so rude." I opened my eyes, fixing them on the Inspector. "I asked him to move out last night, because he took money from my purse. He did leave, taking my TV, microwave, and just about anything else of value with him."

A wave of heat seemed to roll through the room, and I pulled uncomfortably at my shirt collar. How the hell had I not known what Alex was really like?

"Have you seen or heard from him since? We would like to talk to him."

"No. Is he a suspect? I can't imagine him getting into this building and hitting a girl over the head." And I couldn't, no matter how much of a cheating asshole he had turned out to be.

"He is a person of interest, and we would like to talk to him. And Beth, I'm sure that you can understand that given that the victim was in a relationship with your boyfriend, you are also a person of interest."

For a second, I was sure my bagel was going to make a reappearance. "Me? But I could never..." I trailed off as my breathing got shallow, and my head swam. I looked at Mr. Nox. "He knew her."

The words popped out before I could stop them. Something flared bright in my boss's eyes.

"The Inspector is aware of the nature of my relationship with Miss Thornton." Smooth as silk he spoke, his eyes not leaving my mine.

"Indeed. It seems she was a busy girl," sighed the policewoman. "If you hear from your boyfriend—"

"Ex," I interrupted viciously.

"Right. If you hear from your ex-boyfriend, please let me know immediately."

"If you find him first, tell him I want my TV back." Anger was replacing my shock, building with a force that I was struggling to suppress.

The inspector nodded, then left the conference room.

"Sounds like your boyfriend is an asshole."

I looked in surprise at my boss. "Mr. Nox, I don't know why you're getting involved in this, but I don't need *representation*. Thank you." I wanted to be alone, and I couldn't go back to my desk yet. I wanted him to leave me to get my shit together.

"Nox."

"What?" I didn't mean to be rude, but I was at my limit.

Alex had been cheating on me. *For three months.* The

memory of Sarah's large breasts when she'd been in that office filled my mind, followed by a vivid image of her and Alex together. Fury swelled inside me.

"Please call me Nox. No *mister* required."

"Why?"

"Because I have a feeling we're going to be spending a lot of time together." I blinked at him. "The way I see it, Beth, you're in trouble. You're a prime suspect in a murder."

My mouth fell open. "Prime suspect?"

"Do you have any idea how hard it is to get to the top floor of this building? You have an elevator pass, and a timeless motive."

"Oh my god." He was right.

"Hell hath no fury like a woman scorned." His blue eyes sparkled with something that could have been excitement as he spoke.

"I didn't do anything! They can't find me guilty of something I didn't do!"

Nox raised one eyebrow and leaned back in his chair. Good Lord, he looked like he'd stepped straight out of an Armani catalog. "I'm afraid the police have targets to hit. Take it from someone well-acquainted with bad behavior; law enforcement are not all angels, and they don't always get it right."

Panic skittered through my whole body, and I felt another wave of dizziness sweep through me. "What am I going to do?"

"I could help you."

I stared at him. "Why? Why would you help me?"

"She was killed in my office. And I was quite fond of her. I have a personal interest in seeing her killer found."

I swallowed. "Okay. How can you help? Do you know something?" I obviously didn't keep my suspicion from my voice, because his mouth quirked up in a smile. Even through my rising panic, his smile instigated something hot and alien inside me.

"Do you think I killed her?" His voice was soft and sultry.

"I last saw her in your office with you." I dropped his gaze, embarrassment flooding me again. "And when I next saw her, she was dead."

"I left her very much alive, I assure you."

I flicked my eyes back to his but couldn't hold his gaze. I was feeling overwhelmed— anger, panic, and injustice all clubbing together to drown out my ability to think properly. It was hot in the room—too hot—and I was starting to feel like I was suffocating.

"May I have the day off?" I blurted the words out, horrified that my voice was cracking slightly.

"Yes. My driver will take you home."

"What?"

"Would you prefer to take the Underground?"

I couldn't think of anything worse than fifty minutes rammed into other people's armpits, my claustrophobia mounting with my panic and rage.

I shook my head. "No."

"Claude will pick you up at the front of the building in five minutes." He stood quickly and held his hand out across the chairs between us. I hesitantly took it as I stood.

A brief moment of fuzzy vision and wobbly legs took me, and he gripped my hand until it abated, as though he'd known that it was coming.

But as my vision cleared and I saw his face, I frowned. His eyes were wide with shock, and his lips were parted as though in surprise. A tingle of something seemed to pass from his hand to mine, and he abruptly let go. Then, without a word, he strode from the conference room.

SIX

BETH

I managed to hold myself together in the back of the huge town car all the way through start-stop London traffic. It took as long to drive across the city as it would have to take the tube, but I had plenty of space in the car. In fact, there could be three more people in the vehicle with me, and I would still have more space than I needed. The air-con blasted cooling air over me and I leaned back on the soft leather and tried to sort through my feelings.

Mostly there was anger. Anger that I had been taken for a damn fool. Anger that I had meant so little to the man I had been with for three years. Anger that I had been stupid enough to let him take advantage of me. There was a hefty dose of shame and self-doubt in there too, though.

Did he cheat because I really *was* boring in bed?

No sooner had the question forced itself to the front of my mind than Francis' voice drowned it out. *"Ain't no man got the right to attack a woman's sexual prowess."*

Alex was an asshole, just like Nox had said. I wasn't normally a frequent user of the word, and my Mom would be horrified if I said it aloud. But it was a fact. Alex *was* an asshole.

And worse, he'd left me the prime suspect in a murder. I leaned forward in my seat, putting my face in my hands. *A murder.* This was real. Real and serious and terrifying. The police couldn't really think I was capable of killing somebody. Especially so brutally. I couldn't even lift something heavy enough to do the damage that had been done to that girl's head.

Bile burned my throat at the awful train of thought.

"Are you alright, young lady?" The elderly driver wore a worried expression when I looked up and saw his face fixed on me in the rear-view mirror.

"Yes. Fine. Thank you." He nodded, then pulled the car forward as the stop light changed to green.

I was lying. I wasn't okay. I felt dirty—the thought of Alex going from that girl's bed to mine seriously unpleasant. Especially knowing she liked to get her kicks elsewhere, too. If she'd seen both Alex and Mr. Nox yesterday... I rubbed at my arms.

As soon as I got into my apartment, I stripped and got into the shower. I stayed under the running water until it got cold, scrubbing the stain that was my vile ex-boyfriend from my skin, desperate for all traces of him gone.

I knew I would have to try calling him. But not today.

I was too angry. Too vengeful. Mom would be ashamed of the thoughts running through my head. The cursing especially.

When I'd dried off, I put my pajamas on, even though it was the middle of the day. I wasn't going back out. I needed to be alone for a while and work out what on earth I was going to do next.

The most immediate, and easiest, thing on my list was to arrange to get my locks changed.

I made a few calls, discovering that it would cost me two-hundred pounds extra to get a locksmith to come to the apartment the same day, so I reluctantly booked an appointment for their first available free slot, which was two days away.

That done, I decided that curling up on my couch with a good book and cup of tea was my best option to calm down and think clearly. But when I stepped into my living room, tea and Kindle in hand, I froze.

Mr. Nox was standing in the center of the room, looking as out of place in his designer suit as it was possible to look.

"What the hell?" I half-shrieked.

"I didn't mean to startle you," he said, holding his hands up. His deep Irish accent was instantly soothing, even though it shouldn't have been. He'd broken into my freaking apartment.

"How did you get in here?"

"I can pick locks," he said dismissively. "I have decided to make you an offer."

"Then call me! You can't just break into my house!"

"On the contrary, I can. You have poor locks."

"That's not the point!"

"It's exactly the point. You need my help."

"I need you to knock!"

His eyes flared with what I could swear was actual light. "Coming from you, that's quite hypocritical."

Anger and embarrassment bubbled out of me. "If you want to make love to people in your office, then lock the door! My door was locked!"

"Make love?" His mouth formed a wicked grin, that sent heat rippling through me. "I don't make love. I'm the Lord of Sin."

"Lord of Sin? Is that some sort of sex thing?" I instantly regretted asking, set down my tea, and waved my arms before he could speak. "Wait, stop, I don't want to know. You can't break into my home."

He stared at me a long moment. Long enough for me to really appreciate how unnecessarily good-looking he was.

His dark hair was just the right side of too long, making me instinctively want to run my hands through it. His lips were the perfect blend of full and masculine, made for that grin he'd flashed me that was so full of filth. And his electric blue eyes were borderline mesmerizing.

"You are right. I should have knocked. I apologize. And for what it's worth, I have never laid even a finger on Sarah Thornton."

"Oh." I hadn't really expected him to say sorry. I didn't think arrogant millionaires apologized much. I wasn't sure I believed him about Sarah though. "Why are you here?" His eyes moved slowly down my body, taking in my threadbare pajamas. I folded my arms across my chest, still clutching my Kindle.

"I have an offer for you."

Curiosity pricked at me. "Go on." I took a small step closer to my front door, feeling the reassuring weight of my cell phone in my pocket as I moved.

His eyes sparkled. "I have power. I can help you. But I will want something from you in return." Alarm bells rang at the back of my mind, warring with the pull I felt toward him.

This sounded shady as hell. But he did have a point; I *did* need help. "What do you want?"

"For you to spend one night with me."

My mouth fell open. "Who the hell do you think you are?"

"The Lord of Sin."

"You're a damn pervert! Get out of my house!"

"You only have to spend the night with me. You don't have to do a thing you don't want to do." His voice was smooth and calm.

My hands moved to my hips, indignation swamping me. "Oh really? You want me to come and play Monopoly with you all night, do you? As if I would willingly spend the night with someone who calls themselves the Lord of Sin!"

He shrugged. "I'm very good at Monopoly. But I should warn you, I cheat."

I bared my teeth at him in frustration. "Get out."

"Think about it. The terms of my deal are as follows. I help you out of your situation with the police, and you spend one night in my company. Sounds like an easy decision to me."

"Sounds like you're freaking crazy to me. Leave." I pointed to the door with a slightly shaking arm.

"Let me know what you decide," he said. "But before I go, there is something else I'm obliged to tell you."

"What? What could you possibly have left out of your charming offer of help?" I said sarcastically.

"I'm the devil."

SEVEN

BETH

"You're... you're what?"

Tabitha shrieking about the devil flashed through my mind and I shook my head.

The man was clearly deranged.

"I am the devil. Lucifer. The Lightbringer. Lord of Sin. King of Darkness. A fallen angel."

"Right. Of course you are. And you're in an apartment in Wimbledon because..." I kept my eyes fixed on him, moving my hand as slowly as I could to my cell phone, ready to call the police.

He was crazy. Which meant he probably killed Sarah.

"Because I've been kicked out of both Heaven and Hell, and have to make do with the company of mortals." He let out a small sigh. "I have a strong suspicion that one of my fallen brethren is involved in Sarah's murder, and as such, I feel an obligation to help you. The police will never catch a supernatural killer, meaning it's highly likely that you will be the best, and only, option for pinning the crime on."

His words were so crazy that my mind almost halted completely, as though someone had pressed a pause button. "You're mad," I said eventually, for lack of anything else to say.

"No. I wouldn't have mentioned it, but the terms of my power state that whenever the devil offers a mortal a deal, the mortal must be fully of aware of who they are dealing with." He shrugged. "Terms are terms."

"Completely mad," I muttered.

"I'm not mad. But I do have power. And trust me when I tell you that if you do not accept my offer, you will spend the rest of your life in prison for a crime you did not commit."

His words made my skin crawl, the seriousness of them slashing through the absurdity of his nonsense about devils.

Ravings about Lucifer or not, he did have power. Or at least influence. I had nothing.

"I'll think about it," I said quietly.

"Good," he said with a nod.

He took a few long strides toward my door, and I stepped back out of his way quickly. He paused when he reached it, and when he spoke, his tone was deliciously low. "The terms of a deal with the devil are unbreakable. If you choose to spend the night with me, I will not force you to do anything you do not want to do." His eyes were fixed on mine, blue light dancing in them, and for a split second, I was quite sure I'd let him do anything at all to me.

But sense quickly squashed my desire.

"I said I'll think about it, and I will." I made my voice as curt and clipped as I could, and with one final, piercing look, he left.

My heart pounded against my ribs as I stared at the place he had just been standing. Could my life get any more surreal?

I spent the rest of the day trying to pretend that I wasn't really in the mess that I was in. That my boyfriend hadn't been screwing the sandwich girl, and I hadn't found her dead with her head caved in, and mostly, that my gorgeous millionaire boss hadn't broken into my apartment to proposition me for sex whilst telling me he was the devil.

I failed.

I considered visiting Francis, but decided against it, unable to face voicing all the confused and unpleasant thoughts and fears whizzing around in my head.

Try as I might, I couldn't dismiss the tiny bit of me that was terrified that Nox's claims were true.

I had spent every penny I had, and then a lot more that I didn't have, trying to find my parents. But they had vanished off the face of the planet. Before I had given up, there had been a time when my brain couldn't process the fact that they had disappeared, and I had been genuinely convinced that something supernatural had happened to them. There was no other answer for such a complete disappearance.

Later, I had written off the notion as a symptom of grief, an inability to accept my loss. But the idea had been planted, and now that voice was back. There were too many things in life that could not be explained to dismiss the existence of something magical, or divine.

I tipped my head back and closed my eyes. *Your boss is not Lucifer,* I told myself. *He's just an egotistical maniac.* There was a human killer at the root of this bloody business, and the police would find them.

But what if they didn't? What if Nox was right, and arresting me was the only way the London Met could meet their quota of convicted murderers for the year?

The thought sent me cold. The idea of prison was bad enough, but a lifetime of being accused and convicted of a crime I was innocent of? That was unbearable.

If the cost of the help of Mr. Nox, wealthy London powerhouse, was one night in his company, perhaps I *should* take it.

His sincerity was so palpable when he said he would not force me into anything that I couldn't help but believe him. The stirrings deep below my stomach at the notion of *allowing* something to happen with him unsettled me though. I needed to make this decision with my head, not any other part of my body.

. . .

When I got into my bed at the woefully early hour of 8pm, one thought was dogging me above all the others.

What if Nox was the killer?

He had been with her, in that room. He was strong enough to do the deed. And he had just pronounced himself the damn devil.

If a man was unhinged enough to believe himself to be the Lord of Sin, surely he would be able to justify a sin like murder?

I buried my face in my pillow and groaned. Agreeing to spend the night with him would be madness.

I had never, in my entire life, had a dream in which I was aware that I was dreaming. But as I stepped out onto a crystal-clear frozen lake, I knew with certainty that it wasn't real.

"Did you think about my offer?" Nox was gliding across the ice toward me. "You look stunning, by the way." There was a hunger in eyes when he neared me that made muscles clench that I didn't know I had, and I looked down at myself to avoid his predatory gaze.

I was wearing a lemon-colored ball-gown, and I could see my chestnut brown hair falling down my chest in waves. I looked back up and gasped to find Nox just a few inches from me. "Well?"

"Did you kill her?" I breathed. If I was in a dream, then there was no harm in asking outright.

"No. I don't kill people. That's one of the reasons I'm in the predicament I'm in."

"Predicament?" I cocked my head at him.

"I'm cursed," he whispered, and he managed to say the word as though it was filthy. Desire pulsed through me.

"What do you mean?"

"If you agree to the deal, I'll tell you more." His breath was warm against my lips, he was so close.

"I don't know if I can trust you."

"Let me prove it."

"How?"

"I'm a fallen angel. I have powers beyond your imagining." I blinked at him. "Kiss me."

"What?"

"Kiss me. Lust will reveal my true soul."

"No."

He smiled, and those beautiful blue eyes danced with desire and enticement. "It's a dream, Beth. What have you got to lose?"

"You're dangerous."

"More than you know."

"If you're the devil, then you are evil and cruel."

Something dark flitted through his eyes, and he stiffened. "I am not cruel. Wrathful, yes. Fierce, yes. Lethal, yes. But I am not cruel. And I am paying the price for that."

I scowled. "What do you mean?"

"Kiss me, and you will feel my soul. I own Lust."

He smelled of whiskey and wood-smoke, and he

slowly lifted a hand to my cheek. His fingers hovered millimeters from my skin. He was waiting for my permission, I realized. I nodded my head a fraction, and when his warm touch met my cool cheek, a jolt of pleasure shot through me. It seemed to linger in all the right places, dancing down my jaw and neck, circling my now heaving chest, flicking across my taut nipples. As the feather-light invisible touch moved lower, I made a small noise of alarm and it vanished.

"I am the Lord of Sin, and you need me," he murmured. I looked into his eyes, and realized that I desperately wanted to believe everything he was saying to me. I wanted him to be who he said he was, not cruel, but dangerous and fierce and lustful.

Before I could consider the action, I moved my head the tiny distance between us, and as my lips met his, heat exploded in my core. His tongue found mine and the touch was so sensual, so right, I moaned.

His palm flattened to my cheek, and then his fingers were pushing into my hair, drawing me closer to him, our mouths locked in a dance I had no idea I knew the steps to.

He was divine. Perfect. Irresistible. And as I kissed him, I knew with complete certainty that he was telling the truth.

EIGHT

BETH

When I woke, it was to an almost painful throbbing between my legs, and a deep annoyance that I was alone in my bed, rather than on the frozen lake. Kissing the devil.

"What is wrong with you?" I berated myself out loud as I swung my legs out of bed.

The dream stayed with me though, the whole time I showered and dressed for work. Nox's lips, the heat in his touch, the promise in his voice, the expertise of his tongue...

There was no way I was going to be able to look him the eye now. I mean, there were sex dreams about your boss and there was... Well, whatever that dream had been.

Once again, when I reached my desk in the open-plan office, I was watched by the beady eyes of all my colleagues. I sat down awkwardly, avoiding meeting anybody's eye, and switched on my laptop. My desk phone flashed red and I picked up the receiver.

"Beth," I answered, distracted by the alarming number of emails from the day before filling my inbox.

"I need to see you in my office. Now." I almost dropped the receiver at Nox's voice.

"Why?"

"I have information for you."

"Okay. I'll be right up. But..." I felt everyone around me staring and half whispered my request. "Can we meet somewhere other than your office?" I never wanted to set foot in that room again.

"I have moved offices. Room 6B."

"Oh good," I said on a sigh of relief. I also drew a small amount of comfort that *he* hadn't wanted to stay in an office where a woman was brutally killed.

"See you in five minutes. And I hope you're wearing yellow again." He hung up, as an ice-cold tingle worked its way down my spine.

I didn't own any yellow clothes. The only time he could have seen me in yellow was... The lemon ball-gown in my dream.

No. That wasn't possible. It couldn't be.

Butterflies danced in my stomach, and a feeling of things being far beyond my control made my head spin as I stood up from my desk and made my way to the elevators.

. . .

The smell of coffee washed over me as I opened the door of room 6B. It wasn't as impressive as the corner office, but it boasted an expanse of glass, and an absolutely stunning view of the river Thames. Cranes dotted the gaps between the skyscrapers, and I drew as much of a sense of normalcy from the comforting skyline as I could.

"How do you take it?" Nox turned to me from where he was standing at a large coffee machine. The sight of his chiseled jaw, with just a shade of stubble today, and his wicked blue eyes brought the memory of the dream crashing back. I coughed.

"Black, no sugar, please." He raised one eyebrow and turned back to the machine. I wasn't about to tell him that I had to get used to having no milk or sugar because there'd been a time I couldn't afford it.

"Did you sleep well?" Mischief danced across his face as he passed me a cup, then gestured to a large leather chair in front of his desk.

"Fine, thank you, Mr. Nox."

"Please, just call me Nox."

"Is that your first name, or your last name?"

"It suffices as both. Have you thought about my offer?"

I frowned. "I thought you said you had information for me?"

"I do. But I offered you help in exchange for something. That's how a deal works. I can't just give you what you want."

His lips forming the words *what you want* was unnervingly arousing, and I shifted in my seat. "I don't think the police will pin this on me. I can't have done it; I was in the office all afternoon."

"They have a time of death. It was very close to when you came up with the flash reports."

"What?"

"And none of the elevator camera footage is working. Another reason I believe my supernatural brethren to be involved. They're good at messing up technology."

My stomach lurched again, the butterflies no longer dancing but now somersaulting through my gut.

"Take the deal, Beth. I promise you will not regret it." When I said nothing, he sat down in his chair, steepling his fingers together. "I don't want to see you in a prison cell any more than you want to be in one."

"Why not?"

"There's something different about you. I wish to get to know you better."

Good Lord, how was I supposed to make rational decisions when even the way he spoke sounded porno-graphic? His tongue wet his lips, and I took a breath.

He knew about the yellow dress from my dream. It could be a coincidence, or a guess, or something else entirely. But if it wasn't and he really had visited me in my dream, then there was a slim chance that his assertion that this was a supernatural crime was true too. And if that was the case, the police would not catch the killer. I would remain suspect number one.

"You won't force me to do anything?"

"I swear. I was created to punish those who take by force. I do not condone it. In fact, I despise it." Dark shadows swept across his bright eyes, and a faint red gleam glowed against the back of the chair behind him. An instinct to run and hide gripped me, a primal fear that was impossible to suppress.

This man was dangerous. That much was abundantly clear. I could physically feel it.

But I also felt the truth to his words. He would not force me to do anything.

I was in a situation that was already scarily beyond my control. And day by day, it appeared to be getting further beyond my grasp. Maybe Nox was the devil. Maybe he was just completely crazy. But if there was a chance to regain any control over my fate, then I had to take it.

Perhaps I could back out of the deal, once my name was cleared. Maybe I could even offer him a new deal. But right now, if there was even the slightest chance that what he was saying was true, that something supernatural really did exist in the world, then I needed help.

"Okay," I said, looking straight at him.

Delight sparked in his eyes, that irresistible smile taking his mouth. "Excellent."

He held his hand out across the desk, and I put my coffee down hesitantly, before taking it. "We have a deal. My help clearing your name of murder in exchange for one night with me." The Irish lilt in his voice was deliciously seductive, and fiery tingles spread from our contact as we shook hands.

I had just made a deal with the devil.

"You said you had information," I said, pulling my hand back before he could notice how clammy my palm was.

"And I do." Even his eyes were smiling as he picked up a file from his desk. He was definitely pleased that I'd accepted his offer, and I didn't know if that was a good or bad thing. "Sarah Thornton had more than one job." He passed the file to me and I took it.

"Why do you print everything out?" I asked him, flipping it open.

"I told you, supernatural beings don't always work well with technology."

"This building is full of technology," I pointed out.

"I know. It's exhausting. Read."

I frowned at him but did as he bid. My eyes widened a little at the words in the file. "Where did you get all of this information?"

"Money buys knowledge."

"Could you be more evasive?"

"I had my research team dig up everything they could on Sarah in double quick time."

"Oh." I swallowed uncomfortably, not wanting to ask my next question but also wanting to get it out of the way. "Was she just sleeping with you and my ex-boyfriend?"

"I was not sleeping with her."

"I saw you two in your office, and I'm inclined not to believe you."

"I did not have, and have never had, sex with Sarah

Thornton. What you witnessed was her attempt to seduce me." His words were simple, matter of fact.

I felt my cheeks heat. "She came onto you hours before she died? What bad timing for you," I muttered.

"As I recall it, you were the one with the bad timing."

"You should have locked your door," I snapped. "We're not getting into this again." I waved the file at him. "This says Sarah worked at a club in the evenings."

"Yes. In answer to your original question, Sarah had a boyfriend. Which is probably why the police are looking for Alex. If her boyfriend found out she was cheating, he may have killed her. And he may have attacked her secret lover too. Have you heard from him?"

I snorted, feeling angry and dirty all over again. "He stole all my stuff. He's hardly going to call me."

"Does he still have a key to your apartment?" Nox's tone had become serious suddenly, all his usual teasing mouth quirks gone.

"Yes. But the locksmith is coming tomorrow." His mouth became a hard line.

"Tomorrow is not soon enough. There is a murderer out there, connected to you and Alex."

Defensive annoyance stabbed at me hard enough to make me speak without thinking. "Well, if you want to pay for a same-day call out, be my guest."

Nox blinked, then picked up his desk phone. "Get me Geoff," he said into the receiver. I gaped at him open-mouthed as he instructed whoever Geoff was to go to my address immediately and install new locks. "What are you doing?" I said as he put the phone down.

"Protecting my new asset. I have a vested interest in your safety."

I scowled. "I'm not an asset. And I don't belong to you."

"Well, you will for one night, and I'm not going to risk anything happening to you before then." The gleam was back in his eye, the seriousness gone.

"On that subject..." I reached for my coffee nervously. I took a sip, pleasantly surprised at how delicious it was. "That one night only happens once you've cleared my name, correct?"

"Unless you want it to happen sooner."

"Absolutely not."

"Then yes. I will fulfill my end of the bargain first."

I nodded, slightly more confident. "Good."

Nox stood up suddenly, and I straightened in my chair. "We will visit the club Sarah worked at tonight. In the meantime, I have told your supervisor that you are on secondment to my office indefinitely."

"W-what? But what about my work?" My pile of unread emails flashed into my mind. I cared about my work. I was good at my work.

"I'd say clearing your name of murder is more important, Miss Abbott, wouldn't you?"

"Erm... Yeah. I guess so." I frowned. "What am I going to do all day?"

"Go and buy a dress for our undercover date this evening."

My eyebrows rose so high that my forehead hurt. "Buy a dress? Date?"

"Yes. We don't want the police to be aware that we are poking around in the case. So, we will go for dinner and then visit the club, on a perfectly innocent date."

Red light seemed to pulsate from him when he said the word innocent and I felt a shiver of something I thought was either excitement or fear, but I had no idea which.

"I already have dresses," I said.

"Well, by this evening you will have one more." His tone made it clear there was no room for argument. He pulled a thin leather wallet from his pocket, then handed me a jet-black card. A credit card, I realized on closer inspection. "We will be eating at the Ivy, so please purchase something appropriate."

"You aren't serious?"

"Oh Beth." He leaned down toward me, close enough that I could see the light dancing in his eyes and smell the same delicious wood-smoke scent on him that I had in my dream. "I am deadly serious."

NINE

BETH

It turned out, Nox really was serious. No matter how much I protested that I wasn't a character from Pretty Woman, all I could get from my boss was a wicked grin. Eventually I gave up. If I wasn't going to do any work today, then I would do what he had asked, and buy a damn dress. But there was no way on this earth I was keeping it after this was over. I was not a charity case.

Claude was waiting for me in the town car out the front of the building and leapt from the car to open the door for me when I reached it.

"It's fine, Claude, thank you," I told him, and he tipped his black cap at me.

"Mr. Nox says I must treat you as I treat him," he said, and his brown eyes shone with interest.

"Well, I can open my own door. And I would prefer to, if it's alright with you." The high-pitched ringing of a bicycle bell drew our attention, and with a small nod Claude climbed back into the car before the moody delivery cyclist reached the part of the road we were blocking with the huge vehicle.

"It's part of my job to open the door," said Claude, once we were on our way to Oxford Street. He sounded slightly offended, and I sighed.

"I'm sorry. I didn't realize," I said. "By all means, please get the door for me." I felt awkward as hell, but Claude beamed at me in the mirror, happy again. "Does Mr. Nox get you to drive lots of girls around London?" I asked, as casually as I could.

"No, Ma'am."

"Ma'am? Please, call me Beth. That I insist on."

"Oh, I couldn't do that."

"Miss Abbott, then?" I tried. I could not deal with Ma'am. That was what they called the Queen, for heaven's sake.

"Okay, Miss Abbott," Claude said, and winked at me.

"So, not many girlfriends to drive around?" I steered him back to my question.

"Not really, no. None in the last century, anyway."

I felt my face freeze at his words. "None in the last *how long*? It sounded like you just said century."

"Oops! None in the last year. That's what I meant." Claude smiled, then began humming to himself, making it clear the conversation was over. A cold tingle traced its way across my skin.

Either Nox was telling the truth, or his staff were just as crazy as he was.

⁓

I eventually bought a dress from Karen Millen. If I were totally honest, trying on dresses that cost as much as my monthly utility bills was kind of thrilling.

I had worked in London long enough to see how the other half lived; it was everywhere, all the time - in every bar, store window, sports car and insanely well-dressed person that I walked past.

But I knew I would never be among their ranks, and I was okay with that. I made do with what I had, buying clothes second-hand, and appliances used, recycled, and refurbished. People had a tendency to throw out or sell perfectly good stuff. My wage working for LMS was good, and I had actually got myself to a decent place with money for the first time since my parents went missing - finally having just enough leftover every month to start clearing some of my insane debt. That was, until Alex started spending it.

The knowledge that the price of the heavy navy-blue maxi-dress I had chosen would cover two months of my loan repayment was where the pleasure of the shopping experience became uncomfortable.

I could just sell it after the date. That little lump of cash could mean a lot more to me than a dress could. But was that morally questionable?

I wasn't as strait-laced or proud as my mom had been, for sure, but I had a solid enough moral compass and sense of dignity to prohibit me from keeping an expensive dress a crazy man was buying me, didn't I?

You agreed to sleep with him for help. The voice popped into my head as the cashier handed me my bag, which was far too nice to be a shopping bag. I gritted my teeth and gave her a fast nod of thanks, before exiting the shop.

There I was, trying to be all high-and-mighty about a dress, when the fact of the matter was, I had agreed to spend the night with a man I barely knew in exchange for him clearing my name of murder.

How in the hell had I got myself into this?

Claude drove me home to Wimbledon and made a big deal of retrieving my bags from the enormous trunk of the car when we arrived. I thanked him, trying not to show how weird I felt about him acting like he worked for me.

"Oh, and you'll need these," he said, and handed me a metal ring with three identical keys on it. "Mr. Nox said the locksmith has been. Have a nice day, Miss Abbott!"

He turned and eased his frail frame back into the car, while I blinked at the keys in my hand.

Somehow, without me being there, the locksmith had indeed been. A shiny new Yale lock was installed in place of the old mechanism on my front door, and deadbolts had been fitted at the top and bottom, too.

Anger rolled around my gut as I glared at the door. I mean, it was clearly a better lock than I could have afforded, and an undeniable part of me was glad that Alex couldn't walk in at any point, especially if he was connected with a murder.

But this was my apartment! My boss shouldn't be giving locksmiths permission to break into my home.

As I looked down at the keys in my hand, I wondered if Nox had one. I squashed down the fizzing excitement that accompanied the thought of him turning up in the middle of the night and dropped the keys onto the console table with a huff.

When 8pm rolled around, I was starting to feel extremely grateful for the dress. It had wide straps that merged with the plunging neckline, which was tight across my chest, and the heavy velvet skirt draped beautifully to just a centimeter off the floor.

It felt a little like armor. And with my make-up on and my hair braided and curled, I was more prepared to face Mr. Nox, millionaire crazy man, for dinner than I thought I would be.

As far as I was concerned 8pm was far too late to eat, but he had texted me saying that was when he was picking me up, and whether I liked it or not, he was the boss.

There was a knock on my door, and I took a long breath before opening it, schooling my face into an expression I hoped said 'classy annoyance'.

But the sight of Nox almost physically knocked the breath from me. I'd have been lucky if my expression didn't say 'take me now'.

His normal Armani suit and white shirt had been replaced by black jeans and a black shirt, open just enough to see the skin of his chest. He had a black blazer jacket on too, the very model of expensive casual attire.

But his clothes were not what was having such an effect on me.

Something was different about him. His whole body exuded wicked promise, his eyes gleamed and his skin begged to be touched. His lips were almost impossible not to look at, and a hundred images of him doing exceptionally exciting things with them raced through my mind.

"You look gorgeous," he smiled.

"Umph," I said. Totally not the correct response. But my brain had turned to mush. Sex-obsessed mush.

A filthy smiled pulled at his lips. "Ah. This is the first time you've seen me at night."

"What?"

"I'm the devil. I get most of my power from the darkness."

"You become hotter at night?" I was immediately embarrassed at calling him hot, but there was no way this man didn't know what he looked like.

"I become a lot of things at night. Let's go." He held his hand out, and god help me, I took it.

TEN

BETH

The Ivy was beautiful. It was decorated in 1920s art deco style, and I adored it instantly.

The center of the restaurant was dominated by a marble counter-topped bar. Hundreds of martini glasses hung from the mirrored top that was fixed to the ceiling, and baby-pink velvet seats ringed it. The walls were orange, and tropical looking plants added bright green everywhere I looked. Soft light from intricate globe chandeliers danced over round tables, and massive windows along the far wall displayed the lights of London at night against an inky-black sky.

The room fell silent as Nox strode in, and without a glance at a member of staff, he made his way to a table. It was in front of the largest window, and as I hurried after him, I saw that the other diners were watching not-so-indiscreetly. A tall, vividly green palm plant framed each end of the table for two, and Nox let go of my hand to pull out one of the chairs for me.

I sat down self-consciously, and realized that the wall opposite us was made up of tall arched mirrors. More people were watching us in the reflection. I swallowed. The second Nox sat down, a waiter appeared with two menus. One for food, and one for cocktails.

"An espresso martini and a scotch."

I raised my eyebrows as I looked at Nox. "I haven't even opened my menu yet," I said.

"Trust me, you want to try an espresso martini. I saw your face when you drank my coffee yesterday." I narrowed my eyes at him, but put the cocktail menu down. Truth was, an espresso martini sounded awesome, but I wasn't going to say that out loud.

When I read the food menu, my pulse kicked up another notch. I loved food, and I wasn't a bad cook. But my budget limited what I was able to rustle up, and some of the Ivy's dishes sounded divine.

They were also insanely overpriced.

I wasn't paying for this meal, I rationalized mentally as I read the delicious descriptions. I hadn't even wanted to go for this meal. What would be the point in ordering the cheapest thing on the menu, just because it was the cheapest? Nox probably wouldn't even notice what I ordered.

"The cheese souffle and the lobster linguine, please," I said, when the waiter returned. I avoided making eye contact with Nox, just in case he reacted. The dishes were expensive.

"I'll have the same," he said, and I couldn't help looking at him. "You have good taste." He smiled. The waiter took our menus and left.

"You wouldn't say that if you met my ex," I said awkwardly, attempting and failing to make a joke.

"Why is he an ex?"

"He was lazy."

"Ah. Sloth. One of my least favorite sins."

"Dare I ask which one is your favorite?"

His tongue snaked out, wetting his lips as he grinned, and I bit down on my own tongue, in case any drool came out. "Definitely lust. But it's got me in a bit of trouble."

"I imagine it's got a lot of people into trouble," I said, tearing my eyes from his mouth and sipping at my drink. "God, that's good," I exclaimed.

"Gods have little to do with alcohol, I assure you," Nox said. "Or coffee, for that matter."

I cocked my head at him. With so many people around us, and my girl-armor on, I felt a little more confident. "So, have you met God? If you're the devil and all that, I assume your paths cross?"

"There are many gods. The one I deal with most often is... very powerful. He's responsible for my current situation."

"So, he's a man?"

"Whenever he talks with me, yes. I have no idea what he truly is. I doubt gender is even a concept at that level."

I drank more of my drink. "What do you mean, your current situation?"

"I don't want to scare you."

I laughed, surprising myself. Something dangerous flickered in Nox's eyes and my laugh cut off abruptly. "I think you're beyond scaring me. You broke into my house and told me that you're the freaking devil. I already think that you're batshit crazy."

"Right now, I would rather you thought I was crazy than you knew what I was truly capable of." The blue light that I had seen dance in his eyes before was gone, and shadows moved in his irises, as though his pupils had turned to ink.

Perhaps he *could* scare me more than he already had.

"Fine. Then tell me what the plan is to clear my name."

The waiter arrived with our souffles at exactly that point, and for a blissful eight minutes, all I was aware of was the taste of salty, buttery cheese.

Wine had been brought with the food, a crisp and fresh white, and I honestly couldn't remember a time when my tastebuds had been treated so well. A temporary contentment washed through me as I sipped at the wine.

"I see gluttony is making a bid for the top spot on your sin scale," Nox said with a smile.

"It's excellent wine. And food."

"Do you eat out often?" he asked me.

I suspected he already knew the answer. "No. I have some debts I'm working on." I felt ashamed saying the words, but I wasn't stupid. I'd seen his file on Sarah. I had no doubt he had one on me too by now.

"Debts from when you lived in America?"

"Debts from all over." Debts from trying, and failing, to find my parents. Desperation did not make for good, rational decision-making. I should have stopped paying private investigators and gone back to work long before I did. But I didn't, and now I was left with the bill - not just for the useless investigators, but also the time I spent out of work, obsessing over their disappearance.

Nox nodded and took a long drink of his wine. "Do you have any close friends in London?"

"I've been here five years, of course I have friends," I said, a little defensively.

"Anyone special?"

"Yes. She's seventy-five and swears like a soldier."

Nox smiled, and I couldn't help my own lips mirroring his. "She sounds fun."

"She is. But she cheats at cards."

"So do I."

"Why doesn't that surprise me?"

The lobster linguine arrived, and saliva filled my mouth as I inhaled the divine smell. "What's her name?" Nox asked, topping up my wine before the waiter could do it.

"Francis."

As we ate I told him about how I had made friends with my elderly neighbor. The food was utterly excellent. The wine matched perfectly, and by the time the waiter took our empty plates we had just about finished the whole bottle.

I wasn't sure if it was the alcohol, the comfort of great

food, or talking about Francis, but I was significantly more relaxed than I had been at the start of the evening.

"Dessert?" Nox asked as the waiter came back with two tiny menus.

"Damn straight," I said. Nox smiled.

He copied my order again, a tiramisu, and added two French Seventy-fives.

"What's one of those?" I asked.

"It's a champagne cocktail."

"Oh. Thank you."

"It's my pleasure," he said, emphasis on the word pleasure.

I squirmed in my seat, my newly found comfort ebbing away. I became aware again of the other diners watching us in the mirrors. Were they wondering what a man like Nox was doing with a girl like me? They must be. He oozed power, and confidence, and wealth.

I oozed nothing at all. *"The single most shitty, boring woman I've ever met."* That's what Alex had told me I was.

My swing in thoughts must have shown on my face, because Nox reached across the table, lightly touching my hand where it rested on the crisp white tablecloth.

"Are you alright?"

"Yes. Of course. I'm sorry. Tell me something about you," I said, clumsily.

"You'll get all cynical if I tell you about myself," he said, leaning back in his chair.

"I promise I'll act like I believe all your crazy devil stuff."

"OK. What do you want to know?"

"Why does the devil run a financial services company?"

"I run many companies. Greed is a sin I have a very large stake in, and LMS is the company I make decisions from regarding the others."

"What does LMS stand for?"

"My true name. Lucifer MorningStar."

"Are you really a millionaire?"

A flicker of a smile ghosted over his lips. "Oh, yes. I am."

"You said you'd been kicked out of Heaven and Hell. Why?"

"Refusing to obey orders. I'm what you might call a bad boy."

"Are there others like you?"

"There is nobody like me. There are other fallen angels, and many supernatural creatures besides, but there's only one Lord of Sin."

My skin was heating, both at the power with which he spoke, but also an excitement that what he was saying could be true. I shouldn't have been excited. I should have been confused, or scared.

But part of me was actually hoping he was telling the truth.

"Prove it."

Nox raised one eyebrow. "Prove what? That supernaturals exist, or that I'm the devil?"

"Either. Both." My heart was beginning to hammer in

my chest. I had a strong inclination that I was going to regret making this demand.

Nox looked at me for a long moment, his blue eyes alive with light. "Look in the mirror," he said eventually.

I did. "What am I looking for?" Nothing was out of place, or different. I just saw us, the other diners, the waiters, and the bar, all reflected back at me.

"You don't see it?"

I scowled. "See what?"

"If you can't see it, then you're not ready." I snapped my attention back to him, immediately annoyed. How gullible could I be? Of course he wasn't the damn devil.

"Well, that's convenient for you," I said sarcastically.

"Not really," he shrugged. "If you *were* ready, then I could make your panties vanish off that perfect arse of yours right now. Then we'd have a more interesting dessert."

Heat stormed my cheeks, and I opened and closed my mouth a number of times. The right response completely eluded me. Mercifully, the young waiter appeared with the tiramisu, and I began shoveling it into my mouth in a less-than-elegant fashion. Good Lord, the man was sex-on-legs. I had to concentrate, not let his charm or seduction get to me.

But damn it, every time his sparkling eyes caught mine over the delicious dessert, I felt the sudden need to check my underwear was still on.

∾

We left the restaurant as soon as I had finished my French Seventy-five, which was quite frankly the best drink I'd ever had. Who knew there was a way to make champagne better?

Claude and his town car were waiting for us outside, and the fabric of my dress slid across the leather of the seat as I tried to climb into the car gracefully. Nox's arm shot into the car and steadied me, and then he got in after me with an annoying amount of grace.

"Where's the club?" I asked, aware that the champagne and the wine had made my head a little light.

"Not far."

"Evasive and unhelpful," I muttered.

"I can be extremely accommodating when I want to be."

"I don't doubt it. I'm sure Sarah found you very *accommodating.*" Why was I bringing that up? I had definitely drunk too much. Nox smiled as I looked at him sideways, the back of the dark car lit only by the lights of the storefronts and restaurants we were passing.

"Why don't you believe me that I did not have sex with her?"

"You two looked..." I trailed off, trying to find the right word. "Sexy," I finished, lamely. "Like you were about to have sex."

Nox turned fully to face me, and I swear his eyes were actually giving off their own light. "Do you like it?"

"Like what?"

"Sex."

I stared at him, glad he couldn't see how red my face must have been.

"I am absolutely not answering that question," I snapped, folded my arms, and turned away from him.

"I want to know the answer." To be quite honest, so did I. I enjoyed sex, but I had always wondered why people got quite so excited by it.

Although I was starting to wonder less since meeting Nox. The thought of sex with him—hell, even just proximity to him—was more arousing than some sexual encounters I had experienced.

I did not need to share that information with him, though.

"You're like a randy teenager," I said, channeling my mother's scolding voice.

He gave a low chuckle. "You wouldn't be comparing me to a teenager if you saw me naked."

A vivid image of Nox naked filled my mind, dominating my champagne-addled thoughts.

Crap.

"Well, you're not naked, and I am your employee, so behave yourself," I dredged the words up, willing my desire for him to lessen.

"My apologies, Miss Abbott," he said formally, and I jumped in surprise as I felt his hand on mine. I looked at him as he lifted it gently to his face, and planted one soft, and impossibly sensual, kiss on the back of my hand. "The devil can be a gentleman, I assure you."

"You mean you can turn on the charm," I muttered, trying to calm my fluttering stomach.

"And I can offer deals. What would you like in return for the answer to my question?"

I felt my eyebrows lift. "You want to know that much?"

"Yes. How about a month of meals at the Ivy?"

My mouth fell open. "What? Just for me saying something dirty?"

"Yes."

"You've got more money than sense," I breathed.

His eyes darkened. "So? You going to take the deal?"

"For a month of meals like that? Of course I am!"

"Then tell me."

I took a deep breath. I tried to hold his gaze, but I couldn't. "Yes, I like sex," I whispered in a rush. Slowly, his hand moved to my chin. Shivers spread through me from his touch, and I hoped he didn't know that the rate of my pulse had just doubled.

"Tell me again. I didn't hear you." He tilted my head up, so I was looking at him.

"Yes, I like sex."

I could see desire fire in his eyes, and I heard his intake of breath. My body clenched everywhere, an ache building in my core as my mind processed what I was seeing. *He wanted me.* There was no question about it. His teasing and flirting wasn't superficial.

But he was a playboy. He probably wanted everyone. And I wasn't throwing myself at him, which likely just made me a challenge to him. A man with an ego like Mr. Nox must love a challenge.

"Are we nearly at the club?" I asked, praying my voice didn't sound as breathless as I felt.

"Yes." He didn't take his eyes off mine, until the car slowed sharply. His gaze flicked to the window, then he shifted in his seat. "In fact, we've just arrived."

ELEVEN

BETH

W hen I stepped out of the car and looked at the building we had pulled up in front of, my stomach sank.

"The Aphrodite Cub," I said, reading from the vertical neon sign over a narrow doorway. A massive security man wearing a black coat was standing in front of it, and I could hear the sounds of music and laughter coming from both the restaurant to our left and the trendy-ish bar on the right.

"Indeed," said Nox, coming to stand next to me. "I fear you might be a little overdressed."

I glared at him. "What kind of club is the Aphrodite Club?" I asked him though gritted teeth. I suspected that I already knew the answer.

"Let's find out." He took my hand and walked toward the door, the security guy ducking out of the way for him with an overly deferential nod.

We made our way up some steps covered with

threadbare carpet and brown stains that I hoped were beer, until we reached a short landing. A bored looking man in a small booth held out two paper tickets that looked like they had come from an arcade, without looking up at us.

"Ten quid each," he mumbled, and I saw he was playing a game on his phone. Nox gave him a twenty-pound note and then handed me one of the little paper tickets. I gave him a sarcastic smile as I thanked him, then we walked through the heavy red curtain at the end of the hall.

To say I was overdressed was an understatement. In fact, a woman wearing clothes at all in the Aphrodite Club would be overdressed. My cheeks felt warm as I followed Nox to a round plastic table that had a front row view of the small stage. I did my very best to not look at the girl halfway up the pole in the middle of it.

"You've brought me to a strip bar?" I hissed at Nox as we sat down.

"It's not my fault the victim worked here," he said, eyes dancing with light.

"You could have warned me."

"There is no way you'd have come."

"You don't know that!" He was right, I wouldn't have set foot in the place. But I didn't like him making the assumption.

"Yes, I do. You're what some might call a prude."

I scowled at him. "I just have a healthy respect for sex," I whispered loudly.

"So do these women," he said, and a lady came over with a notepad.

"What can I get you to drink?" she smiled. She was completely topless, wearing just a G-string and four-inch stilettos. I opened my mouth and closed it again.

"Scotch, and a bottle of water please," Nox said. She winked at him and whirled away, swinging her bare buttcheeks as she went. An admiration for her confidence filled me as I watched her go. "This place is very interesting indeed," Nox said, his eyes not on the girl's ass but roaming the room.

"Mmmm," I answered awkwardly. The girl on stage had just removed her glittery bra. Another woman led a man by the hand to a door covered by a heavy curtain. She grinned at him as they disappeared through it. A stale scent hung in the thick air—beer mixed with bleach.

"There are many supernaturals here."

I looked at him. I had expected the interesting thing to be the sheer number of nipples on show, not an abundance of pretend supernaturals. "Really?"

"Yes. Lots of shifters."

"Shifters?"

"People who can transform into animals."

"Sure, sure," I said, nodding. I was tipsy enough that going along with his craziness was feeling more like a game than a chore. "Any vampires?"

"Only one."

My mouth fell open. I'd been joking. "What else?"

"No demons. Couple of sprites though."

"Right."

The topless woman returned with a whiskey on ice in a cheap looking glass, and a plastic bottle of water with a straw in it. Nox passed me the water and I took it gratefully. I both wanted the drink, and something to occupy my hands.

"What's your name?" Nox asked the girl as he passed her a note. She tucked it into the strap of her panties.

"Candy."

"Who runs this place, Candy?" A shadow crossed her young face.

"Have I done something wrong?" She pouted prettily.

"Not at all. I'm just curious."

"Oh. Well, Max." She pointed to a large man with no hair and a big beard making drinks behind the bar.

"Thank you, Candy. Did you know a girl who worked here called Sarah?"

"Sarah still works here," Candy scowled. "Thank god. She's one of the only nice people here." She seemed to realize what she'd said and turned her smile up to full volume. "Although all the girls give great lap dances," she beamed.

"I'm sure they do. Is Sarah here tonight?"

"No. She missed her shift, but I'm sure she'll be back tomorrow."

My stomach clenched with sadness. This young woman didn't know her friend was dead.

Nox just nodded and gave her another note, which she tucked alongside the other one before sauntering away.

"Should we have told her about Sarah?" I asked.

"No. It's not our place. And we are supposed to be being discreet. Besides, she could be talking about a totally different Sarah."

I pulled a face. We both knew that wasn't likely.

For a short while, we didn't speak, just sipped at our drinks. I wasn't sure what Nox's plan was, but he seemed cool, calm, and in control enough that I was sure he had one. Or maybe that's just how he always was.

I looked around at the people in the club, dancers and customers alike, and decided to temporarily indulge myself in believing Nox's supernatural fantasies. I tried to work out which one might be the vampire.

I was just deciding that it had to be the severe looking woman with scarlet panties and lipstick to match, when a man's cough drew my attention.

"Candy says you was asking after me." It was Max, the manager, and he was standing beside Nox with his hands fisted on his hips.

"Candy is correct," said Nox. He looked up slowly at the man, and I saw Max's eyes widen.

"How can I help?" His tone had gone from confrontational to deferential with just one look from Nox. I frowned.

"When did you last see Sarah?"

"She never showed up today. Pain in the arse. Always high on some shit."

"So, when did you last see her?"

"Day before yesterday. Her boyfriend showed up and fell out with one of the punters. They went at it."

"They fought?"

"Yeah. Not in here. I chucked 'em out. Scrapping on the street, they were. Sarah was a right mess. Had to let her go home early." Max looked annoyed about that.

"Have you heard from her since?"

"No."

"What's her boyfriend called?"

"Dave something. Works at a garage nearby, I think."

"Thank you."

"Is that all?"

"Yes." Max looked relieved. "Okay. It's just seeing two of you in here tonight set me on edge. I'm not breaking any codes. I'm doing everything by the book."

When Nox answered him, his voice was hard as steel, a tone I'd not heard him use before. It made my skin feel tight and cold.

"Two of us?"

"Yeah. Earlier."

"What did the other one want?"

"Dunno. She never spoke to me. Paid for a dance and left."

"What did she look like?"

"White hair, white skin. Really hot."

Nox stood up abruptly, and I nearly spilled my bottle. "Beth, I will see you tomorrow. Claude will bring the car around the front for you now."

Without another word, Nox turned and strode from the room.

"Wait!" I called after him, but he didn't stop, and within seconds he was gone from sight. Max raised his eyebrows at me and gestured at my bottle of water.

"Another one for the road?" he offered.

"No, thank you."

He shrugged and ambled back to the bar.

Great. Now I was confused as hell and alone in a strip club.

Claude was indeed waiting for me when I hightailed it out of the Aphrodite Club minutes later. I spent the whole drive back to my apartment trying to work out what Nox's conversation with the club owner meant.

The stuff about Sarah was straightforward and very helpful. An interested punter and an aggressive boyfriend? Hope that the police might very well have better suspects than me surged at the news.

But the other stuff was downright weird. The fact that Max had gone from aggressive to helpful when he saw Nox's eyes was strange enough. The way he'd said 'two of you' was creepy.

If Nox's crazy claims were true, then what Max had said could make sense. He may have meant that someone else like Nox, a fallen angel or something, had been in the club.

But if Nox was just crazy, which was a million times more likely, then I couldn't make any sense of the conversation at all. Nox had said he owned lots of businesses, I thought, scrambling for an explanation. Maybe he owned the club? Or the building? That might explain Max' nervous deference. But then who was the other woman that had made Nox so angry?

Whenever I spent time with mysterious boss, more of me started to believe him. But then I would get some time to myself and remember that it wasn't possible for his claims to be real. It simply wasn't.

Hopefully he would be able to explain it all to me when I saw him the next day. After I gave him a piece of my mind for abandoning me, that was.

TWELVE

NOX

Leaving Beth was the last thing I wanted to do. She was at that perfect point, just tipsy enough for her inhibitions to lower and for her imagination to relax around me. She was humoring me when she asked about the supernatural world, but I could feel that she wanted to believe.

That wasn't the only thing I could feel. There was something different about her, and every part of my body seemed to know it. *Every* part. For the first time in years, I had felt something more than useless lust. I didn't know what it was, or why she had triggered it, but she had, that first time we touched in my office.

And now, I found her to be utterly fascinating. I was interested in everything about her, and not only did I find myself enjoying watching her face, hearing her laugh, seeing her shock and embarrassment, I found myself wanting to protect her.

I had cared for very few mortals in my life. With good

reason. But Beth was like a damn beacon, calling parts of my ruined soul to her. And she was no siren, no incubus, no demon. She was human, pure, and shy. I should have no interest in her.

Fuck, I wanted her. I wanted her lips on mine, I wanted her skin under my fingertips, I wanted my desperate cock to feel her arousal. I wanted to see her beautiful face in blissful ecstasy.

Soon, I told myself. *Soon*.

THIRTEEN

BETH

Whe I found myself stepping onto the frozen lake in my dream that night, my first reaction wasn't surprise or fear.

It was unadulterated excitement.

This was a dream. A dream in which I'd experienced the hottest kiss of my life.

"But what if it's real?"

Nox's voice came to me on a cool breeze, sending shivers across my bare arms. I was wearing the yellow dress again.

"It's not. It's a dream," I answered.

"I'm a god of the night, a god of lust. Dreams are my playground." With a wave of warmth, he shimmered into being before me. He was wearing the black jeans and shirt from dinner, but the top three buttons on his shirt were open, revealing smooth, hard pecs. I lifted my hand, the instinct to trail my finger down the center of his chest so strong that I couldn't stop it. He stepped into me, and my touch met his skin.

He let out a hiss of breath and looked down into my eyes. They blazed with blue fire, and my heart hammered in my chest.

"You do something to me, Beth. I didn't want to leave you tonight."

The conscious part of my brain berated myself for dreaming that Nox didn't want to leave me. This was clearly my self-confidence trying to make up for being left alone without a kiss on a date.

The rest of my brain screamed at me to take the kiss I was owed.

Now.

I reached up, tentatively running my fingers through his dark hair, then bringing the backs of my fingers down his face, feeling his coarse stubble. He was stunning. Too stunning. My mind couldn't accept a man who looked like this.

"Do you want to see the real me?" he whispered.

I paused in my exploration of his face. "How do you know what I'm thinking?"

He dropped his head, moving closer to me, and spoke quietly. "I'm creating this dream. I am a god of darkness and fantasies." His lips almost touched mine as he said the word fantasies, and heat fired through my core, making me feel both weak and fierce at the same time. "You've let me in, Beth."

"Show me the real you." I should have been scared, or

at least wary. But I felt like I had permission to test my boundaries here, in this frozen, made-up world.

Nox stepped back from me, staring into my eyes with an intensity I didn't think I could bear if it were real. "Soon."

A deep disappointment speared my gut. This was *my* dream—he couldn't say no!

"I want to see you." I wanted so much more than to see him. I wanted to touch him, kiss him, feel his heat, his weight, his length, his hardness. My thoughts were spiraling into the obscene as I stared at him.

"Good," he said, and vanished.

"I don't care how good your coffee is, it's not going to make me forgive you for leaving me alone in a damn strip club!"

Nox smiled as he pulled the proffered coffee back. "I'll pour this away, then."

"Don't you dare," I snapped, and took it from him hard enough to almost spill it. I set it down on the desk and marched over to his office window, staring out at the view of the river.

I had woken even angrier with the arrogant ass than I had been when I fell asleep. There was no way I was going to bring up the dream, though. I wasn't going to give him the satisfaction of thinking I was starting to believe him.

Even though I was.

"I'm sorry that I left so abruptly. It was unavoidable." His voice was deep and soft and made me want to look at him. I resisted, keeping my eyes on the iconic London skyline.

"What was so unavoidable that you thought it was okay to just walk out? We're supposed to be working on this together." If he was telling the truth, and he really had visited me in my dreams last night, then he knew my anger was tinged with a different kind of frustration.

Frustration of the type I should not be feeling in connection with him; my boss and potentially a total lunatic. *And my best shot at avoiding a murder charge.*

"The woman that the club-owner told us about is a new and very interesting lead. I could waste no time checking into it."

I turned to him, my annoyance temporarily forgotten. "A lead?"

He nodded, then strode to his chair, and sat down. He was wearing a navy suit, his white shirt open at the collar. My eyes moved to his lips as he began to speak. "You remember I told you that I have my favorite sins?"

"It's 9am. How are you bringing up lust already?"

He raised an eyebrow at me, wickedness flashing in his eyes. "Lust is appropriate at any time of day, Beth." I swallowed. "But that is not my point. My point is that not all sins are so much fun. In fact, they can be very troublesome indeed."

"I'm not following. Unsurprisingly, because you're talking nonsense."

"I think I like it when you're this feisty," he said. "Remind me to make you angry more often."

I narrowed my eyes at him. "This is not feistiness. It's confidence. I've given up being intimidated by you." That wasn't strictly true. My mood that morning was primarily fueled by the new and distracting ache between my legs, which outweighed the intimidation.

"I can't decide if I'm pleased or disappointed by that."

"And I don't care," I lied. "Tell me about this lead."

"You won't like it."

"I'll be the judge of that, thank you." I folded my arms and jutted my hip out, in my best attempt at sass.

Nox raised one eyebrow, then shrugged. "When I came to the mortal realm, I decided to..." he rubbed a hand across his stubbled jaw as he searched for the right word. "*Relocate* responsibility for the sins I didn't care for."

I opened my mouth, then closed it again.

"The woman who was in that bar yesterday is the fallen angel who is currently hosting of one of the more unpleasant sins."

I blew out a long breath as I replayed his words. "Okay. In order for this to work, I'm going to have to pretend like I believe you. Because there are about a hundred questions that go with that statement and I can't ask any of them if I'm spending all my time telling you that you're crazy," I said.

He held out a hand toward the chair opposite him.

"I'm glad we agree on something. Ask away. I am completely at your disposal."

A knock on the door interrupted the uninvited stream of thoughts running through my head at the idea of Nox being completely at my disposal. There were many, many things I would have that man do if that were true, and none of them involved answering questions about fallen angels. Most of them involved those wicked-looking lips.

"Come in," he called, and I blinked.

Inspector Singh entered the room, and all the pleasant thoughts vanished from my head, replaced by flashes of Sarah, dead on the floor.

"Inspector," Nox said, standing slowly and reaching to shake her hand.

"Mr. Nox," she nodded, quickly moving her gaze to me. I saw a uniformed officer come into the room behind her. Anxiety coiled my stomach into knots. "It's actually Miss Abbott we're here to see."

"Hello," I said, my mouth dry as a desert all of a sudden.

"Do you want him present, or would you rather talk alone?" the inspector asked me. I flicked my eyes to Nox, and my nerves lessened ever so slightly at the steady calm on his perfect face.

"He can stay." Whatever this was about, I would have to tell him anyway if he was going to help me.

"Fine. We need to know a bit more about the day of the murder. Specifically, what you were doing that day."

I swallowed. "I already told you."

"Then tell us again. And leave nothing out."

"I took the flash reports upstairs-" I started, but she cut me off. Her eyes were calculating and serious, but not accusatory. I couldn't decide if I liked her or not.

"Before that. Please tell me about your whole day."

"Erm. Okay. Well, I got to work at eight, and I worked on a presentation for one of our customers all morning. My colleague, Anna, had an appointment at lunchtime and asked me to take some papers up to Mr. Nox's office." I wasn't going to tell Nox that Anna was on a date, and I hoped Inspector Singh wouldn't push for more.

"The flash reports?"

"No, this was earlier. At lunchtime."

"Ah. This was when you saw Sarah and Mr. Nox together." I nodded, unable to stop myself looking at Nox. He was staring at the Inspector, his expression severe. There was no supernatural sparkle to his eyes, no sense of sin rolling from him. Just a powerful sort of presence.

"I worked on my presentation all afternoon, until Anna texted me and asked me to take the flash reports up," I said.

"May I see those messages?" I nodded, pulling my phone from my purse and handing it to her, praying Nox wouldn't see them. Both for the sake of Anna's job, and my own embarrassment.

He made no move though, staying on his own side of the desk.

The Inspector was quiet as she scrolled through my

texts and then handed me the phone back. "Thank you. What next?"

"Well, you know what next. I went into the room to put the reports on the desk and found the body."

"After that?"

I frowned. "Why do you need to know that?"

"We are interested in the movements of Alex Smith that day. Any conversation you had with him may contain something useful."

"You've not found him then?" Nox's voice was hard.

"Not yet. We're confident he's still in London though."

"What about Sarah's boyfriend?"

"Got an airtight alibi. Not that it's any of your business." The Inspector gave him a look and a muscle in his jaw twitched. "Back to you please, Miss Abbott. What happened when you got home?"

I took a gulp of coffee, followed by a deep breath, before I answered her. "We had a fight. I asked him if he had taken money from my purse and he said yes. I asked him to leave, he swore at me, so I left instead. When I got back, an hour or so later, he was gone, and so was my stuff."

A flicker of what I thought was genuine compassion showed on the Inspector's face for a heartbeat. "I'm going to need more detail than that, Miss Abbott."

I felt my own jaw clench. "What do you need to know?"

"Exactly what you said to each other. Anything he let slip may help."

"He didn't let anything slip, except the fact that he's a jerk."

"Please, Miss Abbott."

I sighed. "When I got in, I told him about finding the body."

"Did you tell him who it was?"

"No, just that she was the sandwich girl."

"Was he interested?"

"No. If anything he showed remarkably little interest, given how often people are murdered in the workplace." I could hear the bitterness in my voice, and I didn't like it.

"Then what?"

"Then I asked him if he had taken the twenty from my purse. We'd had a bunch of fights before about him not getting a job and spending money that I don't have."

I was regretting saying Nox could stay. I felt pathetic talking about my relationship with Alex. I sounded like a doormat, even to me.

"And you fought."

"Yes. I told him I wanted him to move out. At first, he was super nice, asking me to give him another chance. But when he realized I was serious, he turned nasty."

Heat rolled up my body suddenly and Nox spoke. "How nasty?" He had the same icy gravel to his voice as when the woman was mentioned in the club the night before.

"Oh, he wasn't violent or anything," I said quickly. "Just... mean. He said I was self-righteous and boring." I felt my cheeks heat. Saying it out loud now, it didn't sound that nasty. "He said it in a meaner way than that. With some swearing," I added.

Oh god. *Could I sound more pathetic?*

"Right. So, why did you leave?"

"Because I was angry, and I didn't want to be around him anymore. I didn't want to stoop to his level." I lifted my chin, trying to drag some dignity around myself.

"Where did you go?"

"Over the lawn to the retirement home. I talked with my friend there, Francis, and we played cribbage."

"And you haven't seen or heard from Alex since?"

"No."

"Is there anything else at all you can think of that might be useful?"

"No. He said nothing about where he was going or where he'd been."

The Inspector looked at me for an uncomfortably long moment, and then turned to the uniformed officer, who had been scribbling on a notepad the whole time.

"Go and talk to the security guy and see if they got that footage working yet," she said. The officer nodded, then left.

"Miss Abbott, I hope your ex-boyfriend can be found soon. Because as much as I don't like the sound of him, I can't find any way for him to have entered this building. You, on the other hand, were already in it when Sarah was killed."

My heart skipped a beat. "I didn't do anything. I *couldn't* have done something like that."

"We'll be in touch," she said, and left the room.

FOURTEEN

BETH

"Why is it so hot in here?" I was flustered, and I felt like I was burning up, my skin clammy and unpleasant.

"I'm sorry." Nox's voice was low and hard, and quite frankly, a little scary.

"Why are you sorry?" At the same time I spoke, the air around me seemed to cool, and I paused in pulling uncomfortably at my shirt. "Wait... You're the reason it's hot?"

"Human police are morons," he growled. "They make it hard for me to control myself sometimes. As do people like your ex."

I felt my brows rise. "You're saying it gets hot when you're mad?"

Nox said nothing, and the butterflies started up their jig in my stomach again. "It really sounds like the Inspector thinks I did it," I said, deciding to abandon the many questions I had about fallen angels and their powers over temperature. "Nox, they're going to pin this on me."

I swear I saw shadows swirl through his eyes again, before he leaned back in his chair and ran a hand through his hair. His bicep bulged in the suit as he lifted his arm, and he left his dark hair ever so slightly tousled. For the first time in ten minutes, I felt the ache back in my core.

Not now, stupid body. I'm suspected of murder!

When Nox spoke again, his teasing calm was back. "Then it's a good job that you made a deal with the devil. We need to go and speak to the boyfriend."

"The one with the airtight alibi?"

"Yes."

I bit down on my lip, nerves making me feel sick. "Do you think Alex did it? I mean, I clearly misjudged him but... Have I been living with a murderer?"

"No. I do not believe Alex did it. But I do believe he'll wish he was dead if the police don't find him before I do."

The harshness of his words didn't sit with his casual tone. There was a danger to them that was impossible to miss, an undercurrent of something that made my fearful instincts kick in.

"Why?"

"I told you before. I have a vested interest in your health. That man has made you unhappy."

"I don't need protecting. I kicked him out on my own, like a big girl." I stood up, putting a hand on my hip as I spoke. I didn't want him to think I was weak.

Even if I was.

"And besides, you heard what I said. He wasn't even that nasty."

Nox stood up, moving around the desk toward me. I let him come. I couldn't will myself to put distance between us, not when his eyes were filled with such intensity. His voice was husky and sensual when he spoke and filled my body with a feeling that was completely new to me, and so much better than the fear that it was replacing.

It was a confidence bordering on alarming, and it was *physical*. I felt taller, slimmer, prettier, as he stared into my eyes. "However that man made you feel, and whatever he said to you that made you doubt yourself, he was wrong."

"He just called me boring," I said. "Nothing that bad."

"Cruelty comes in many shapes and forms, Beth. If the man made you feel like shit, then the man is a piece of shit." The blaze of anger in his eyes that accompanied his words softened as he stopped a foot away from me. I stared up at him. "And for the record, you are the least boring woman I have ever met."

I felt my lips part in surprise. "Well, now I know you're lying about being the devil. Lucifer himself must have met some pretty interesting women."

"Many. But none like you."

I sucked in air. "Prove to me who you are." I whispered the words before I could stop myself. I swear I could see the magic in his eyes. I needed to know if he was crazy, or if this was real.

"The proof is in front of you. When you're ready, you will see it."

I clamped my mouth closed.

That was a cop-out.

There was no such thing as magic. What I was experiencing was a just a pathetic response to a gorgeous man.

A gorgeous man who was admittedly turning out to be quite different than I had thought he was.

If the man made you feel like shit, then the man is a piece of shit. His words echoed through my head. That was not the way I expected an arrogant millionaire to think. Or the devil, for that matter.

I took a step back from him. It took every ounce of willpower I had, and I immediately missed that delicious wood-smoke scent. "Thanks for the confidence boost," I said.

"I hope to make it permanent." Before I could ask him what that meant, he turned, striding to the door of his new office. "We have a mechanic to visit," he said.

With a small shake of my head, I followed him through the door.

One of the few things I didn't like about England was the weather. And April was the worst. It was either too warm to wear a sweater, or pouring rain and cold, with little variation between.

Nox strode through the pouring rain as though it weren't even falling, as I pulled the big, black umbrella he had given me low over my head, fighting the wind that was pulling at it.

Fortunately, we didn't have far to go. Cannon Car Repairs was a large repair shop set behind the terraced shops on Cannon Street in Whitechapel. I hadn't owned a car since living in London. There was no need. Parking cost more than a car would be worth. But I missed driving. Auto repair shops in England were largely the same as the ones I'd grown up with in America, it seemed. The concrete and corrugated metal hangars were just smaller, with more packed into them.

The wide garage doors that fronted Cannon Car Repairs were rolled up and open, the sound of rain pinging off the metal just audible over the radio. Cheesy eighties hits were blaring, and a male voice sang along loudly as I hurried into the dry garage after Nox, shaking my umbrella and looking around.

The smell of motor oil filled my nose, and I could see a car at the back of the busy room rising into the air on a hydraulic lift. Three other cars were raised on jacks, and the whole space was lined with racks of tires and tools. I spotted a man in blue overalls, who appeared to be the one singing, but before we could make our way over to him, a voice called out.

"You here for the Audi A4?" The London accent came from the other side of the room, and Nox and I turned as a well-built guy in his early twenties emerged from behind the raised car.

"No. I'm looking for Dave."

The man paused, suspicion crossing his face. He was

reasonably nice looking, with dark blond hair and brown eyes set in tanned skin smeared with oil. His overalls were too tight, I thought maybe deliberately, to show off his muscular frame.

"Why do you want Dave?"

"Ooo, what have you done now, Davey-boy?" yelled the guy who was singing, before laughing and belting out the chorus of A-ha's Take on Me.

Muscley-blond-guy's jaw clenched tight. "Is this about Sarah?"

My stomach clenched at hearing the dead girl's name.

"Yes. It is. Can you tell me when you last saw her?" Nox replied.

"Why? Who are you?"

Nox didn't miss a beat. "Her employer."

Dave snorted, slapping a rag against his palm, then turning back to the car on the lift. "Max was her piece of shit employer." He glanced pointedly between Nox and me, then lifted the hood on the car as he carried on, speaking loudly so that we could hear him. "You two don't look much like you work in a shithole like the Aphrodite Club."

"She did lunch runs for my company." Nox moved closer, clearly unwilling to shout over the banging and singing, and I followed behind him.

Dave stopped squinting at the car engine and looked at Nox. "Wait, is it your office she was killed in? The big place she delivered sandwiches to?"

Nox nodded. "Correct." Something dark flashed on

Dave's face so briefly I almost missed it, and my chest squeezed in anxiety.

Dave crouched to pick up a wrench, then straightened. "I don't know what the fuck it's got to do with you mate, and I don't care. Sarah was screwing someone else. Probably more than one person, knowing her. I was through with her."

My stomach flipped. Sarah had been screwing *my* boyfriend, but I didn't want this guy to know that. He made me nervous as hell. A louder bang than usual came from somewhere else in the garage, followed by a loud cheer and laughter.

"Did she know you were leaving her?"

"Yep." Dave brought the wrench crashing down on something inside the hood of the car and I couldn't help flinching. "Not that she ever fucking listened. She was always too high to hear anything I said."

Clang. He smashed the wrench down again. I was no mechanic, but I was pretty sure cars didn't get fixed by beating them with bits of metal.

"What did she take?"

"What didn't she take, more like." *Clang.* "Said she needed it to drown out the voices."

"What voices?"

"Fuck knows. She was nuts." Dave turned to us abruptly, wrench still in hand. I thought I felt a little flash of heat come from Nox, but dismissed it, looking instead at Dave. There was pain in his eyes, I was positive. He may have been playing the big man, saying he didn't care about her, but I wasn't so sure.

"I'm so sorry about what happened," I said.

"Really? Why? You do her in?" Dave's response was sharp, and bitter.

"It must be hard," I said, as gently as I could and still be heard in the loud garage. Singing-guy was onto Tina Turner now.

"It used to be hard. Now she's gone, it'll be easy," Dave said.

I raised my eyebrows. "What do you mean?"

He waved the wrench animatedly as he answered, and I stopped myself taking a step back as Nox moved closer to me. "Do you know how many times I tried to leave her? Sarah was... good at getting her own way. But this time, it's really over. She's gone for good."

Was that a motive for murder? Ending a bad relationship once and for all?

"I would appreciate it if you could answer my original question," said Nox. Dave looked at him.

"If it means you'll piss off and leave me alone, fine. I saw her when I left for work in the morning. She was asleep. I yelled at her that she'd better not be there when I got back, and I left. Police called round later that night to tell me she was dead."

"What time did you leave for work?"

"About quarter to eight. Now, will you leave me to do my job?"

"Of course. Thank you for your time." Nox nodded, and looked pointedly at me. His meaning was clear. We were leaving.

"Erm, thanks, Dave," I said.

"Whatever," he said, and turned back to the car.

I opened my umbrella as soon as we got outside again, and half offered it to Nox. He was almost a foot taller than me, so I was grateful when he gave me a small smile, then shook his head.

Plus, I kind of wanted to see him wet.

"So? What do you think?" I said as we began to walk down the street to where Claude was waiting with the town car.

"I think that Dave has a temper."

"Yeah. Remind not to ask him to fix my car," I muttered.

Nox looked at me. "You don't have a car."

I frowned. "Firstly, that's the sort of thing you shouldn't know until I tell you. If you're going to learn all about me from your files, at least pretend you don't know some stuff. Secondly, I meant it figuratively."

"Alright. Here's something I don't know. If you were to have a car, what kind of car would it be?"

"Easy," I said. "Lamborghini Countach."

"Really?"

"The one the Prince of Monaco has." Nox chuckled, and I gave him a sideways look. "You didn't say I had to be realistic."

"I'm amused because that's not the sort of car I thought you'd choose. It's the sort of car a ten-year-old boy draws with crayons."

"I know. That's why I love it. It's all eighties and angles and bright red and just... Not boring."

"Well. My files can't tell me everything, it seems." We had nearly reached his car, and Claude leapt out of the driver's seat when he saw us, rushing to open the back door.

"What's your dream car?" I asked Nox, smiling gratefully at Claude as he took my umbrella and I clambered into the car.

Nox slid in elegantly after me. "Not so much a dream, and more of a reality," he said. I scowled.

"I forgot for a moment there that you're a millionaire."

"I must be losing my touch."

He said the word 'touch' sinfully slowly, and the ache returned in full force, like a suckerpunch to the ladybits.

"What's the car you have?" I said, too quickly.

Nox smiled, his eyes dancing with that blue light. "I like Aston Martins."

"That's what James Bond drives, right?"

"Right."

"Spies are good. I like spies," I babbled, turning away from him and looking out of the window as I tried not to squirm on the leather seat. How could him just saying the word *touch* make me feel so ridiculously aroused? I heard him give another low chuckle, but he said nothing.

I needed a serious word with myself when I was alone.

FIFTEEN

BETH

"No. I'm not going on another date with you."

"Did you not enjoy the last one?" I was standing outside my apartment building, the umbrella sheltering me from the worst of the awful weather. Nox had gotten out of the car, too, and seemed totally oblivious of the beating rain. Water dripped from his thick hair and ran down the olive-toned skin of his face. I longed to reach out and catch the drops, to stroke them from his cheek, feel his warmth.

I gripped the umbrella harder.

"I enjoyed the food, yes. But you took me to a strip bar and then left me there on my own."

"What if I promise to try harder?"

"You owe me a month of meals at the Ivy. I don't need you for a good dinner anymore," I said, swallowing and trying to stop myself replaying him saying the word harder in that sultry baritone. *Jeez, what was wrong with me?* I needed a cold shower, stat.

"I didn't think that through," Nox said, putting both his hands on his hips and letting out a long breath. "I have somebody to track down this afternoon, so if you're unavailable this evening I'll see you tomorrow." He fixed his eyes on mine. "I hope you have a lovely evening, Miss Abbott," he said, then turned and walked back to the car.

I screwed my face up as I tried to force down the disappointment that he didn't push harder for that second date.

He had respected the fact that I said no, and not pushed me. *That's a good thing,* I told myself as I rammed the key into my new lock a little too hard.

Then why did I want him to have pushed me? Why did I wish he had insisted, giving me no choice but to spend another evening in his company?

"Get it together, Beth," I said aloud as I dumped my purse on the couch, then threw myself down after it.

Listening to a completely unattainable man say normal words in a way that made my insides turn to liquid and my toes curl would not help relieve this frustration. It would only make it worse.

Is he unattainable though?

The question flashed into my head and I groaned. He was a millionaire. And my boss. I was confident that he would sleep with me—the hunger in his eyes I kept seeing was undeniable. But that did not make him attainable. That made him as randy as I felt, and nothing more.

I looked at the time on my cellphone. 3pm. I considered trying to do some work for my proper job, but my laptop was at the office. Besides, every time I tried to think about anything other than Nox, Inspector Singh's questions began to replay in my head, followed by vivid images of Alex with Sarah.

I stood up from the couch, picked up my umbrella and headed back out into the wet English spring weather.

"Beth, am I sure glad to see you! Heather is terrible at Monopoly and I'm bored to tears."

"Hi Francis."

"Honestly, she just doesn't understand how to play the game." Francis was reclined in her La-Z-Boy in the recreation room of Lavender Oaks, shaking her head, her wrinkled expression one of annoyance.

"She wouldn't let you be the banker, would she?"

Francis paused before answering. "No. She wouldn't."

"Which means you couldn't cheat."

She flashed me a look as I flopped into the armchair beside her. "What's new?"

I filled her in on everything, from Alex stealing my stuff when I was last with her, right up to visiting Dave the mechanic that day. I left out the part about Nox claiming to be the devil, and what I had agreed to in return for his help, though.

"Woo-ee, you've been busy."

"Yeah. And I might be in prison by this time next week, so we'd better make the most of my visits." I scrubbed a hand over my face, careful not to smudge my eye make-up. Eye make-up I'd taken a little more care over that morning than I usually did.

"This Nox, you say he's good-looking? And he took you to dinner?"

"And a strip club, yeah."

"I'll bet that was sexy." Her dark eyes were filled with mischief.

"No, it wasn't. It was awkward."

"Was he awkward, or was it just you?"

"No, it was just me," I admitted. "But I guess he's used to seeing boobs."

"Does he want to see your boobs?"

I blew out a sigh. "Francis, if I tell you something, will you promise not to judge me?"

"Honey, I'm beyond judgement. If I could tell you some of the things I got up to in my youth—"

I held out my hand to stop her. "I don't doubt it. That's why I feel I can tell you this."

She leaned forward, eager. "Go on."

"My boss didn't offer to help me out of the kindness of his heart. I... I had to offer him something in return."

Francis leaned back in her chair, a knowing look on her face. "You gotta show him your boobs."

"No! Not exactly. I agreed to spend one night in his company." I felt my face burn as I said the words, my cheeks tingling with embarrassment. "But the important thing is that I don't have to do anything I don't want to. He said we could just talk, or even play Monopoly, if that's what I wanted." I could hear the slight desperation in my voice.

"Well, I'll be honest, sex is more fun than Monopoly. I'd choose the sex," Francis said thoughtfully.

"That's what I'm worried about," I groaned.

"Why are you worried? Is he a nice guy?"

"Yes. I think so." My mind flashed on what he'd said to me in his office that morning, and how angry he had seemed about Alex making me feel bad about myself. "I feel weirdly confident when I'm with him," I told Francis. "And, erm... Well, sexy." I dropped my voice to a whisper, even though hardly anyone else was in the huge recreation room.

"That's how a guy's supposed to make you feel."

"But it's almost like he's too sexy."

"I don't follow." Her wide face creased in confusion.

"Well, what if it's as good as I think it might be? It's only one night, and then that would be it, all over. What if a night with Nox sets the bar too high? I mean, who else could live up to the memory of a gorgeous millionaire sex-god?"

"Sex-god, eh?"

I flushed again, dropping her twinkling gaze. "I think he might be quite good at it."

"At sex?"

"Yes. Although, if he's not, then that's even worse. He could have stayed a gorgeous sex-god in my mind, that I could enjoy forever, instead of being disappointed by him in real life."

Francis considered me a moment. "I think that keeping a sex-god in your mind is a bad decision, if you have an actual one to play with," she said eventually.

"Even if you could only play with him once?"

"Yes," she said with vigorous shrug of her shoulders. "When is this night of passion occurring?"

"It's not a night of passion! And only after he's cleared my name of murder."

"Well, that's exciting."

"It's not exciting, it's terrifying."

"See, that's your problem. You shouldn't be terrified of sex."

"I didn't mean the sex, I meant being a suspect in a murder case."

"Oh. Well, I suppose that is a little alarming."

I bit the inside of my cheek, not wanting to admit that she was probably closer to part of the problem than I wanted to think about. I *was* scared of sex. Not the actual act, but the fact that I couldn't possibly be what a man like Nox wanted. He may think he wanted me now, and if I was being perfectly honest, I liked that. I liked the confidence that came with his attention.

But if he found out how, well, *boring* I was in bed, he would just be disappointed.

"So, who do you think killed her? Was it her boyfriend?" Francis asked. She sounded excited.

"I don't know." I couldn't tell her that Nox thought it was a supernatural murder. Sitting in the retirement home, with everything around me so normal, the idea of supernaturals was even more absurd. "He definitely has a temper, but Inspector Singh says he has an alibi. Which I don't, because I was in the building where she was murdered and none of the elevator footage is working."

"Why does she think you did it? Cos your low-life ex was sleeping with the dead girl?"

I nodded. Hearing the words put like that made my stomach twist into knots. It must have shown on my face because Francis patted me on the knee, her signature comforting gesture. I smiled at her. "I'm okay. I'm glad I got to kick him out before I found out, or I might actually have committed murder," I said ruefully.

Francis gave a snort. "I'd have hauled my ass over there and helped you bury the body."

"Thanks, Francis."

"Anytime, honey."

Covering my pasta in cheese didn't provide the same pick-me-up that cheese usually gave me later on that evening.

I had a hollow feeling in my gut, and a restlessness that refused to let me settle. After reading the same paragraph of my book for the fourth time, I gave up. I stared at Nox's number on my cellphone screen, my finger hovering over the big green 'call' button. What was he doing now? Images filled my head of him at ritzy parties or blasting down the highway in his fancy Aston Martin. A beautiful blonde with enormous boobs like Sarah's was next to him in all my visions, and I blew out a sigh.

A man like Nox was out of my league. And crazy.

He was probably relieved when I turned him down for another date.

I screwed my face up and pressed into the back cushion of my couch. *Get it together Beth. You're suspected of murder. You should be concentrating on that.*

I knew I hadn't killed Sarah. And I was ninety-five percent sure it wasn't Nox or Alex.

But somebody had. My awful interview with the Inspector swam back into my head. The longer the investigation went on with no new suspects, the more I looked like the most likely culprit.

Francis' question repeated itself in my head. "Who do you think killed her? Was it her boyfriend?"

He had definitely cared about her more than he wanted anybody else to know. And he definitely had a temper. But did I think he killed her?

I flopped sideways, so I was laid flat on the couch, staring at the ceiling.

I wasn't sure. I certainly didn't know how he could have got into the building. And the Inspector said he had an alibi.

But there was the guy who the club owner had told us about, who Dave had fought with. Did the police know about him?

The more I thought about it, the more it annoyed me that Nox hadn't mentioned him all day. When he had dropped me off in the pouring rain, he said it was to track somebody down, and I had been too distracted by his damn accent to ask who. I was willing to bet it was the 'lead' that he abandoned me in the strip club for. The one he claimed was a fallen angel.

I sat up straight, some of the restless energy solidifying into a plan. I didn't need Nox's help. Especially not if it centered around hunting down made-up nonsense. Somebody killed Sarah, somebody made of flesh and blood, and we had information the police might not have.

A sense of indignant righteousness filled me as I stood up. I would prove to Nox, and the stupid Inspector, that I was both innocent and not in need of any help.

SIXTEEN

BETH

Skinny jeans, black heels and a sparkly, low cut t-shirt were the best thing I could come up with for visiting a strip club.

My pulse was racing, and anxiety was making my stomach squelch as I asked phone-playing guy for a ticket in the entry-hall of the Aphrodite Club. On hearing a woman's voice, he peeled his eyes from the screen of his phone. A lazy smile spread across his face.

"Single women go in for free," he drawled.

"Oh. Right." I wasn't going to complain about that. That was ten pounds I could put toward a new TV.

Trying to hide my nerves, I gave him a small nod as he passed me the little cardboard ticket, and I strode as casually as I could to the red curtain.

The smell of beer and the overly loud music rolled over me as I stepped through. It was ten o'clock, and pretty quiet. I felt my cheeks blush as my eyes swept over the topless lady on the stage, and I made my way a small table near the back.

I half-expected everyone to be suspicious of me, a woman on her own in a strip club, but the drinks girl from last time flounced right over to me with a smile on her face.

"Hi sugar, what can I get you?"

I was about to ask her for some water but decided something stronger might settle my nerves. "A gin and tonic, please."

"No problem."

I took a deep breath and tried to relax into my chair. The confidence I had built up in my apartment, stamping around as I got ready, telling myself I didn't need the help of my arrogant, completely mad boss, was leaking away the longer I looked around the club. An irrational fear that I would see somebody I knew kept wafting into my head, and I tried to channel Francis.

Own it. Who cares? You can be in a cheap, seedy, strip bar on a weeknight if you want to be. You're a grown-ass woman.

Besides, if I saw someone I knew in the Aphrodite Club, they would probably be equally as embarrassed as I was.

The girl came back with my drink, and I took it gratefully. She had a glittery bra on this time.

"Thanks. I erm, like your bra," I said.

She beamed at me. "Thanks! We're only allowed to keep them on 'til midnight, but I like the bling."

"It was Candy, right?"

Her face darkened a moment with suspicion, and then cleared. "You were in here the other night with that hot-as-hell Irish guy!"

"Yes."

"Ah, I'm real sorry to tell you this, but the girl you were looking for? Sarah? She's dead. Someone killed her."

My heart beat a little harder in my chest, my anxiety ratcheting up. I wasn't good at lying. I wasn't good at talking to girls in their underwear, either. "I heard," I said, settling somewhere between a lie and a truth. "Who do you think did it?"

"Well," she said thoughtfully, chewing on her thumbnail. "Her boyfriend, he's over there, and he's real cut up about it." She gestured over her shoulder and I leaned out of my seat to look.

Dave the mechanic sat in a dark corner, a pretty, topless girl grinding against his lap.

"He doesn't look too cut up about it," I said doubtfully.

"That's men for you, sugar. They hide their emotions behind booze and sex." She spoke with an authority that belied her young looks, and I wondered if she was right, or if that was what you had to tell yourself to work in a place like this and not end up hating men.

"So, not the boyfriend then. Didn't her boyfriend punch someone recently?"

"Oh, Dave punches quite a few people. But he did have a proper fight with Mr. Jackson."

"Who's Mr. Jackson?"

Candy shrugged. "A regular. He loans money to all the girls in here. Doesn't charge interest, just wants extra dances instead." Panic crossed her face suddenly, and she dropped her voice, bending closer to me. "Don't tell Max."

"Of course not."

"He wouldn't approve of giving extra dances and not charging. I heard he loaned money to one of the girls once, but it didn't go so well. So now they go to Mr. Jackson."

"Did Sarah owe him money then?"

"I dunno. I just know that Dave hit him."

"Is Mr. Jackson in here tonight?"

"No. He comes in on Fridays and weekends."

"Okay. Thanks."

"Why do you want to know?"

"Oh, I, er," I flailed around for an answer, feeling myself begin to sweat instantly.

"She's just doing some research for me." A twenty-pound note appeared between us, and I followed the hand holding it up to Nox's perfect frame.

My pulse skyrocketed. What the hell happened at night to make him so much more attractive? Shadows played in all the right places, making the light that fell across his hard jaw and reflected in his eyes look freaking magical. He was wearing dark jeans and a black shirt, and I found myself unable to swallow as my eyes traced their way up and down his body, fixing on the exposed skin of his collarbone.

"Oh. Well, let me know if you need anything else." Candy grinned as she took the banknote from him.

"We will."

As Candy wiggled away, Nox sat down in the plastic chair opposite me. "So, you turned me down for this?" he said.

My mouth was dry, and I reached for my gin, downing half of it in a panicked attempt at rehydration. "I felt that you had overlooked the lead about the guy Dave punched."

"Oh. So you're here for work, not pleasure?"

I scowled at him, the playful gleam in his eye both unsettling and ridiculously hot. "Of course I'm not here for pleasure," I hissed. "Why are you here?"

"Have you found anything out?" He ignored my question completely.

"Yes. Dave the angry mechanic is consoling himself with a naked lady over there, and the guy he punched lends money to the dancers here. In return for extras."

Nox quirked an eyebrow. "What kind of extras?"

"Dances. He comes in on Fridays and weekends. His name is Mr. Jackson."

"You've been very thorough, Miss Abbott."

"Unlike you."

He gave me a frown, mock hurt on his beautiful face. Even his hair seemed different at night, less perfect somehow, more tousled. "I assure you, I have been working hard."

"On what? Your fallen angel lead?"

"Exactly."

I felt my lips purse. "Nox, I am suspected of murder. You get how serious that is, right?"

The playful gleam vanished from his eyes. "Beth, you've made a deal with the devil. Do you get how serious that is?"

I gulped, then lifted my drink back to my lips. "If you want me to believe your madness, then I need proof."

"The switch has been flipped, Beth. It's ready for you, whenever you want to see it."

"What are you talking about?"

"When you're truly able to accept it, you'll see it. I've made sure of that."

I ground my teeth. "So, I might just never see it? That's very convenient for you, don't you think?"

"I assure you, there is nothing convenient about any of this. Getting permission to lift the Veil for a non-supernatural is not easy. It took my assistant two days."

He was actually mental. "Lift the veil?" I repeated. "Also, how have I not met your assistant already?"

"You won't see my assistant until you can see the supernatural world. She's a pixie."

I froze with my glass against my bottom lip. "A pixie?"

"Yes. One of the few species who can't exist in both worlds."

"Right." I tipped the rest of the gin and tonic into my mouth and swallowed. "I'm going home."

"On the night bus?"

"Yes." I glared at him. "Did you follow me here?"

"The night bus is dangerous."

"The night bus is not dangerous."

"Have you eaten?"

"It's half past ten, of course I've eaten."

"Good. Let's go dancing."

SEVENTEEN

BETH

"You're insane." I shook my head as I stood up.

"What's insane is you turning down the chance to go one of the best Latin clubs in London."

I paused. I loved Latin dancing. Really and truly adored it. Did he know that?

"It's nearly eleven," I protested a little less vigorously than I should.

"It's half ten. And I'm sure I can smooth things over with your boss tomorrow if you're late for work." Amusement danced over his features and my insides squirmed as my mind filled with the idea of dancing with him, my body pressed against his.

I wanted to dance with him. There was point denying it to myself, heat was trickling down my spine, heading straight to all the right places just thinking about it.

Which was why I shouldn't. "No, I should get home."

Our eyes locked, and I could feel him probing my face, searching for something.

"I insist."

My brows raised, but as I opened my mouth to argue, he pushed his chair back with a loud scrape and stood.

"I need to tell you more about my world, and so far, you have been more receptive when full of good food and drink."

I cocked my head at him, now a foot taller than me. "I told you, I've already eaten."

"But you haven't eaten a Cubano's quesadilla."

"No." I had eaten a hugely dull bowl of pasta with some cheese.

"Then allow the sin of gluttony to give you a happier end to your evening. Please."

If the pull of Latin music wasn't enough, the lure of South American food was. Add in the gorgeous hunk of arrogance standing before me using the world *please*, and I didn't stand chance. "Fine. Since you asked so nicely. Just an hour, though."

"Or you'll turn into a pumpkin?"

"Something like that."

Claude smiled as he opened the car door for me when I stepped out of the narrow entrance to the Aphrodite Club.

"Hi, Claude," I said.

"Good evening, Miss Abbott," he grinned back.

Nox slid into the car behind me, and now that we were out of the pungent club, I could smell his delicious smoky scent. My stomach skittered, and for a brief moment my confidence plummeted into my shoes. I was in the town car of a guy about a hundred miles out of my league. For heaven's sake, what was I doing?

"You asked me about the Veil. Would you like to know more?"

I snapped my eyes to Nox, sitting beside me on the soft leather, the colored lights of London playing across his face as the car moved slowly through the streets.

"Sure." *Out of my league and completely crazy,* I reminded myself, trying to pull some of my confidence back.

"The magical population of London are hidden by what we call the Veil. We have to petition those in charge to get it lifted for a non-supernatural, like yourself. Once it has been lifted, your brain needs time to adjust, to accept what it has spent a lifetime not seeing. But I assure you, you will start to see. And the sooner you allow yourself to believe, the sooner you will see."

"Who do you have to petition? Who has more power than the devil?"

"The gods."

"Do they live in London too?"

"They do not live on earth."

"Okay." I wasn't sure what else I was supposed to say to that.

"There are five major cities in the world populated by

supernaturals, but London has the most. That's why I'm here."

"Because you like being around them?"

"Because I'm supposed to keep the wild ones in check."

I shifted in my seat, moving to face him as I frowned. "I thought the devil would cause trouble, not keep everyone well-behaved."

"The role of the devil is widely misunderstood, Miss Abbott."

"If you say so."

"I may be the root of all evil, but I am also it's keeper." He looked away a moment, the light dimming in his bright blue eyes. "Or I was, anyway."

"Have you considered writing fiction? I think you'd be very good at it."

He flashed me a look. "I've written many books."

"Of course you have."

I blew out a long breath and looked out of the window.

Hot as hell and batshit crazy.

Cubano's was not the dark, swanky club that I was expecting. Nox gestured me to go ahead of him when we reached a palm covered front courtyard with bright red and green chairs dotted around, people smoking and laughing. The rain had cleared, leaving a cool, but not cold, spring evening. I pulled open a large door and a smile leapt to my lips. I couldn't help it. Mint and citrus dominated my nose, and my hips tried to sway of their own accord as the pounding beat and smooth Spanish voice washed over my ears. All the furniture I could see was pale wood, and all the metal and plastic was painted mint green or red. But none of the furniture was being used. Dancers filled the space. Women in huge flamenco skirts alongside men with shirts open to their waist, as well as folks dressed like me in jeans and heels. All were spinning, gyrating and swaying in time to the upbeat tune, and every one of them looked happy.

I felt a hand on the small of my back, and I didn't need to turn to know it was Nox who gently guided me through the throng of bodies. The fizz of electricity I got from his touch gave it away.

We exited the dance floor to find a long bar across the back of the room, where men and women shook metal cocktail tubs and filled trays. To the right was a red metal staircase that led to a narrow mezzanine row of small tables, overlooking the dancers.

Nox strode to the bar, and a particularly good-looking guy looked up at him and smiled. "Nox! My man. What can we get you?"

"Two mojitos and some quesadillas to share, thanks. Upstairs, if there's space," Nox called over the music. A cheerful feeling was pulsing through me, the energy of the place infectious.

"For you there's always space. I'll bring them up."

Nox turned and I followed him up the stairs, taking

advantage of the short time that he couldn't see me to wiggle my hips enthusiastically.

We found an empty table against the rail, boasting a great view of the dancefloor below. Our drinks and quesadilla's arrived seconds after us, and I excitedly sipped at the mojito. It was perfect.

"You know, I could watch your face when it looks like that all night." Nox's sultry voice carried across the music, and I felt heat flood first my face, then head south.

"Looks like what?"

"A mask of pleasure," he said, and his eyes seemed to actually spark with light.

"It's a good cocktail," I said, dragging my eyes from his mouth. "Why don't you try yours?"

"I get as much pleasure from watching you."

Oh god. Tingles spread through my chest at his words, images of him giving me pleasure firing through my head in a parade of lust. My nipples hardened, and I put the drink down on the table, launching myself at the quesadillas for a distraction.

"What's in these?" I spluttered awkwardly.

"Cheese. And peppers."

"Huh." I bit into one. Salty, tangy, spicy goodness melted into my mouth, and I made a small, involuntary noise of happiness.

Nox straightened in his chair, his cool demeanor slipping ever so slightly. Had I caused that? By eating gooey cheese?

"Are you going to have one?" I asked him. I wasn't keen on the idea of stuffing my face while he ate nothing, but that wouldn't stop me from eating the entire plate. They were freaking delicious.

He smiled. "I'm not going to let you have all the fun."

The divine cheesy-triangles-of-joy, as I was now calling them, didn't last long, and when the plate was empty I felt like I was buzzing with more restless energy than I had before I'd decided to leave my apartment. Probably because the sexual tension I had spent all afternoon talking myself out of was now back in full force, adding to the now-permanent hum of anxiety that went with being suspected of murder.

"Do you want to dance?" Nox said.

"No," I lied. "Thank you."

"Why not?"

"I don't think I'm as good as these people."

"You don't need to be. They're not looking at anyone else. They're just enjoying the music. That's why I like this place. There are no show-offs."

"Isn't one of the sins pride? Shouldn't you be into people showing off?"

"Pride is one of the sins that I let go."

"Let go?"

"Yes. I told you. I relocated some of the sins when I settled here."

"Right. Your lead from the strip bar is a fallen angel who hosts one of your sins," I nodded, remembering what he'd said. *Crazy.* "Is that who you gave pride to?"

"No."

"Oh. Which sins did you keep?"

"Lust." I swallowed as his eyes darkened. The music

seemed to intensify, a sexy samba beat filling the air, making my skin vibrate. Nox ran a hand through his hair. Golden light flickered behind him, making his skin glow. "Would you like to dance?"

This time it wasn't a polite offer. Somehow, it was the sexiest damn invitation I'd ever had.

I took his outstretched hand instinctively, the need to touch him overpowering everything else. My breath caught as the zap of energy moved between us, his eyes flaring briefly as it did. Then he was pulling me to my feet and guiding me ahead of him, toward the stairs. His fingers laced through mine as he followed me to the dance floor, and I felt the music seeping into me, forcing out the self-consciousness. I let my hips sway, even though he was behind me and could see every movement. When we reached the edge of the throng of dancers, he lifted his arm, spinning me around, then catching me with his other.

My brain fizzled to a halt as he pulled me into his body, pressing my chest to his and dipping his head close to mine. Desire and passion burned in his gaze, unmistakable. Then I realized with a tiny gasp that there were flames in his irises. Actual blue flames, dancing with life.

The only time we had been this close was in my dreams. In real life, he was even more intoxicating. Mesmerizing. I couldn't look away. I couldn't breathe.

Before my stupid brain could shut down completely, he spun me back the other way, and I sucked in air, as though the only way I could breathe was with distance between us.

Those flames... Could it be true? Was I dancing with the devil? The god of lust?

He had some sort of power, there was no doubting that.

The music changed to something lively, with whistles and drums and a lady singing fast and high. Nox lifted my arm higher and then I was spinning around and around. A laugh bubbled from my lips as he caught me, and dizziness washed through me. "I haven't spun like that since I was a kid," I gasped, and he extended his arm with a grin, rolling me along it.

"Dance like nobody is watching, Beth."

That same sense of confidence I'd felt earlier in his office settled over me, and I swung my hips in time with the music as the woman's singing got louder. Nox mirrored me, moving his own hips in time with mine. With a surge of confidence, I rolled myself back along his arm, thrusting my hip against his thigh, before spinning back out and letting go of his hand.

For a second I felt an inexplicable sense of loss at the removal of contact, but I closed my eyes, and let the music take all of my focus. It was as though all my nerves and tension were building into something that I could no longer control, and before I stopped to consider what I was doing, I raised my arms, tipped my head back and let my body do whatever it wanted to do. I swayed fast to the music, my feet moving me across the floor, my heart rate rocketing as I began to dance the pent-up energy out of my body.

I opened my eyes when I felt a hand on my waist, the

spark confirming it was Nox before I saw him. He was standing behind me, and I took the hand he'd planted on me and swirled, lifting it and moving under it in time to the music.

I didn't know how long we danced. Tune after tune passed, beats and melodies that made me feel invincible, and as sexy as I ever had in my life, sank into my body, taking root. Every time my body pressed into Nox's, my skin fired to life, a delicious anticipation that I wasn't sure I'd ever experienced becoming my sole focus. I moved so that I brushed against him every few beats, and those seconds became all that mattered.

He moved like he was on ice, gliding over the floor, his hips swaying perfectly with mine whenever we were close. Each time his breath whispered over my neck or cheek, I couldn't catch my own breath, and a surreal dizziness made me feel like I was in a dream.

Something different began to play, slow and sultry. A tango, I realized. Nox pressed against my back, wrapping his arm tight around my stomach and pulling my ass into him. A pulse of desire so strong it almost hurt assaulted me as I felt him pressing hard against me.

He wanted me. No freaking question.

Slowly, he moved his hand down my ribs, brushing his fingers over the lose fabric of my shirt. I closed my eyes, leaning my head back into him, and breathing in his intoxicating scent.

His hips rocked against me in time to the song, and I pushed back, desperate. His palm flattened to my hip, and then he was tracing his hand back up my body. I swayed into him, hardly able to breathe as his touch neared my breast. Exquisitely slowly, he ran his fingertips up the curve of my chest, then my bare collarbone. As his fingers met my skin, waves of need beat through me, and I arched against him instinctively. His other arm snaked around me, pulling my body back against his, his erection grinding into my ass cheek. A moan escaped my lips, lost to the music, as his feather-light touch continued up over the sensitive skin of my neck. His fingers rolled against my jaw, then he gently pulled my head to the side and dropped his own.

The moan that left me when his lips met my neck was louder. Too loud.

Crashing back to earth with a jolt, the surreal haze lifted, and I realized what I was doing.

My boss, my crazy boss, was kissing me in a club. Without my job, I had nothing, and this man could fire me. He could sleep with me, regret it, and fire me, and it would likely mean nothing to him. Even worse, if he got he wanted before helping me clear my name of murder, he might decide not to help me with the police anymore.

With an effort of will I didn't know I possessed, I stepped away from his embrace.

"Wow, I'm so hot! From all the dancing! I'm going to grab my purse and get some air!" I shouted overly cheerily, without meeting his eyes.

"I'll see you outside," he answered, his voice somehow cutting through the surrounding sound as it always did, as I whirled and raced for the staircase.

EIGHTEEN

NOX

The need to touch myself, to check what was
happening was real, was torture.

For the first time in centuries, my body was
responding to a woman. And not just responding. I was
so hard I ached.

She was... She was like a drug, and I couldn't get
enough of her. Fierce intelligence shone in her eyes, she
was quick and funny, and fucking beautiful to look at.

But the innocence of her soul... She was good.
Morally good. And it was a draw I simply could not
resist.

I had to corrupt her. I had to open her eyes to a world
she didn't know existed. I had to make her body dissolve
in a pleasure she wasn't ready to take, then spend the rest
of my life rebuilding her from tiny fragments of bliss.

"Sorry about that." Her awkward tone cut through
my thoughts as she pushed her way through the doors,
out to the courtyard I was standing in. Cool air bit at my

skin, but it did nothing against the inferno of excitement that tore through my body on seeing her. Sweat shone on her chest, and my enhanced senses could hear her heart race.

"It's easy to lose yourself to the music here."

"I, erm, yeah." She looked at the ground, kicking her shoe at nothing. "I was a bit restless earlier. I feel better now. Thanks."

I was so tense that I could feel the tick in my jaw. There was nothing in this world I wanted more than to pull her to me, to press my lips against hers.

But I was devil. The fallen guardian of hell. I had more control that that.

"Do you want to leave?"

Indecision flashed in her eyes before steely resolve settled over her face. "Yes. Please."

She wasn't ready. And if I pushed her, I would lose her. Innocence didn't equate to weakness. I knew how far this woman had pushed herself to find her parents. She was tenacious and stubborn.

I felt a trickle of guilt, knowing so much about her when she hadn't told me herself. But there would be time. She would come to trust me, and to tell me. And then I would change her life.

NINETEEN

BETH

M y desire had not lessened at all since widening the distance between us. Nox's presence in the back of the car next to me was almost overwhelming, and I glued my eyes to window to stop myself drinking him in.

"Beth."

His voice was a command, not a request. I turned to him.

"We will tell the police about this new suspect of yours tomorrow. I do not wish to wait much longer before fulfilling our deal."

A predatory hunger sparked in his eyes. If I felt even a fraction of this desire when I spent the night with him, there was no way I would be able to stop myself.

"Who do you think killed her? Do you think it might be this new guy?" I asked, clinging to the sobering and very unsexy topic of murder.

"No. I think it was my lead."

"The fallen angel?"

"Yes."

"Then why don't we go and see her?"

"I can't take you with me until you can see through the Veil."

I frowned. "You understand that you sound crazy, don't you?"

"You know there is more to this world than you can see. You are bright and have enough experience in the unexplained to want to believe." My stomach clenched. "When you believe what I am telling you, I will be able to..." He trailed off. Curiosity fired through me. What would he be able to do? Then reality, with a lashing of doubt, washed over the spark of interest, dousing it.

There was no such thing as angels and shifters and vampires. Or freaking pixies for that matter.

"I can't believe with no proof, Nox. It's unfair to ask me to."

"Then I will give you proof. What do you wish to dream of tonight?"

I raised my eyebrows involuntarily. *You.* My brain supplied the answer instantly, but mercifully I didn't give my response aloud. "I don't know," I lied.

"Then I'll tell you. You will dream of me. On a frozen lake. And you will be dressed for the part."

I felt my heart beat hard in my chest at his words. I had never told him about my dreams. About the frozen lake.

Please, please, let him be telling the truth. Let there be a world alongside this one that was full of magic.

Let there be some place I haven't already searched for my parents.

"A frozen lake?" I said, forcing my words to come slowly. "Why a frozen lake?"

"Ice and fire. Cold and hot. Extremes. They are where my power is most intense."

"No flame-filled, burning underground lairs for this devil, then?"

"I told you. Much about me is misunderstood."

That, at least, I believed.

I worried that it would take me forever to fall asleep, with Nox's promise of dreaming of him playing on my mind, and the demure kiss on my hand when he'd dropped me off leaving me wholly unsatisfied. But the physical energy I had exerted dancing my ass off ensured otherwise. I was asleep within moments of my head hitting the pillow.

I was on the lake immediately. As though somebody had been waiting for sleep to take me, and then pounced. The lemon ball gown was absent, a striking scarlet dress, made for doing the tango, in its place. It left my left shoulder bare, and an almost hip-high split exposed my opposite leg.

I felt the unmistakable presence of Nox behind me, then hand curled around my waist, pulling me into his body.

"I told you that you would be dressed for the part," he murmured into my hair.

"Dreaming about the tango proves nothing," I said, breathing deeply and savoring his woodsmoke scent. "This is just my imagination filling in the gaps left by this evening."

"The gaps? You mean the things you wanted me to do to you? The things you stopped me from doing?"

He pressed into me, hard and large and delicious, and his other hand skimmed my jaw, tilting my head. This time, when his lips met my neck, I was ready for the moan that left me. The freezing air against the heat of his mouth caused tingles to run over my skin, and my nipples to tighten.

His mouth moved higher, and I leaned into him as his tongue flicked over my earlobe. One hand still firmly against my stomach, keeping me pressed to him, he moved the other, stroking his fingers across the tight top of the dress. Slowly, his fingers dipped under the fabric, his electrifying touch skimming the skin of my breast.

Longing spread through my body, heat pooling between my thighs. I felt his teeth against the sensitive part of my neck and gave a tiny gasp. At the same moment, his hand moved lower, flicking my hard nipple so fast I wasn't even sure he had done it.

I pushed back harder into him, raising my own hand and reaching behind me, feeling for him.

He paused, lifting his mouth from my neck. "Not yet. This is your dream. It's about you."

"If it's my dream, then I should be able to do what I like."

"Beth, do you have any idea how long I've waited for this? I am not rushing it."

"Waited for what?"

"You."

Before I could answer, his hand pushed the fabric of the dress down, exposing me to the icy air. His warm breath skimmed over my shoulder and his fingers encircled my nipple, squeezing. Pleasure, pent up for days, and now having somewhere to focus, coursed through me.

My soft moan was echoed by him. "Fuck, Beth. You're stunning."

Stunning. He thought I was stunning.

His deft fingers moved faster, and the ache between my legs built alarmingly as his tongue flicked against my neck.

I needed his mouth on me, lower. I needed his tongue flicking my nipples, my stomach, my thighs.

I tried to turn to face him, but his grip around me was iron.

"Please," I murmured.

"No. Piece by piece, you're going to learn just how good every single part of your body is." He nipped my earlobe, the sensation close enough to pain to make me shiver. "I am going to enjoy each and every inch of you before you even lay eyes on me."

I sucked in a breath and closed my eyes.

He squeezed hard on my nipple. "Are you wet?"

A small squeak escaped me.

"Is that a yes?"

"Yes," I whispered.

His hand left my breast and skimmed quickly down my dress. It stopped, heavy and still, right between my thighs. I tried to push myself against him, but he moved with me, allowing me none of the pressure I was so desperate for.

"What do you call this?"

"What?"

"I want to tell you everything I am going to do to do, when you fulfill your end of the deal and spend the night with me. And I need to know what to call this. I'm going to be referring to it a lot."

Oh god. Oh god. He was going to find out how boring I was. I couldn't tell him I called it my ladybits. "What do you want to call it?" I said, avoiding answering.

His hand moved, stroking back up my stomach, and over my ribs. "How is pussy?"

My whole body throbbed with need at his words. Apparently, it approved. "Yes."

"Say it."

"What?"

His fingers found my swollen nipple and squeezed. "Say it."

"Pussy," I breathed.

"Tell me how wet your pussy is."

Oooooh god.

Dirty talk was not something I had ever done, or even thought about doing. But my god was it turning me on hearing him speak like that. Words that would normally make me cringe with embarrassment turned into something I craved when spoken by him.

"It's a dream, Beth. What have you got to lose?" His lips fell on my neck again, hot and slow and sensual, his fingers to my other breast, teasing and pulling at my nipple.

I could feel the slickness between my legs. *He had said I was stunning.*

"Wet," I whispered, closing my eyes to the frozen landscape around me and letting the confidence he was causing to build up inside me take over. "I'm wet for you."

I heard his intake of breath, and swore I felt him stiffen further against me. "Good girl. Come to my office tomorrow morning. There's something I want to show you."

And just like that, I awoke.

My mom would have been ashamed of the curse words that poured from me when I found myself alone and ready to burst in my bed.

"If he's telling the damn truth, and he actually got me that wound up and left, I swear to god there'll be another murder," I snapped, tearing the sheets off and throwing my legs out of bed. "One I'm actually freaking responsible for!"

I didn't need to get out of bed—it was 3am. But I couldn't lie still.

I wasn't exactly averse to dealing with my needs myself. But too many years listening to preachers at strict churches had made me less than comfortable with it. Which was probably why I wasn't very good at it. An awkward embarrassment, even though I was alone, would always descend over me, and my climax — if I even got there — wouldn't really make me feel any more satisfied. Plus, I always spent the next day thinking that everyone I saw knew what I'd been up to.

Irrational, maybe, but that was how it was.

I stamped down the stairs, unsure where I was going. "Stupid damn church," I muttered, throwing in the *damn* deliberately. At least, after a decade of practice, I could blaspheme without feeling guilty.

I made myself a cup of tea and took it back to bed, where I tossed and turned with a book until my alarm rang at seven.

With some relief, I showered and dressed. The Nox in my dream had told me to go to his office in the morning. Real Nox hadn't said anything at all about when I would next see him, but I was his employee, and he did run the company, so sense dictated that his office was where I should go, dream or none.

I spent the entire commute into the city drifting between toe-curling thoughts of my dream, and a weird excitement that he might be telling the truth. It was too vivid, too real, too much like him. I didn't believe that my imagination was capable of what I had dreamed last night. There was no way my subconscious was getting me to say the word *pussy*. Not a freaking chance. Just thinking it made my cheeks heat.

Nox was capable of creating what I had dreamed last night though. The man was sex-on-damn-legs. I had no problem believing that he would behave just like that in real life. Could it really have been him? Inside my head as I slept? Using magic?

I was flip-flopping constantly between the idea being too absurd to consider, and too exciting to ignore.

"'Scuse me," grunted a voice, as I poured myself off the packed underground train alongside the river of other commuters. I tried to shift out of the way, looking in the direction of the voice. My head jerked back in surprise. The guy was covered in hair. I blinked as he nodded. "Cheers."

Fur, I realized. It wasn't hair, it was fur. I gave him a weak smile as we were carried along the underground station corridor in the tide of people.

I rammed my ticket into the barrier machine when I reached it, still doing my best not to stare at the guy covered in fur. He had headphones in, and was completely ignoring me, but I couldn't help my curiosity. He didn't seem self-conscious at all.

Beep. My ticket was spat back out at me and I hissed in annoyance.

"Come through here," called the attendant from the end of the row of machines. I backed my way through the line of people behind me, apologizing awkwardly, and handed my train pass to the attendant. My mouth opened slightly as she took it. She had claws. Not long nails, but claws.

"All the machines are playing up today," she said as she checked my ticket. You can go through." The manual barriers opened when she pressed a button and handed me back my train pass.

"Thanks," I breathed.

What the hell was going on?

I hurried through the rest of the station, half scared to look at the people around me. There was a man to my right, that I could just see in my peripheral vision, who I was fairly sure was glowing green.

When I reached the top of the steps to the Underground, emerging into the cool spring air and bright sunshine, I felt a bit better. I was tired. I had hardly any sleep. My sex-starved brain was just playing tricks on me.

Or the veil Nox told you about really has been lifted and you're starting to believe. I couldn't squash the tiny voice in my head.

"Got any spare coins?" My attention snapped to a homeless woman sitting in the doorway I was passing. She was wrapped in a torn blanket, and her blonde hair was in dreadlocks.

"No, I'm sorry," I said. I wasn't lying, I didn't have any cash. Her eyes flashed bright yellow and a strange sensation spread through my chest, then she smiled.

"Have a nice day," she said, her eyes returning to their normal color.

"You too," I stammered.

I half jogged the rest of the way to the office, barely stopping to say hi to the security guy as I badged my way in. I didn't hesitate to hit the button for the top floor when I reached the elevator bank, shifting my weight impatiently as I waited. I kept my eyes either on the floor, or the screen showing where the elevators were, refusing to even acknowledge the other people milling about, waiting for their own elevators.

I didn't know what was going on, but I could not handle finding out any of my colleagues were vampires. At least not until I spoke to Nox and got this straightened out in my head.

Mercifully, the only guy who got in the same elevator as I did looked totally normal. When I reached the top floor, I raced down the corridor to Nox's new office. I was about to fling the door open, but paused. It could never be said that I didn't learn from my lessons in life.

I knocked, loudly.

"Yes."

"Something is happening, and I don't like it," I said as I pushed my way into the room.

Nox was sitting behind his desk, a newspaper in his hands, a pristine navy suit on, and not a hair out of place. My mind filled with the image of him in the open black shirt, body moving against mine to the thrilling beats of the Latin music, hands through his hair, tight jeans across his ass-

"Good. Come with me."

He stood up, and I blinked the vivid images away. "Where are we going?"

"I told you. On the lake. I want to show you something."

No, no, no. He couldn't know about the lake. "The lake?"

He strode toward where I was still standing in the open doorway. "Yes. The lake." He paused less than a foot away from me, and I stopped myself from inhaling deeply. My pulse quickened. His tongue darted out, wetting his soft lips. His stubble seemed thicker, darker. Rougher. "The lake where you told me how wet your pussy was for me."

Jesus Christ almighty. My knees did a small trembling thing that they had never done before. This wasn't a dream. Nox had actually just said that in real life. Heat crashed through me, my face and my aforementioned pussy both flaming instantly.

Desire blazed in my boss' eyes, and he reached for my hand. "Come on. I need to show you this. It's important."

Mutely, I followed him.

TWENTY

BETH

He led me down the corridor and through a heavy fire door that he had to use a card to open. I said nothing as I followed him up a concrete, unglamorous staircase.

This was real. He was telling the truth. There was more to London, to the entire world, than I thought there was.

Or I was having a breakdown. I mean, it *was* possible. After the trauma of losing my parents, maybe being suspected of murder had tipped me over the edge? Maybe I had decided that this world was too shit to live in and invented a new one. Maybe I was in some hospital bed somewhere, and this was a coma-induced dream.

Nox unlocked another door with his card and held it open for me.

The skygarden. We were on the roof. If my mind hadn't been so buzzing I would have worked out where we were headed sooner — after all, we had taken the stairs up, and his office was on the top floor. There was nowhere else to go.

The space was incredible. Like a giant greenhouse, all the walls and ceilings before me were made of glass, massive metal struts lining them like ribs. The whole of London was spread before us, framed by lush green plants that stretched up into the cavernous roof.

Bright sunshine flooded the room as we walked closer to the panoramic view, and for the first time that day, a slight calm worked its way through my frantic thoughts. The smell of damp earth and rich coffee washed over me, and I realized as I searched for sounds that there were none.

Nobody else was in the skygarden. "Where is everyone?" I whispered into the quiet.

"It won't open for another hour. I've had some breakfast sent up for us."

Along the main glass wall of the room were tables, and there was a counter hidden amongst the ferns and ficuses. Nobody manned the counter though. Nox led the way to a table set with two coffees and a bagel.

"Sit."

I opened my mouth to argue with the command but found I didn't have the words. I sat down.

"Do you like the view?" he asked, as he sat down opposite me.

I cast my eyes over the magnificent vista. Even the muddy brown of the Thames seemed more blue from here. "Yes, but-"

"Beth. Eat the bagel. Drink the coffee. Take some

normality where you can get it. Because this is going to be an interesting day for you. One you will never forget."

Nerves caused my stomach to skitter. Did I want an interesting day that I would never forget?

Yes. The answer flashed into my head immediately.

How the hell could anything be worse than living on my own, in my dead family's apartment, paying off endless debt? And that was the best-case scenario. The worst was that I would be spending the next twenty years in prison for a crime I didn't commit.

I picked up the bagel and forced myself to take a bite. "Nice," I mumbled around it, nodding at Nox. "Thanks."

"You are starting to doubt."

"Huh?"

"You are starting to doubt the world around you, and you are seeing what is behind the Veil."

"Erm, yeah. I think maybe I am."

A slow smile spread across his face, and my heart fluttered. Christ, it wasn't easy conversing with this man.

"This is good."

"It's alarming, is what it is. Are you sure I'm not having a breakdown?"

"If you are, then we are having it together."

I considered his words and decided that a mutual breakdown was better than going solo.

"Right," I said. I took another bite of the bagel. "If you're telling the truth, then I have a lot of questions."

"As I would expect."

"For example, why are fallen angels even a thing? Where have you fallen from?"

"The idea that Heaven and Hell are above and below earth is actually quite accurate. But anyone cast from either place is termed as fallen."

"There are things cast from hell?"

"Other than myself?" He gave me a wicked grin. "Yes. Demons escape sometimes."

My mouth dropped open. "Who catches them?"

"Creatures who are trained to do so. But some evade capture and stay here forever."

"There are demons living here? Among normal people?"

He gave a low chuckle. "You're more worried about running into a demon than drinking coffee with the devil?"

I did some more fish-like opening and closing of my mouth as I scrabbled for a response.

"Beth, the easiest way to answer your questions is as they come up. We could be here a long time otherwise."

"This is too crazy," I said, feeling myself begin to sweat slightly in the warm space. I turned, focusing on the city below us. I could just make out people, scurrying about like tiny ants, all with their own purposes. *All with their own freaking species.* "I saw a homeless girl this morning and her eyes glowed yellow and my chest felt weird."

"A veritas sprite."

"A what?"

"A sprite who knows if someone is lying."

"What happens if you lie to her?"

Nox shrugged. "I'm assuming you didn't, so don't worry about it."

Panic was starting to mingle with the confusion, and I wasn't sure I wanted to be in the glass room anymore. I wanted real air. "Nox, can we go outside?"

He reached across the table in a swift movement, scooping up my hand. "I like hearing you say my name," he said, his voice low.

"Well, I like breathing fresh air," I said, my chest getting tight as his energy tingled through me, like it always did when he touched me. Was that magic too? "Please, can we go outside?"

He stood up, pulling me with him, and I saw that there was a door onto the patio along the outside edge of the glass. "How are you with heights?"

"Fine."

I gulped down cool morning air as soon as we got through the doors and leaned back against the cold glass. We were high enough that I couldn't smell the constant London fumes, and could only just hear the car horns, the sirens, the buskers, the cranes, and the shouts and calls that made up the permanent song of the city. A low hum was all that made its way so high.

"It's honestly all real?" I said, looking at Nox. "You're the devil?"

"Do you still want to see me?"

The blue light sparked to life in his eyes, flames dancing. He wanted me to say yes. I could feel it with every fiber of my being. That addictive confidence I so often felt around him coiled up through me, making my tense muscles relax, and my churning thoughts slow.

"Yes."

"There's no going back from this, Beth. This is it."

"Show me."

He took a step back, then another. My breath caught as he reached the rails, then unbuttoned his jacket.

"What are you doing?"

He didn't answer my question as he draped it carefully over the railing, then began to unbutton his shirt too.

"Please tell me you haven't staged all of this just to get naked." My casual tone belied my racing heart and somersaulting stomach.

His lips quirked into a smile, but he still didn't speak.

When he slid his shirt off his shoulders, I became seriously grateful for the glass support behind me.

He looked like he had been sculpted from marble, he was so perfect. Olive toned skin stretched taut across cords of muscle, and his shoulders seemed somehow bigger, now that they were bare. His biceps bulged as he draped the shirt over the jacket, and I let out a breath as I got a glimpse of his broad, powerful back.

I tried to keep my gaze high when he turned back to me but failed. My eyes were dragged inexorably down to perfectly defined abs and a V of muscle over his hips that drew my gaze lower still.

I needed him. I needed to feel him, to touch him, to caress him, to—

"Are you ready?"

Unable to trust myself to speak, I nodded.

"Open your mind. Your soul. Believe because you want it to be true."

I wanted him. I wanted him to be true. Did that count?

Light flared around him suddenly, and I gasped. "Nox," I started to say, but the word never made it out.

Wings, made of pure gold light, erupted from his back. My heart almost stopped beating altogether as they expanded, rippling as they settled, spreading out behind him. They started high above his head and trailed down to his feet, and they were, without a doubt, the most beautiful things I'd ever seen in my life.

"Nox," I tried again, this time the word coming out as a faint whisper.

The light dimmed enough that I could make out huge feathers, shining like liquid metal, gleaming with an ethereal light that I knew was not of this world.

They rippled again, widening for a moment and giving me a view of the hundreds of smaller feathers lining the underside. "Nox, they're... they're..."

"They're real."

I pushed myself slowly off the glass.

I knew they were real. I knew it as surely as I knew my own damn name. They were the most real, most right, most perfect things in the world.

"Can I touch them?"

He paused, and with a mammoth effort I forced my eyes from the golden feathers to his face.

"No. Not yet."

"Can... Can you fly?" I tilted my head as I gazed at his wings, and they fluttered a little in response. When they moved, the light seemed to move like liquid across them, the gold color intensifying in waves. At the bottom of each huge wing, where they tucked back into his body, the feathers looked softer, and lighter. More like real feathers. I was *desperate* to touch them.

"Yes."

"I've always had dreams about flying." I murmured the words, not really aware I was saying them. Images of soaring through the skies, so high I could escape anything or anyone, raced through my mind.

"Do you believe me now?"

"Yes."

"Good." His eyes fixed on mine. He looked... godly. There was no other way to describe him. The poise and elegance he always had about him had given way to something otherworldly, and power rolled from him in waves, drenching me in awe.

I let out a long breath as I drank in the sight of him, shirtless and glowing, golden wings utterly breathtaking.

He had been right. There was no going back.

"Today will be difficult for you. You will see things that you are not expecting everywhere." With a quick stretch and a final flutter, the wings vanished.

"No! Wait—" I started, but Nox cut me off.

"I have something that needs attending to, then I will come to your apartment. You should stay there and wait for me."

"But I only just got to the office." *And you have no shirt on and freaking wings,* my brain added. I didn't want to go back home. An almost childlike excitement was building inside me that needed someplace to go, along with about a thousand questions. "You have wings, Nox. Wings!"

The serious expression on his face slipped ever-so-slightly. "Big wings," he said.

"Bigger than other fallen angels?"

"The biggest."

"Oh my god, I can't believe you were telling the truth. Magic is real? Actual magic? Can you read minds?"

"Only when you're dreaming."

"Can you snap your fingers and go anywhere?"

"No."

"Can you wave your hand and make stuff come to you. Like this bagel?" I held up my half-eaten bagel hopefully.

"No."

"Oh. Are there any other magical things who can?"

"Yes. And they're not called magical things. We call them supernaturals."

"Right. Got it. How many are there?"

"Many. Beth, I can't answer all of your questions now."

"But you have wings!" I was not acting quite as cool about the whole situation as I would have liked, but I also wasn't totally losing my shit. Which made me wonder if I had subconsciously started to believe in the idea of another, magical, world earlier than now. Maybe I'd even started to believe it all those years ago, when I thought it was the only avenue left to me to find my parents.

"I'm glad they've made such an impression on you."

"An impression? Are you kidding? They're the most incredible things I've ever seen."

Heat rolled from him, his eyes alive with electric light. He reached for his shirt. "Thank you. Now, go home and take some time. It's a lot to process. Then, we'll have a chat with our respective leads."

"Oh. Yeah." I was a suspect in a murder case. My boss having giant gold wings had removed that from my mind, for a short while at least.

"Rory will ride back to your place with you and fill you in on a few things you should know."

"Who's Rory?"

"My assistant."

"The pixie?"

"Yes." He began to button up his shirt, and the action drew my eyes to his hands. And the exposed skin of his chest that they were moving over.

"Right," I said. I did not have room in my head for magic, murder, *and* muscles. Something was going to have to give. And I sure as hell hoped it was going to be murder.

TWENTY-ONE

BETH

Nox gave me one last searing look, then strode back into the building, leaving me alone on the skygarden balcony. A surreal feeling washed over me with his departure, and I took a long breath, grateful for the moment alone. I stared out over the sunlit city far below and gripped the railing, my mind racing.

Magic was real. Which meant...

My parents may still be alive.

I couldn't help making the mental leap. If there was a whole world I was only now aware of, then surely that's where they had gone? I always knew that they couldn't have vanished without trace. It simply wasn't possible. But nor were outrageously hot Irish millionaires with wings made of gold light - until ten minutes ago.

I had to concentrate on clearing my name of murder. Then, if Nox still had any interest me in me, maybe he would help me look for them. I mean, who was more likely to know where to start than the damn devil?

A surge of guilt and fear made my bagel taste sour at the word devil. I had spent many years learning just how evil, cruel and corruptive the devil was. But Nox didn't seem to be any of those things. Well, maybe he could corrupt me a little... My recent dreams flashed into my head and I felt my knees go slightly weak again. If magic was real, then did that mean the dreams were, too? Had Nox really stood behind me with his hand in my dress and asked me how wet my pussy was?

An unintelligible noise escaped me, and I shook my head firmly. What was important was finding the murderer. And getting my head around magic existing.

"Are you ready?" A bored-sounding female voice drew my attention to the balcony door. A woman was standing there looking at me, and my jaw dropped for the tenth time that day.

She was gorgeous. Not just attractive, but full-on, supermodel beautiful. She was six feet tall, with wide hips and a full chest, and the most beautiful skin I'd ever seen, a rich coffee color. Her hair was baby pink and fell in thick waves around her shoulders.

"Er, hi," I said, stunned into awkwardness.

"Let's go." She whirled on her heels, and I moved fast to catch her up.

"Are you Rory?"

"Yep. Short for Furor. So don't piss me off."

She had a British accent, clean and clipped, and she already sounded pissed off.

"Furor?"

"Latin for angry." She didn't turn to look at me as I finally caught up to her. "You not go to school?"

"We, er, didn't study Latin at my school."

"No, I don't suppose you did. Well, most supernaturals are named after Latin words, so you'd better learn. Now that you've been invited in."

She did not sound happy about my invitation. "Where are we going?"

"Elevator, and then wherever it is that you live."

The frosty reception from someone so intimidatingly beautiful was sufficient to keep me silent as I followed her the rest of the way to the elevators. I had enough going on without needing to work out why a pixie named after anger seemed to have a problem with me.

We rode to the bottom floor in awkward silence, more and more questions stacking up in my head.

"Thanks for sorting out the whole veil-lifting thing," I tried when we got to the bottom. "Nox said that it took you a while to sort it out."

"That's because humans shouldn't be able to see behind the Veil. It's there for a reason." Her eyes settled on my face, accusingly, before she turned and strode from the elevator into the main lobby of the building.

"Oh." I trotted after her. Was that what her problem was? That I was human? The very idea that she *wasn't* human was weird enough. Maybe that's how she walked so fast in four-inch heels. "Nox said pixies can't be seen by humans," I said, remembering what he told me.

"Nope. Relegated to the Veil."

"Does that bother you?"

"Let's just get this sorted now, shall we?" She turned to me, and I saw a red glow ringing her dark irises. "I am not your friend or your employee. I'm here because Mr. Nox asked me to be. I'll answer your questions about the Veil and nothing more."

"Right," I said.

"Good." She pivoted, and we were off again.

Claude smiled at me when we got onto the street, holding the door to the town car open. "Hi, Claude," I said quickly as I climbed into the car after Rory.

"Good luck, Miss Abbott," he whispered with a grin.

"So. What do you want to know?"

"Huh?"

"Christ, Nox normally has better taste than this. What do you want to know about the Veil?" She looked at me like I was stupid, and my dignity finally began to bristle.

"Look, I'm a little on the back foot here," I said, straightening in my seat. "There's no need to be rude."

Rory rolled her eyes. "There's always a need to be rude. I'll start, if you can't come up with anything."

"I-" I began, but she talked over me.

"The magical world that I am from, *and you are not,* is nicknamed the Veil, after the magic that hides it. London, and a few other heavily populated cities in the world, have the most supernatural inhabitants. They tend to stick together, to feed off each other's magic. They are no threat to humans, for the most part, as there are more powerful entities keeping them in check."

She picked at her long pink fingernails as she spoke.

"Entities like Nox?" I asked, remembering what he said about wild ones.

"Once, yes. Now, not so much."

"What do you mean?"

"It's not important. What is important is that you don't freak out when you see a vampire or a wolf shifter and fuck everything up for the rest of us."

I blinked at her. "I think I saw a wolf person this morning."

"Good for you. Did you freak out?" She gave me a look. How could anyone with resting-bitch-face be so attractive? "Brilliant," she said with a sigh. "You freaked out, didn't you?"

"No. I was just a bit... starey."

"Starey is fine. Freaking out is not. That clear?"

I nodded. "Yes."

She cocked her head at me, her gaze intensifying suddenly. "Why is he so interested in you? You are supremely ordinary."

"I'd rather be ordinary than rude," I retorted. I thought I saw a small quirk at the corner of her mouth before she looked away.

"Being rude has many advantages. Spend much more time with the devil and you'll learn that for yourself."

· · ·

I had so many questions but found myself un-inclined to ask the moody pixie anything else as we wove our way through the city traffic to Wimbledon. I wanted to talk to Nox, not to her.

She gave me a cursory glance when we reached my home, so I employed my best kill-'em-with-kindness voice, thanked her for her help, and told her I hoped she had a lovely day. She just rolled her eyes in response.

It took less than an hour for me to grow bored of being alone, the restless impatience returning in full force. Only now, it was even worse. Now there was magic outside. Potentially around every corner. A thrilling sort of fear welled up in me every time I thought about all the things I'd done in my life, now knowing there had been another world just out of sight the whole time.

My mind raced through my own memories, casting teachers I disliked as evil sprites, and replaying every coincidence I had ever experienced as a wild act of magic.

I had hundreds of questions, and every time I thought of one, another took its place. I couldn't keep track of them. Who was in charge of the gods? Was there a king, or queen, or president? Did our kings and queens and presidents know about supernaturals? Who created the magic in the first place? What did Rory mean about them feeding off each other's magic? Who policed them? Why couldn't pixies be in the human world? Where did the shifters turn into wolves in a packed urban city like London?

After my third unhelpful cup of tea, I gave up churning through my list of questions, and did what I always did when I was unsettled. I made my way across the lawn to see Francis.

I decided not to tell my raucous friend about the veil, or supernaturals. Not because I thought she wouldn't believe me. She probably would. But because I thought that giving my million-mile-an-hour thoughts a chance to slow down would do me some good. I wanted to talk about something normal, something to offset the crazy.

I made my way into Lavender Oaks cautiously, half-expecting everyone I saw to be covered in fur or have glowing eyes. If Francis was a supernatural, I didn't know what I would do. Not a lot, I realized, as I considered the possibility. Nothing would change the way she'd looked out for me for last five years. And she was already nuts - what difference would some fur make?

I stalled as I walked into the recreation room and spotted Francis in her La-Z-Boy.

She wasn't alone.

"Cooo-eeee!" She waved as she saw me in the doorway. The man beside her stood up and gave me a slow smile, and my body reacted to him instinctively. Heat washed through me, and my heart skipped a beat.

What the hell was Nox doing in Lavender Oaks?

"I thought I might find you here," he said as I reached them, and I could swear his Irish lilt was stronger.

"Did you now?" I smiled through gritted teeth. He gestured to the chair he had been sitting in, next to Francis. She beamed at me.

"Mr. Nox has been telling me all about what a good job you do," she said.

"Is that right?"

"Yes. And I told him how good you are at Monopoly." She gave me an exaggerated wink, and my stomach clenched as I sank into the chair.

Oh god. What had she told him? *Please don't let her have talked to him about sex,* I prayed silently.

"Francis tells me that you never cheat," Nox said, taking a seat opposite us. Amusement sparkled in his eyes. I fixed mine on his, determination settling over me. This was my space. My world. My friend. The only place I had a hope of not being intimidated by him.

"She's right. I don't. You know this isn't normal, right?"

"I don't know what you mean."

"Traditionally, it's normal for people to introduce you to their friends, rather than you tracking them down and introducing yourself."

He held his hands up, and his perfect suit jacket fell open. "I was halfway to your door, and just thought I'd take a look, and see why you liked it so much. I'm sorry if I've overstepped."

He spoke slowly, and I couldn't tell if his apology was sincere or not. It didn't seem to matter to Francis though.

"Honey, don't you dare give this nice man grief about visiting me! Hell, I ain't had nobody that looks like him visit me since..." she trailed off, casting her eyes ceiling-ward as she thought hard. "Since 'sixty-four. And he was actually nicer looking than you. Had an enormous-"

"Well, we'd better be going!" My voice was a little shrill as I cut her off. The heavens only knew what her visitor in 'sixty-four owned that was enormous, but I was not about to discuss it in front of Nox.

"But you just got here." She looked genuinely sad, and guilt pulled at me.

"I'm sorry, I just wanted to check in on you before what might be a long few days," I told her.

She nodded sagely. "With the murder investigation. Mr. Nox here said you were investigating up two leads."

"Erm, yeah." My lead was human, his was a fallen angel. This was going to take some getting used to.

"Miss Abbott? Mr. Nox?"

The voice carried across the massive recreation room and we all turned to look. Inspector Singh and a uniformed officer I hadn't seen before were striding toward us.

My eyes flicked to Nox in alarm, and his expression turned dark. He stood up as they reached us. I stayed where I was, trying, and failing, to stop the fear that they had come to arrest me from making my throat close up.

"Your driver told us we could find you in here," the Inspector said to Nox, then turned to me. "I need to talk to you both about something we found at the scene of the crime. Do either of you recognize this?" She had pulled her phone out of her pocket and turned it around to show us a photograph.

It was of a long white feather, a yellow police marker next to it showing how large it was. One foot, according to the marker. One side of the feather seemed to be tinged a darker grey.

I shook my head. "It's a feather," I said. "Who would recognize a single feather?"

Even as I said the words, my mind exploded with the sight of Nox's wings. *The fallen angel that Nox suspected.* Could this feather belong to her?

I wasn't sure I hid the widening of my eyes from the keen gaze of the Inspector, but I schooled my face into mild confusion. She frowned at me and then looked to Nox. "Did you have a feather like this in your office before the murder?"

"No." His voice was hard, the sensuality often in his tone when he spoke to me nowhere to be heard.

Inspector Singh sighed and put the phone back in her suit pants pocket. "Have you heard from Alex?"

"No. I told you that I would let you know if I did."

"Be sure that you do."

"I'm surprised you haven't found him yet," said Nox.

She raised her eyebrow at him, in a *don't push me* kind of expression. "Druggies and petty thieves are good at moving around. There's bloody hundreds of them in London." Her words sank like lead to the pit of my stomach. I had been living with what the police considered a 'druggie and petty thief'.

And now you can live in a world with magic, without

him. My inner voice was more confident than I had heard it in a long while.

I stood up.

"You'll be the first to know if he makes contact," I said. My palms were sweating but I wasn't going to let myself look weak. "And please, let me know if there's anything else I can do to help."

"Can you tell me why there was a big feather at my murder scene?"

Shit. She *had* seen my expression change when I made the connection to angel wings. How was I supposed to explain that? I shook my head.

"Then the only thing you can do, Miss Abbott, is give your passport to my constable."

"What?"

"You're a flight risk. I wouldn't want you to follow any urges to fly back home to America any time soon."

I tried to swallow, but there was a lump the size of a golf-ball in the way and my mouth was abruptly void of any liquid. Unlike the rest of my body, which had started sweating profusely.

"We will go and get it for you now," said Nox. I snapped my increasingly frantic eyes to his.

We. He had said we. I wasn't on my own. I didn't need to go to pieces. Not yet.

"Fine. We'll wait by your car."

As soon as they were gone, I sank back into the chair, gratefully taking the glass of water Francis thrust at me.

"You weren't wrong, honey. She does not like you."

"They haven't arrested you. We have time." Nox's voice was low and soothing, a balm to my frazzled nerves.

"Yet," I said, looking up at him. "They haven't arrested me yet. They want my damn passport!" It hadn't even occurred to me to leave the country. Maybe it should have.

Nox dropped into a crouch in front of me, moving himself so I couldn't look anywhere other than into his face. Warmth wrapped around me. "We have a deal, Beth. I intend to keep my half."

TWENTY-TWO

BETH

Nox waited outside my front door when I went to get my passport. I supposed I should have been grateful that it wasn't one of the things Alex had stolen. The police would never have believed me if I told them I didn't have it.

I pulled it from the drawer I kept it in and felt a pang of sadness as I looked at the little blue book. I hadn't used it since abandoning the search for my parents and coming to London. As soon as we were able to prove that I didn't kill Sarah, I was going to talk to Nox about my parents' disappearance, I resolved.

If we could prove I didn't kill Sarah.

The Inspector nodded her thanks when I handed over my passport, then the two police officers got in their car, and left. The second they were gone, Nox turned to me.

"We need to escalate our own investigation," he said.

He was right.

He had been telling the truth about magic this whole time. If a supernatural had killed Sarah then I really was in trouble - the police weren't going to find the real killer. And freaking out about going to prison, or magic existing for that matter, wasn't going to help.

I had to put my big-girl pants on and find the killer myself. Or at least, with the help of the devil. He was still my best chance at clearing my name, and he was committed to helping me. *In return for what could be the best damn night of your life.* I screwed my face up and pushed that particular train of thought to the back of my mind, to deal with later. *Murder before muscles, Beth,* I told myself firmly.

"For once, I agree with you," I said, turning to face Nox and forcing as much authority into my tone as I could muster. "But if a supernatural is involved, how do we convince the Inspector to believe us?"

"If we can prove it, then the Veil authorities will deal with it."

"How?"

"If my suspicions are correct, then I will report the fallen angel responsible, and get permission to use magic to make the police abandon the case."

I gaped at him. "Abandon the case? How?"

"There are some very persuasive sprites in the city. They can make anybody forget anything."

I did not like the sound of that. But if they could make the police forget about me...

"Do they do what you tell them to?"

"If I were to force a sprite to do something as serious as get involved in a murder case, I would be cast from this world by the gods."

"I'm glad you mentioned the gods," I said, holding up a hand and putting the other on my hip in a gesture I hoped conveyed that I was serious about getting answers. "They're in charge, right?"

He frowned, his face still beautiful even when it was creased up. "Did Rory not tell you this?"

"Erm, not really, no. Anyway, I want to hear it from you."

"We'll talk on the way." He moved to the car, and Claude leapt out to open the door for him.

"On the way where?"

"To interview my lead."

"We do not know how many gods there are, nor if there is one in particular in charge," Nox said when we were on our way back to the city. "They have strict rules for the supernatural. If they are broken, then the offender can't live here anymore."

"Where do they go?"

"It depends. But not this world."

I blew out a breath and decided that processing the idea of other worlds was too much. I'd come back to that when I'd got my head around more immediate issues. "Rory said something about them all living in just a few cities because they feed off each other's magic. What does that mean?"

"Magic is not limitless. But it lasts a lot longer when it's near other magic."

"Right. We'll talk more about that later," I said, not really understanding.

"Will we?" He smirked at me, eyes darkening, and my insides wobbled.

"Yes. We will," I snapped. I needed to keep control, not let my stupid, randy body dictate my relationship with this man. I did not want to go to prison. First step passport, second step arrest. I was running out of time. "Are there magic police?"

"There are enforcers of the rules."

"You said before that fallen angels are the most powerful?"

"Yes."

"And you have to stick to the gods' rules as well?"

"Even more so."

"What are the rules?"

He looked away from me, out of the car window. "There are many. As many as your world has. We live by the same standards and morals as the human world."

"But you're the devil."

He moved his head slowly, until he was looking at me again. A little tendril of discomfort coiled around my gut. "Angels have the power to influence. Fallen angels are no exception. But my function in life is not to make people want to kill each other, I assure you."

"So..." I bit down on my lip as I tried to word my question. "What *is* your function in life?"

Dark shadows swirled across the bright blue of his eyes before he answered me. "To punish those who abuse the seven deadly sins. The scum of humanity." A dangerous, bitter edge laced his words, and I wanted to sink back into the leather of the seat. But I knew I had to keep pushing him if I wanted answers.

"Okay. So, if you're in charge of punishing the scum if humanity, then..." I gulped. "How come you don't already know who the killer is? By magic?"

His eyes turned onyx-black, and heat swamped the back of the car. "I am no longer in charge of punishing anyone. That honor was removed from me when I gave up my power over four of the seven sins." He said the word honor as though it was anything but, and barely-contained anger simmered in his voice.

"I'm guessing you don't want to talk about this?" I was becoming seriously uncomfortable, both the heat and the anger radiating from him making me want to roll the window down and jump out.

Some of the darkness leaked from his eyes, sparks of blue returning. "I am sorry. I find it harder than usual to control myself around you."

"Really? Why?"

He ignored my question. "I still own Lust, Greed and Gluttony. I punish nobody. That is all you need to know for now."

"Okay," I nodded. "Which sin is murder?"

"None of them, directly, though a murder will always have been motivated by one of them." He took a deep breath. I had never seen him look so unsettled. The air in the car felt heavy, a dangerous thrum ringing through it that made something intense and restless course through me.

"Just one more question," I said, and he nodded curtly. "The woman we are visiting, what sin does she own?"

"Wrath."

I swallowed. "Wrath. That sounds pretty murdery," I said quietly.

The car stopped in front of a building I must have walked past a thousand times on my many commutes through London City center. Everybody called it the Gherkin, because, well, it looked like one.

Rising from its concrete mount like a giant bulbous bullet, it was made entirely of smoke colored glass; except for the black lines that curved their way up and around the structure like geometric vines. The rounded peak at the top was made from darker glass and I'd heard there was a restaurant and bar up there.

"Wrath works in the Gherkin?" I asked disbelievingly, as we got out of the car.

"According to my research team." Nox pulled his jacket sleeves down, and my eyes skimmed his muscular frame. "Most of the people she keeps around her are supernaturals. Are you ready for this? You can stay in the car if you'd rather."

"No, I'm ready," I said, even though I wasn't sure I was.

A flicker of approval crossed his face and then he strode to the entrance of the building.

The building exterior was made up of sections of interlocking triangles, giving the rounded shape it's geometric look, and the ground floor was accessed through massive cut-outs in the bottom layer of triangles.

When we walked into the building my senses were assaulted by gleaming white. Other than the chrome reception desk and matching metallic columns, white was everywhere, from the floor all the way up to the very high ceilings.

The security guard nodded at Nox as we made our way to the reception desk.

"I'm here to see Miss Madaleine," he said to the smart looking guy behind the counter. There was nobody else in the room, I realized as I cast my eyes about the minimal space.

"Do you have an appointment?"

"She will see me. Please let her know that Mr. Nox is here." A sultry power had slipped into Nox's voice and the receptionists face softened.

"Of course, Mr. Nox."

As he picked up the phone, I hissed at Nox. "Is he a supernatural?"

"No."

"Then why is he doing what you told him to?"

"I think you're forgetting that I'm quite well known in human circles too," he replied quietly.

Oh yeah. My boss, the millionaire. "Right," I muttered.

A moment later the guy got off the phone and came around the desk to us. "Follow me, please." He took us to a white hallway filled with elevators, and I expected him to press the button on the large console to call one. Instead, he kept moving until we reached a small, unassuming door beyond the shiny chrome elevators. Pressing his badge to the unit on the door, he turned and smiled at us. "Have a good meeting," he said, then turned and made his way back to his desk.

Nox pushed open the door and I followed.

Once again, I was faced with something I didn't expect. The stairs behind the door led down, instead of up. "I didn't know there was anything under the Gherkin," I said.

"That's because there's not supposed to be."

The steps were, somewhat unsurprisingly, white, and it took what felt like an age to descend them. I found myself watching the way Nox's shoulders moved as I followed him down, and my mind cheerfully pictured them moving in different ways. Moving as he pressed me against a wall, my hands held high above my head in his strong grip, his biceps bulging, his bare chest against mine...

"Do not speak, even if she speaks to you," Nox said.

"Isn't that rude?" I answered, shaking the images

from my head and glad he couldn't see my guilty expression.

"No."

"Well, it seems rude to me."

"Most things seem rude to you."

"It's not my fault I was brought up properly," I retorted.

He threw a glance over his shoulder at me, and I almost poked my tongue out at him. The look in his eyes stopped me though. "You'll need to redefine rude when I'm done with you."

Oh god. The heat was back, rushing straight to my core. I could see my desire mirrored in his gaze before he turned back to the stairs.

I kept my mouth clamped shut until we reached the bottom, trying not to squirm as I walked.

A white marble door set in large ornate archway was waiting after the last step, totally at odds with the super-modern lobby of the building.

"Remember, say nothing," Nox said, then knocked on the door.

If I had thought stairs going down instead of up were a surprise, boy was I unprepared for what I saw when the door swung open.

TWENTY-THREE

BETH

The only colors in the cathedral-like room were white and chrome. The whole thing appeared to be made of marble; floors, walls and ceilings alike, and against the back wall was a water fountain twice the height of me, running into a pool that ran most of the length of the room. The water glistened, reflecting all of the white and metal. Palm trees made entirely of shining chrome dotted the space along the edge of the pool, and white loungers and chairs sat under their metal fronds. A long couch with fluffy white cushions lined one side of the room, and woman was reclined on it, a magazine in her hand.

"You're supposed to make an appointment, Nox," she said, without looking up. He walked toward her, and I quit my gaping and moved to keep up with him. My footsteps were silent on the marble and I was grateful I'd worn flats instead of heels.

Movement caught my eye and I saw somebody sit up

from one of the pool loungers to look at us. He had jet-black hair, and equally dark eyes. And *horns*. They jutted, short and sharp, from his forehead, and I squeezed my mouth shut to keep my jaw from dropping again. He had no shirt on, and his chest was covered in hair. He gave me a slow smile when he saw me looking at him. I snapped my eyes back ahead of me.

"Madaleine. Always a pleasure. It was harder to find you this time. Well done," Nox said, coming to a stop in front of the woman. She sighed and sat up, swinging her legs gracefully off the couch.

Her eyes fell on me before Nox, and there was a beat of silence as we took each other in.

She was wearing a white suit, cut beautifully, and clearly expensive. She had no shirt on under the jacket, which fastened perfectly at the widest point across her chest, and an expanse of porcelain cleavage was on show. She had white hair braided back from her face, white eyebrows, and cheekbones that could cut glass. The only color about her at all was a hint of amber in her mostly gray irises.

Even if I hadn't been told that she had the power of Wrath, I would have known there was something... wrong. There was a presence about her, a dangerous gleam in her eyes, and a fierceness that didn't speak of courage, but of fear, emanating from her.

"I'm glad I gave your team a challenge. And who is this?" she purred.

"A new assistant of mine." I suppressed my scowl.

"She's human."

"Yes."

"Can she see through the Veil?"

"Yes."

"Good. I fucking hate what this place looks like to those miserable mortals. Look what they've made me do to it."

She waved her hand and the pool and metal palms vanished, a clean white office appearing in its stead. The couch she was on became a large leather office chair, white of course, and a long desk appeared between us.

She waved her hand again and shook her head as it all vanished, the pool returning. Her eyes glowed red. "It's enough to make one quite angry."

"I thought all this lack of color kept you calm?"

"It did, until you two strode in, all glowing and bright." She glared at my pale blue shirt.

"I need to ask you something." Nox' voice was serious.

Madaleine stood up and I jumped in surprise as the horned guy stepped out of nowhere and handed her a drink. I had only been able to see his top half when he sat up on the lounger, but now that he was standing, I could see that he had nothing on at all. I snapped my eyes up from his middle and fixed them on Madaleine.

Please don't blush. Please don't blush.

"Oh, how cute. Your new assistant is uncomfortable around demon dick."

A low rumble sounded from Nox, and I stood straighter as she smiled at me.

"This is Cornu. My new pet," Madaleine said,

gesturing at the horned guy. "They're letting quite a few demons out at the moment, Nox. You should invest. They're ever so good at some things." Her eyes dropped pointedly to Nox's waist, and I felt an unexpected spark of hatred for the woman.

"Thanks, but I'm not in the market."

"No. I don't suppose you are." There was a gleam in her eyes, and I felt a pulse of heat come from Nox. "What do you want?"

"Did you hear about the woman who was killed in my office?"

"Of course."

"Do you know anything about it?"

"No."

"May I see your wings?"

"Absolutely not."

Nox straightened, more heat rippling into the room from him. "A white feather was found in my office, Madaleine. And some valuable property of mine is missing. I want to know if you had anything to do with it."

I looked at him sharply. *Why the hell hadn't he mentioned missing property before now?*

"Are you threatening me?"

"Yes. Show me your wings."

"You have no authority, Nox. I need to do nothing you tell me to." She put her hands on her hips, her eyes narrowed.

"You don't need to, no. But I strongly advise that you do." He seemed to be filling more space somehow, and an undeniable power was seeping into the air.

My senses were firing everywhere, my fight or flight instincts kicking in of their own accord. I shifted my weight anxiously, unable to keep still, and unable to move away.

She regarded him for a long moment, the color in her eyes shifting between red and amber. Eventually, she shrugged and looked at me. "Don't you get fed up with men and their constant fucking need to show everyone how big and strong and powerful they are?"

"Wings. Now," Nox barked, before I could say anything.

"For fucks sake, there's no need to be an asshole about it." There was a brilliant white light behind her, and when it faded, large white wings framed her body.

Nox was right. His were bigger. And far more beautiful.

But still... She looked angelic. The feathers looked harder than the gold ones in Nox's wings, almost as though they were cut from ice. They fluttered and she held her hands out. "Satisfied? No missing feathers."

Nox stepped forward, looking closely at her wings. "They have been damaged recently," he growled.

"Cornu likes to play rough," she said with a sickly-sweet smile. "Don't you, you naughty boy."

Cornu gave a low chuckle. I managed to keep my eyes on his face as I looked at him, and he held my gaze, licking his lips slowly.

"If I find out you have stolen from me, I will not take it to the authorities," Nox said. "I will deal with you personally."

"Oh, I love being dealt with personally," she answered, eyes flashing red again, and her wings extending behind her. She emanated her own aura of danger, and it occurred to me that if these two ever fought it would be both spectacular to watch and utterly lethal. Another inexplicable bolt of jealousy gripped my chest at the idea of them close, even in combat.

"I mean it Madaleine. I want what is mine returned."

"Nox, if you're careless enough to lose shit that's important to you, then that is your problem. As is being stupid enough to kill a girl in your own office. Now fuck off. I'm busy."

A blast of heat rocketed out from where Nox was standing, and she hissed and stumbled backward. A pink flush covered her extraordinarily pale skin, and her wings pulsed red so briefly I thought I might have imagined it. "Get out, now, or I might lose control of Wrath," she said, and her lazy drawl had gone, a primal snarl replacing it. "And whilst you might enjoy the challenge, I doubt your human friend would survive. You wouldn't want two dead girls to deal with, would you?"

"You forget your place. I will make it my mission to remind you," Nox growled, then turned, taking my elbow and practically marching me out of the room.

As soon as we were on the stairs, I snatched my arm back. "Was she really going to kill me?"

"No." His face was a mask of anger and I raised my eyebrows at him. "When I am with you, nothing can

harm you. She forgets who I am. How powerful I am."
He was furious, I realized, as an actual sizzling sound
came from him. As though it were contagious, I felt my
own temper simmering up, adrenaline from the exchange
with the embodiment of Wrath fueling my emotion. My
hands were beginning to shake, and I balled them into
fists.

"Look, if you want to march around reminding
people how powerful you are, you can do it on your own.
This morning, I didn't even believe in magic, and now
fallen angels are talking about killing me."

His eyes bore into mine, dark with shadows. An overwhelming feeling was bubbling up inside me, all the
pent-up frustration and fear coming together into something I couldn't keep inside.

"I'm fed up with feeling like an idiot. Everyone
around you thinks I'm too damn weak to speak for myself,
and you're no better. Why didn't you tell me, or the
police, that something was stolen from your office? Is this
a game to you? Do you think so little of my future, my
life?"

My eyes were burning, and my voice was getting
louder. I swallowed, trying to control myself. I was angry.
I felt so weak and out of my damn depth, and crying
would be the worst thing I could do.

"I am working to clear your name of murder. The
games I play are with my own life, not yours." Nox's
words were cold, and my insides seemed to turn cold
with them, as though the warmth and confidence that his
presence usually filled me with had been sucked away.

"We need to leave." He started up the stairs, and I closed my eyes, sucking in a breath before I followed.

We didn't speak until we reached the car, and the longer we spent in silence, the angrier I became. The murder might be connected to a theft that he had kept a secret. There was more to this than I, or the police, knew, but he had known the whole time.

"Why didn't you tell me something was stolen? We were supposed to be working together," I said, as Claude climbed out of the car.

"I need to leave."

"What?"

Nox spun to face me, and I couldn't help taking a step backward. There was no blue left in his eyes at all, and searing heat rippled off his skin like hot asphalt, making it look like it was moving.

"Claude will take you home. I will see you tomorrow." He turned and was lost in the thrum of commuters in seconds.

I saw a flash of horns and a smattering of fur as my eyes swept the crowd, but no Nox.

Claude's voice reached me. "We should get going, Miss Abbott."

"You're damn right, we should," I hissed, and swung back to the car. "But I'm not going home."

TWENTY-FOUR

BETH

"Miss, I really think that we should head back to Wimbledon," said Claude from the front cab.

"Claude, are you magic?" If he wasn't, I was at least sure that he knew about supernaturals. He'd let too many things slip.

"Yes, Miss Abbott."

I nodded. "I assumed as much. Claude, up until this morning, I didn't believe magic existed. Since then, I have seen my boss sprout golden wings, had my passport removed by the police, been given grief from an angry pixie and been threatened by an even angrier fallen angel. And your boss's reaction to this has been to march off and leave me to sit in my apartment and wait to be arrested. Everyone seems to expect me to stand quietly and nod politely at people who all know more about everything than I do. Well, I'm done with that. Done, Claude."

A fury that I suspected might have been building

since Alex left was crashing through me in unstoppable waves. All the restlessness of the last few days was coming to a head, I could feel it. And to my surprise, I was relishing it.

My whole life, mom had told me to take the high road, to react to unpleasant situations with dignity, be the better person. So I did. I was polite, and I often did as I was asked. I made an effort to make other people's lives easier. I was a decent person.

And where the hell had it got me? I'd lost my parents, I was neck-deep in debt, my ex was an asshole cheat, and I was about to be arrested for a murder I didn't commit. Nobody had any damn respect for me.

If Nox thought for one minute I was about to become his little human pet, there to *ooh* and *aah* every time he turned up the heat or got his wings out, he had another thing coming.

I didn't need his help. I didn't need his stupid deal. Whether magic existed or not, I didn't need him.

The police could not prove that I had done something that I hadn't. It simply wasn't possible for them to find evidence that I was their killer. The only thing they had going for them was the fact that I was the only person other than her boyfriend who had a motive, and I didn't have an alibi.

If I could find another suspect without an alibi, then they couldn't pin it on me. There would be too much doubt for a conviction.

It was time to find my lead and pray to whatever

damn gods existed that he didn't have an alibi for when Sarah was killed.

The Aphrodite Club was weirdly quiet when I walked through the red curtain. There was a girl in a cowboy hat on stage, and just two guys sitting at their own little tables watching her. The music was still unnecessarily loud, and it smelled no better than usual. I made my way straight to the bar, where Max was drying pint glasses with a slightly gross-looking rag.

His eyes went straight over my shoulder, and I guessed he was looking for Nox.

"Just me today," I said with a smile. His shoulders relaxed and he focused on my face.

"Want a drink?"

I was about to say no, but I shrugged my shoulders instead. To be fair, I had earned myself a drink. Even if it was only four in the afternoon. "Sure. Gin and tonic, please."

I leaned my elbow on the bar as he began making the drink, thinking. Nox had said the bar was run and frequented by supernaturals. I watched Max, wondering what kind of supernatural he was. There was nothing obvious to give it away. I glanced over at the dancer, looking for anything to suggest she wasn't human. I was about to give up, when tiny glittering wings unfurled from her back as she sank to her knees and arched her back in a sultry movement.

A new thought occurred to me as I watched, captivated. Was Sarah a supernatural? The more I thought about it, the more I couldn't believe I hadn't asked Nox already.

"Here you go."

I turned back to the bar owner and took my drink from him. "Thanks. What do I owe you?"

"Four quid."

I pulled a five-pound note out of my purse and laid it on the bar. "Are all the girls in here, erm..." I trailed off, looking for the right word.

Max chuckled. "New to the big V, huh?" I stared at him blankly. "The Veil," he explained.

"Oh! Right. Yeah, I guess."

"Most of the dancers are human. It's the customers who ain't."

"What about Sarah?"

He frowned at me. "Sarah's dead."

"Oh, yeah, I know. But was she human?"

"Why you askin'?"

I scrabbled for something to say, and in the end settled with a half-truth. "She was sleeping with my boyfriend."

Max's suspicious expression cleared. "Ah, shit."

"Yeah," I nodded, taking a sip of my drink.

"Sarah was a siren. Made great tips. Your boyfriend human?"

I almost choked on my gin. "I don't know." The realization was like a punch to my already overwhelmed gut. Boy, did I need to take some time to work this out.

Max shrugged, and picked up another glass and started drying it. "Makes no difference really. We all live the same at the end of it."

"Right," I said, trying to marshal my thoughts. "I remember you saying that Sarah's boyfriend hit a guy. Do you know who he is?"

"Dave hits lotsa people," he said darkly.

"I heard."

"You hear a lot." The suspicious expression was back.

I gave him a weak smile. "Just trying to get some closure," I said, trying a small pout. Pouting was not something that came naturally to me, but it seemed to work.

"He punched one of the regulars. Guy who comes in on Fridays."

Which was why I was there. Candy had already told me that, and it was Friday. "What time?"

"In about an hour, usually. Look, my customers don't want no interrogations," he said, putting the rag down and looking intently at me.

"I won't upset anyone, I swear," I said.

"Fine," Max said, not looking all that fine about it. "Seeing as you got friends in high places and all that."

"Thanks. I'll wait in that booth over there," I smiled at him.

∾

I sat in the booth for another fifty minutes or so, scrolling absently through my phone but not really taking in anything I saw on the screen.

Could Alex be a supernatural? Could any of my exes? How about my friends? Anna at work?

I realized as I thought about it, that it really didn't matter. I mean sure, I was curious, but just as when I'd considered the possibility that Francis wasn't human, it didn't change the past. If someone had been nice to me, unpleasant to me, kind, or cruel, then my opinion of them was unchanged. My friends were my friends, and Alex was an asshole, human or not.

Accepting it made me feel just a little bit more in control. No more powerful, unfortunately, but less like I could have the rug pulled out from under me at any moment.

Whenever my thoughts strayed to Nox, my anger bubbled back up. Normally, I would try to suppress it, walk it off. But the new, more confident voice that kept sneaking into my head was embracing the anger.

It was useful. It was keeping me from sinking into shock or fear. Because the truth was, Madaleine and her pet demon *had* scared me. And it wasn't even the fact that I had gone from no magic to naked guys with horns, and death threats from winged women in a day.

The whole room had felt wrong, her presence a lethal, electrifying pressure, squeezing the confidence out of me, and letting fear and anger take over. Nox had a lethal and electrifying presence too, but his did the opposite to me. His presence seemed to give my confidence free rein, and my fears and doubts melted away instead.

He didn't trust me, though. He told me to keep my mouth shut, walked away when I needed answers, and kept crucial information from me. I didn't want to rely on him anymore.

Plus, if I cleared my own name of murder, our deal was null and void. A pang of disappointment made my stomach clench, and I closed my eyes and took a slow breath.

"I'm in charge. Not you," I muttered.

"Who are you talking to?" I jerked my hand in surprise at the voice, spilling my gin and tonic as I snapped my eyes open.

A small man in a tatty suit was smiling down at me. He had thinning brown hair and a glint in his eyes that was vaguely unsettling.

"Oh, no one," I said in a rush. *Note to self — don't talk to my lady-bits out loud in a strip bar.*

"I'm Gordon. Max said you wanted to talk to me?"

"Oh," I said, sitting up straight. "You're the guy Dave punched last week?"

His face darkened. "I thought you wanted to borrow money."

"No, I just wanted to ask you a few—"

He turned away before I could finish my sentence. "Not interested."

"Wait, please. My ex was sleeping with Dave's girl-friend, before she died."

I had to shout the words over the sound of Hot Stuff

blaring from the club speakers. Gordon stopped, then turned back to me. Danger gleamed in his eyes as he stepped back to my table and leaned over me. "Your ex was sleeping with Sarah?"

"Yes. Alex. Do you know him?"

"If I had known Sarah was sleeping with more than one guy..." He trailed off, shaking his head.

"Then what?"

"Then I wouldn't have offered her such a good deal," he snarled. I raised my eyebrows, hoping he would go on. He didn't.

"What deal?"

"She couldn't pay me the money she owed. So, I offered her a different way to pay. She acted like I'd asked to her screw half the men in London, yelling and swearing at me. I mean, how can a stripper be so fucking high and mighty? I've seen it all before anyway."

Hatred for the man oozed through me, but I kept my face mild. "That's why her boyfriend punched you?"

"Yeah. And now it turns out his high-and-mighty princess was screwing around." A nasty smile took over his face. "Hypocritical dickhead."

It took no leap of imagination whatsoever for me to picture Gordon as the killer. I just needed to find out where he was when Sarah was killed, and hope he came across just as creepy to the police.

"Did you hear she was killed?"

He tensed and the nasty smiled slipped. "Probably her boyfriend did it. If she was cheating."

"Where were you when it happened?"

Gordon's eyes narrowed. "What?" I shifted in my seat uncomfortably, aware that something had changed but not sure what. Then I saw a faint glow around him, dark blue. "Are you suggesting I'm a fucking murderer?"

His voice was a low hiss, and I could see fur starting to form in the light around him.

"No shifting in here." A hand appeared over his shoulder and yanked him backward, and relief loosened my tight chest as I saw it belonged to Max. "And you," he said, pointing at me. "I told you not to bother my customers. Out."

"Wait—" I started but Max shook his head. Gordon was still glaring at me.

"You're done for the night. Out."

I stood up. I wasn't going to get anything more out of Gordon, that much was clear. But I had enough to get the police to at least check him out. Sarah owed him money, and he was clearly bitter that she had turned him down. "Fine. Goodnight."

I strutted from the club as though I hadn't just been kicked out, and was surprised to see Claude and the town car still outside.

"Back to Wimbledon now, Miss Abbott?" Claude asked hopefully.

"Yes. Please. Thank you."

I felt guilty for making him disobey orders, but it had been worth it. If Madaleine the angry angel wasn't the culprit, then I was pretty sure that Gordon was.

TWENTY-FIVE

BETH

I asked Claude to drop me off at the little grocery store near my apartment so that I could get some dinner. I had settled on some nice bread and mid-range cheese, until a woman walked past me, pushing along a pushchair with a grinning toddler in it. The baby's skin was pale blue, and small, translucent wings the same color glittered out of the back of the woman's jacket. I put the cheese back on the refrigerator shelf and headed to the alcohol aisle instead.

When I let myself into my apartment armed with a cheap bottle of red wine, it was with every intention of sitting alone for the evening, working through what I had learned, and convincing myself that I did not need, or want, Nox.

An unnecessarily loud banging on my door just fifteen minutes later put an end to that.

My first thought was that it was the police, come to arrest me. Heart in my mouth, I tugged open the door.

"Alex?"

"Beth, thank fuck," Alex said, then barged past me into the hallway, throwing a furtive look over his shoulder.

"Woah, wait right there! You can't come in!" But I was too late, he already was.

"Beth, there is some weird shit going on. Like really, really weird." His eyes were wide, and his hair was a mess, like he'd just woken up. As I took in his disheveled form, all the anger that I had built up spilled inexorably through me.

"You stole all my stuff." My voice almost didn't sound like my own. There was no trace of my usual calm patience, just a cold hardness.

"I was going to pay you back." He reached for me, and I slapped his hand away.

"Don't you fucking dare touch me." Rage was burning through my veins, growing hotter every moment. "You lied to me, cheated on me, and stole from me. Get the hell out of my apartment, now."

"None of that matters, Beth, seriously. Something is happening. I don't know what, but it is messed up."

"You are messed up, Alex! Can you not hear me? Get out!" I yelled.

"They're after me. I need help. Please." His plea was so meek that my anger stuttered a second. I realized there was real fear on his face.

"Who's after you?"

"I don't know, but they're... They're not human." He whispered the last few words, glancing furtively out of the still-open door behind me. I blinked, sucking in air to try to keep myself from losing my shit. This could be important. The police were looking for Alex, and if he knew something about supernaturals...

"If they're not human, what are they?"

"Wolves. They've been following me. I know that sounds crazy, but I'm not making this up."

My head was reeling, and my thoughts flip-flopped between getting as much information as I could out of Alex and punching him hard enough to break his nose.

"Did you kill Sarah?"

Alex's mouth fell open. "Are you fucking serious? I may not have been honest with you, but you can't honestly think I could kill someone?"

I couldn't help my fingernails digging into my palms as my hands fisted in anger. "Alex, I didn't think you were capable of cheating on me or stealing my stuff," I hissed though clenched teeth.

"It wasn't really cheating, just the odd... visit," he shrugged.

Without pausing to consider what I was doing, I slapped him. The sound rang out as I yanked back my stinging palm, adrenaline coursing through me. I'd never slapped anyone in my life.

Anger flashed in his eyes, but then drained away immediately. "It doesn't matter now. What matters is that someone is trying to kill me. Wolves. And there are people out there who aren't normal." The fear was back in his voice, evident in his eyes.

How was Alex seeing supernaturals? At least it

answered my question about whether or not he was human. There was no way he was faking his fear — this was the first he knew about magic.

Someone must have lifted the Veil for him, and Rory had made it clear that it wasn't easy or common.

I moved so that he was closer to the door than I was, and folded my arms tight across my chest, not least to stop myself from hitting him again. "Why have you come here?"

"I don't know. You're the most normal thing I could think of."

I felt my eyebrows shoot up. "You came here because I'm normal?"

"Yeah. Everything out there is crazy. I thought seeing you, and this place, would help calm me down."

"Because I'm so boring?" My words were a venomous hiss.

"No, no," he said quickly. "Not boring. Normal."

"Get out. Now."

"But I've got nowhere to go! The police are looking for me so nobody will let me stay—"

"Get out of my house!" I screamed the words, shoving him hard in the chest, forcing him back through the open door. He stumbled, and it was enough for me to slam the door into him, and push him the rest of the way out. He banged on the door after I got it closed, calling my name through the wood.

"Beth, please! Just let me stay one night, I'll be gone tomorrow, I swear!"

I bared my teeth, rage seething through me. Did I

have doormat written across my head? Did he really think I was so soft that I would help him after what he had done to me?

"Asshole!" I shrieked through the door. His banging stopped. With a vicious kick at the door, I turned and stormed into the living room. More anger than I was capable of containing was flooding through me, and half of me wanted to open the door and hit him again.

But I was a suspect in a murder case. An act of violence of any kind would be exactly what the police needed. At the thought of the severe Inspector Singh, I tugged my cellphone out of my pocket.

"Inspector? It's Beth Abbott," I said as she answered the phone with a clipped grunt.

"Yes?"

"Alex is here at my apartment. Now. Banging on my door, saying people are after him." I left out the part that they were wolves.

"We'll be right there," she said, and hung up.

Alex was gone when the police arrived eight minutes later. But he didn't have much of a head start, and the Inspector had bought a brigade of officers with her, who fanned out from my building immediately, looking for him.

"They'll probably get him at the train station," said the Inspector. She was sitting awkwardly on my couch, having just written down what I had told her about my exchange with Alex. Minus the supernatural bits.

"I hope so," I muttered.

"You know, Beth..." The Inspector pursed her lips, before continuing. "You don't have to do what Mr. Nox tells you. If you know anything that might help us, you should tell us. Don't be intimidated by a man like that."

I looked at her. Even she thought I was a damn pushover. "Mr. Nox is the dictionary definition of intimidating," I said.

"So, he is intimidating you?"

"Insofar as he's my boss, incredibly wealthy, and rather attractive."

She gave me a look. "I mean it, Beth. Don't lie for him just because he's powerful."

She had no idea how powerful he was. He was the devil, for Christ's sake. I shook my head. "I'm not lying for him."

"I have something to tell you."

We both spun in our seats at the cool tone of Nox's voice. I leapt to my feet as he strode into the room. The black-eyed iciness from when I'd last seen him was gone, and instead, his piercing blue eyes bore into mine, and that warmth that came with him caressed my skin and coiled around me. I tried to hold on to my anger with him, but instead my traitorous heart gave a small flutter of relief. *He was back.*

"Who do you have something to tell, Mr. Nox?" asked Inspector Singh, also standing up.

"And how did you get in here?" I added. He held out

a piece of paper to show both of us, holding the corner with a crisp white kerchief.

"This was pinned to your front door."

I looked at the note.

Your skull will crack slower than Sarah's. You're next, pretty girl.

Nausea swam through me. "Alex couldn't have left that."

The Inspector pulled on gloves from her pocket and took the note from Nox carefully. "Is it his handwriting?" she asked me. I forced myself to look, the words warping a little as I squinted at them. It was scrawled messily, the letters long and elaborate.

"No," I shook my head.

"I wanted to report a theft to you," said Nox. "When I called the station, they said you were here."

Suspicion sparked in me at his words — the station wouldn't have handed out information like that. But I pushed the lie aside.

He was telling the police about the theft. Which was exactly what I had asked him to do.

"A theft?"

"Yes. From my office."

The Inspector's eyebrows knitted together. "And why didn't you tell us earlier?"

"I only realized now that it is missing. It is not something I consult often."

"Consult? What was stolen?"

"A book. A very old, very valuable book."

Inspector Singh regarded him a long moment. "Where was this book?"

"In a locked drawer in my desk."

"And you don't know when it was stolen?"

"No."

"Right." She turned back to me, lifting the note. "Is there anyone you think might have written this?"

The sneering anger on Gordon's face flashed into my head. Could he have followed me home?

With a sideways glance at Nox, I spoke. "I went to the club that Sarah worked in a couple of times and found out that she owed money to a really sleazy guy called Gordon Jackson. When I asked him a few questions earlier this evening, he got angry with me."

Inspector Singh's lips tightened. "That was unwise, Miss Abbott."

"I was worried that you weren't looking for any other suspects." I folded my arms again, holding her accusatory stare.

"Police work is best left to the police."

"Will you check him out?" I asked.

"We were already aware of him," she said quietly, and I wasn't sure if she was telling the truth or not. Either way, she was aware of him now, and that had to be a good thing.

"Ma'am, there's no sign of the suspect at Wimbledon station," said a voice on a crackly walkie-talkie on the Inspector's hip.

She sighed. "I need to leave. Mr. Nox, call in the description of that book first thing tomorrow morning. Miss Abbott, I strongly advise you not to stay here on your own. If you want to be difficult and insist on it, then the best I can offer you is an officer within five minutes of your apartment. I do not have the resources to put a man on your door based on one threat."

Before I could answer, Nox spoke. "There will be no need for that. Miss Abbott will be staying with me until we know she will be safe."

"Miss Abbott will be doing no such damn thing," I said, turning to him and dropping my hands to my hips.

"Look, for all I know, you two have cooked this note up to make you look innocent," said the Inspector, moving toward the hallway. "But if, on the off chance it has actually been written by the person who murdered Sarah, then take my advice. Go and stay somewhere safe. Don't let pride get you killed." She gave me a pointed look and disappeared into the hall. I heard the front door slam shut and stared at Nox.

"She's right. Pride is a real bastard of a sin."

I swallowed. "Do you think Madaleine wrote that note?"

"I don't know." Shadows flickered through his eyes. "But if anyone comes anywhere near your skull, they will live to regret it."

"Don't go all angry on me again."

"I have regained control. That is why I came. To tell you that it will not happen again."

It wasn't an apology, but it was sincere.. I cocked my head at him.

"You told the Inspector about the theft."

"I did not want the loss of the book to be public knowledge in the Veil. But I want you to trust me more." He took a step froward, and delicious, tingly warmth stroked up my body. A peaceful calm that I had not felt since seeing his wings on the balcony seeped into me.

Had that been only that morning?

"Are you using magic on me to make me forgive you for being a dick?"

His mouth quirked into a smile. "Do you know how many people get away with calling the devil a dick? I can count them on one hand."

"Answer the question."

"No. You seem to soak up a lot of my magic on your own."

"Why do you want me to trust you?"

"Come to my place. I will tell you everything."

I looked at him disbelievingly. "Everything?"

"Yes. About me, the book, everything."

"I... I don't know if I'm comfortable staying at your place." What I meant was, *I don't know if I can stay at yours without trying to have sex with you*, and I had a sneaking suspicion that he knew that.

"I will not lay claim to you until my end of the deal is fulfilled."

"Lay claim to me?"

A predatory smile took his face, and heat trickled through my core.

"An old-fashioned expression," he said dismissively. "Would you prefer something more modern? How about, I will not make you scream my name and beg for mercy as I ruin you for all other men?"

Oh god. "This isn't making me more comfortable about staying with you," I croaked, as the now-familiar ache returned. I wouldn't last a damn hour alone with him if he kept saying things like that.

"The way I see it, Beth, you have a choice. Either you take your chances with me, or you stay here alone and see if someone tries to kill you."

I stared at him. "So, it's sleep with the devil or die?"

His eyes glittered with promise as he gazed back at me. "I know which I would choose."

TWENTY-SIX

BETH

The town car pulled up outside the oldest, and grandest-looking, four-story house on Grosvenor Street. I swallowed as I peered out of the window. The architecture of the whole row of impressive townhouses was distinctly gothic, the dark stone standing firm and ancient. The ground floor had tall but narrow windows stretching up either side of the huge black door, and the next two floors had three large picture windows with intricate stone arches, warm light spilling from them into the street below. The top floor had three circular windows, like portholes, and no light came from them at all.

"Welcome to Morningstar House." I turned away from the window to look at Nox.

"Which floor is yours?" I was guessing the top floor, given that penthouses were always the best. Plus, the dark round windows stood out the most.

"The whole building is mine."

My mouth fell open. Real estate in central London was like pure gold—nobody owned whole buildings. Even a garage in London cost more than a house in the rest of the country. "How?"

"Money," he shrugged. "You knew I was wealthy."

"Yeah but... I didn't think anybody owned property this size in London, except the people who rent them out. And celebrities."

"I bought this building eighty years ago."

My eyebrows shot up. "How old are you?"

"Old."

"Right. I have so many questions for you."

"And I intend to answer them all. Once we've eaten."

I followed him into the building somewhat apprehensively. Claude insisted on carrying my small case. I'd thrown enough essentials in it to last me a day or two, at Nox's suggestion.

We walked down a long corridor with a rich, dark wooden floor, and pale gray walls. Smoky glass pendant lights led us past doors and up a short staircase.

"On the left is the garage and stairs to the basement. On the right is the gym. There is my study." He gestured to a grander-looking closed door than the others, and then the space opened out abruptly. I inhaled as I stared around.

We were in a kitchen with a glass ceiling. It was the kitchen of my dreams; super-modern but with a slight art deco touch that matched the character of the house. The same rich wood lined the floor, and the counters and long island in the middle were topped with grey-veined marble.

"How is there nothing above us?" I asked, gaping up at the huge skylight and the night sky beyond.

"The top three floors have a gap in the middle. To make a large roof terrace lower down, hidden from view."

"So, the house is like a giant U shape?"

"Exactly."

I blew out a long breath.

"Through there is the dining room and my second study, and the stairs to the back floors. Where the bedrooms are."

His voice dipped as he said bedrooms, and I squirmed a little.

"Will that be all, Sir?" asked Claude.

"Yes. Thank you," Nox said, and the elderly man bowed his head and retreated from the kitchen. "Oh, Claude?" Nox called after him as he gestured for me to sit at on the of the stools at the kitchen island.

"Yes, Sir?"

"Please let Beelzebub in."

"Yes, Sir."

I jerked my head back in alarm. "Beelzebub? Please, please don't tell me that you have a naked pet demon too," I said, screwing my face up. I heard a scratching sound and spun on the stool to face it, my heart rate quickening.

A black labrador bounded into the room, his paws sliding on the shining wood because he was moving so fast. He barreled into Nox, his tail wagging at a hundred miles an hour, and Nox bent to scratch the dogs' ears, chuckling.

"Just a regular pet, I'm afraid. No demons here, except me."

His eyes met mine as he straightened, and sparks shot through my whole body. He pushed a hand through his hair where it had fallen over his forehead, and a wave of need crashed through me. He was gorgeous. Unearthly levels of gorgeous. And now he had a gorgeous dog too. How was I supposed to deal with that?

I cleared my throat, and slid off the stool, crouching. The dog instantly left Nox's shins and scampered toward me. "Well, hello," I laughed as it tried enthusiastically to lick my face. "Beelzebub, is it?"

"Well, the devil has to have some private jokes," Nox said.

"Girl or boy?"

"Boy. He's four."

"He's lovely," I said, as Beelzebub rolled onto his back and looked happily at me as I scratched his tummy.

"Red or white wine?"

I looked up at Nox, in time to see him slip off his jacked and unbutton the top of his crisp white shirt. More rumblings of desire made my muscles clench and I fidgeted uncomfortably. "Erm, you choose," I mumbled.

"Do you like pasta?"

"Very much."

"Good."

I blinked as he pulled open a silent drawer and lifted out a frying pan. "Are you cooking?"

"Why do you think I have a kitchen this nice?"

"You live in a freaking mansion, I thought you might have a chef."

"I have power over gluttony. I have to be able to cook." That deliciously mischievous look was back in his eyes, and I straightened. Beelzebub jumped back to his feet, tail still wagging furiously.

"Can I help?"

"Yes," he said, pushing up his sleeves and exposing toned forearms.

Forearms are not sexy, get a grip!

"Glasses are on this side of the island. The wine refrigerator is at the end. Choose a white."

I did as he asked, selecting a cold bottle at random and pouring us both a glass. I settled back on the stool and watched him as he moved around the kitchen deftly, filling pans with water, dicing tomatoes, frying onions. Bealzebub lay down at my feet.

"Where did you learn to do this?" I asked eventually, breaking the surprisingly comfortable silence.

"Italy. Do you like the wine?"

"It's delicious." And it was. "Do you?"

He paused over the frying pan, a darkness flickering over his features. "In the first dream I visited you in, I told you I was cursed."

"Okaaaay. Not really the answer I was expecting."

"I would like to tell you about my curse. And then I do not need to lie to you. There are some things you need to know first, and there are some things that you never need to know." He turned to face me fully. "I need you to trust me that I will tell you only what is safe. Do you trust me?"

I waited for an answer to leave my lips, but none came. I had no idea whether I trusted him. I picked up my glass and took a long sip of the crisp wine. "I trust you to tell me what I need to know," I said carefully. I wasn't going to tell him that I outright trusted him. I barely knew anything about him, beyond him claiming to be the devil. Flashes of my dreams came back to me, and the way I could feel his soul through the touch of his lips seared through my center. I shoved the thoughts deep, deep down.

He cocked his head at me, a gesture of respect, I thought. "Good answer. You're not as naive as you let people think you are, Miss Abbott," he said quietly.

I frowned. Did I *let* people think that about me? I had never really considered how much I could change what others thought of me. "Would you like to eat formally in the dining room, or in here?" Nox changed the subject, and I glanced around the kitchen. The smell of frying onions and pancetta filled the room, and a pleasant heat from the stove had warmed the space. The padded stool seat was comfortable, and Beelzebub seemed settled.

"I'm happy in here."

"Good. We eat, then we talk."

· · ·

We ate in silence at the island, and food was fantastic. Nox had taken the stool closest to mine, but kept a respectful distance between us, which I was grateful for. An apprehension built inside me as I ate. I didn't know what he was going to tell me, or even whether it would impact my own situation, but it was clearly important to him. And if it was important to the devil, it was probably a big deal.

Seeing Nox like this, cooking, with a dog at his feet, had thrown me somewhat. He still oozed that masculine grace, but it was at odds with the lethally beautiful man with glowing golden wings standing over the London skyline that I'd seen just that morning.

And if I was being honest, the fact that he could be both excited me in a way that wasn't appropriate. Why did I care if the man could cook or liked dogs? It wasn't like I could actually date him. For a hundred reasons. Firstly, he was the devil. Secondly, he was a millionaire playboy who was only interested in me due to...

My thoughts stumbled to a halt. Why *was* he interested in me? He'd claimed it was because he felt a responsibility for me as an employee, involved in a murder he knew I was innocent of. But that suggested that he had a conscience. Did the devil feel guilt? I thought it was more likely that he was either bored and playing with me, or he liked the challenge I presented him by doing my best to resist his charms.

I glanced up at him as I forked spaghetti into my mouth. He glanced back, and took a sip of wine. "I love watching you eat."

I looked away awkwardly. "You know that's a little creepy?"

He took a deep breath. "I can't taste food. To see your enjoyment of it is intoxicating."

I lowered my fork slowly, staring at him. "You can't taste food?"

"No. Eighty years ago, I made a mistake. I decided to relinquish the responsibility of punishing those guilty of the abusing the seven deadly sins. I gave up the four that caused me the most trouble, that brought out the worst in... people. Wrath, Pride, Envy and Sloth. But I kept the three I enjoyed having power over. Lust, Greed, Gluttony." He looked at his empty plate, then back to me. "When power over the sins was carved up, the ability to use them fully, and therefore to punish those guilty of them, was broken. When I realized this, I should have taken them back and resumed my proper place as Lucifer, the punisher of evil. But I didn't. I enjoyed the freedom too much. The gods, in turn, punished me for reneging on my duties. They cursed me so that I am never able to enjoy the sins that I kept."

"So... You can't taste food because you kept Gluttony?" I half whispered the question.

"Correct. I can't taste this wine either, although I know it to be excellent. I also can't keep my wealth for more than one day, due to Greed. I have had to build up an empire of companies in order to rebuild everything I lose overnight. Every night."

"And... Lust?"

"Lust. The worst punishment of them all." The blue

light in his eyes was fierce, dancing across his irises as his gaze intensified. "I have not responded physically to a woman for seventy-eight years. Until now."

My mouth went dry. "Responded physically?" I reached for my wine, feeling my cheeks flush.

"Yes. I think you know what I mean, but I can make it clearer if you would like."

"Erm, no, I get it." I gulped my wine.

"It has been nearly eight decades since I have been able to have sex with a woman."

"What changed?" I asked as casually as I could, trying to avoid making eye contact with him.

"You."

"Me?" My eyes snapped back to his.

"I felt you, in every part of my body, the second I first touched you."

I thought back to the look on his face when I had first shaken his hand in his office, and I felt my own eyes widen. I opened my mouth to ask more but realized I wasn't sure what to say.

There was no question he had *responded physically* when we had danced together, the memory of his hardness pressed against my ass was seared into my brain.

"I do not know what connection you have to me or my curse yet. But I will tell you about the book that was stolen."

The book? I didn't want to know about the damn book. I wanted to know why this god of a man could only get a hard-on since meeting me. It made no sense. I was the most ordinary, boring woman in London. What the hell did I have that turned on the devil?

Nox spoke again before I could splutter a protest, though. "The book contains the power of the devil. Like the opposite of the bible, I suppose. It is what allowed me to share the power of the sins in the first place. There is a page for each, and control of them is shared via those pages, and with my consent. I tore out the pages for the sins I no longer wanted and handed them out, and in doing so, destroyed the ability to use the devil's power as a whole. I have never been told how to break my curse, but I have long suspected that the only way is to retake control of all seven sins."

"Why haven't you done that already then?"

Shadows descended over his face. "A number of reasons. Not least because I do not know who has the pages any longer."

"But Wrath is here in London. You can get her page back, can't you?"

"She does not have the page I gave her anymore. The page is needed to conduct the transfer of magic, but it is not required after that. And pages from that book are worth a great deal of money in the Veil — it is one of the most famous artifacts in our lore."

"Are you saying she sold it?"

"Yes. And it has likely been sold on again since. The black market in the Veil is prolific."

"Do you need the page to take the sin back?"

"Yes. It is needed for the transfer," he repeated.

I blew out a breath. "And now somebody stole the whole book? With your three sins still in it?"

"Yes. They can't take those sins without my consent. But without the book, I can't restore the devil's full power. Or break my curse."

"Who doesn't want you to get your power back?"

"Any of the four supernaturals I gave sins to, for a start."

I shook my head. My mind was brimming with questions, and I wasn't really sure how to get them all out. Start *with the ones about sex,* confident me yelled internally.

"This, erm, lust thing," I said.

He raised one eyebrow at me. "Yes?"

"Can we talk about that some more?"

TWENTY-SEVEN

NOX

Beelzebub whined at Beth's feet, and I pulled my gaze from her wide-eyed, flushed face. Even just looking at her now, biting her lip nervously, my cock ached. *Decades.* It had been decades since I'd felt like this. Images of claiming her in every way it was possible to tore through my mind vividly, and I swallowed down a growl of desire.

I had to control myself. That was true now, more than ever. Wrath's threat to Beth's life in her office had awakened the darkness in me, a deep and lethal fury that I had not needed to contain for years. But when I had walked away from Beth, I had been too close to the edge.

The darkness had lain dormant for as long as my ability to find pleasure in life had, but the need to protect Beth had caused it to rear its head. Was the curse lifting? Was I starting to feel my true power again?

The dog cried again. "Does he need to go out?" Beth asked, looking at me.

I nodded, and stood up. "Let's go to the roof."

She and Beelzebub followed me up the stairs at the back of the house. Walking was almost uncomfortable my cock was so hard. Fuck, I needed her. I needed her more than I needed damned air right now.

And even that felt different around her, as though the air was made of something else when she was in the room. Something that made everything... better. Brighter. More intense. But she was human. How could she cast such a spell over me?

We reached the roof terrace, and Beelzebub raced to the lawned area that ran along the right hand-side, sniffing at one of the potted palms.

Beth stopped in her tracks, staring open-mouthed at the swimming pool. Glowing intensely blue in the dark night sky, I supposed that it was quite striking. Marble tiles ran round the edge, and ornate gold taps kept a steady trickle of water flowing.

"Do you like to swim?"

She nodded, looking at me. She was beautiful, her heart-shaped face always showing her every emotion. I was Lucifer, God of Sin — I knew that she was thinking about us together in the pool. I could hear her heart race, feel the waves of lust rolling from her. But even if I wasn't in possession of lust magic, I would have known what she was thinking. Some folk thought about, or practiced, sex so much that they became masters of hiding their desires and imaginings. But Beth.... Beth was not one of those people. The thoughts she was having were taking her by surprise, and she clearly had no experience in trying to hide them. The knowledge that I was the cause of those thoughts made it even harder to contain myself.

"Your house is amazing." She curled a lock of hair around her finger and gazed between at the houses either side of us. Dark brick loomed high, illuminated by strings of lights that cast a warm glow over the long terrace. The light from the kitchen below shone up through the glass in the center.

I waved my hand and took a step closer to her. The fairy lights flickered and then each one burst into a hundred fluttering fireflies. She gasped, her eyes lighting up. "It's cold. We should go inside."

"Yes."

She followed me back to the kitchen, the dog bouncing excitedly around our feet as we went. I refilled our glasses of wine, and then led her to one of my studies. Bookshelves lined three walls, and a long couch took up the fourth. A long, curved nineteen-twenties floor lamp gave the room a deep, warm mood. "This is my reading room," I told her. She ignored me, walking straight to the shelves.

"So many books," she breathed, running her fingers over one of the shelves. I would kill to have her run her fingers over my flesh like that.

I ground my teeth.

"You like to read?"

"As much as I like to eat."

I smiled. Her curiosity was infectious. *She* was infectious. "Come and sit with me. Ask me what you need to." She turned back to me as I sank down onto the couch. Suspicion clouded her beautiful brown eyes.

"Why are you telling me everything now? What changed?"

I considered her, wondering how much to say. "Wrath's power rubbed off on me today. When I lose my temper, bad things happen. Once I had calmed down, I realized that I am less likely to lose my temper if I have an ally."

"An ally?"

"Yes."

"You want me to be your ally?"

"Only if it's true that you don't cheat at Monopoly."

A smile pulled at her lips, and I saw her shoulders dip as some of the tension left them. "It's true that I don't cheat at games. But I also don't have magic, consort with demons, or know how to..." She trailed off and the flush returned to her cheeks. She took a deep breath. "I make an unlikely ally for the devil," she said eventually, with a small shrug.

"On the contrary. Where there is dark, there is light, where there is good there is bad, and where there is sin, there is always innocence. I believe you might be the devil's perfect companion."

She took a step toward the couch. "I'm not completely innocent."

I smiled. "I have a feeling your definition might differ from mine."

I bit down on my tongue—her chest heaved with

another deep breath. She moved the rest of the distance to the couch, and sat down, holding her wine glass carefully. "You may be right." She was two feet from me, but I could feel her everywhere, as though electricity was jumping the gap between us.

"For someone with no magic, you have quite a presence, Miss Abbott."

She looked at me with a mix of alarm and doubt on her beautiful features. "You're the first person to suggest I have a presence."

I felt a deep anger rumble up inside me at her words. "You should ignore what that man you lived with said."

She looked down at her drink, and then back at me. A flicker of doubt shone in her eyes, then her shoulders squared, her breasts pushing out as her perfect little tongue darted out and wet her lips. "Well, if it's true I have such an effect on you then... Maybe you're right."

I wanted to take her show of confidence and wrap her up in it, teach her to wear it like armor. I wanted her to know she could do, or be, anything.

The strength of my thoughts surprised me. I had never, never felt like this about a human. About anyone, in fact. Need pulsed through me, reminding me that I had also never gone nearly eight decades without the feel of a woman around me. The strength of my reaction to her was, no doubt, linked.

I steeled myself, forcing down the fierce protectiveness and allowing lust to take over my thoughts instead. I needed the release I had been denied for so long. "Do I have a similar effect on you?" Her flush deepened, moving down her neck, coloring her pale skin deliciously. "I meant what I said, Beth."

"Which part?"

"All of it, actually. But right now, I'm referring to the part where I told you that I would ruin you for all other men. Once you spend just one hour with me, you will never be able to go back. I will be seared into you mind, your body, your soul. The pleasure I can inflict upon you will never, ever be matched."

She swallowed, her eyes widening a little and her grip tightening on her wineglass. I felt my hard cock twitch and stifled a groan. Fuck, I'd almost forgotten the feeling. "One hour?" Her voice was quiet, but steady.

My eyes moved to her lips. "One hour is enough for you to know that there is no lover in the world like me. A lifetime wouldn't be enough to take you everywhere your body is capable of going under my touch."

She drew in breath again, and I could see the desire in her, warring to be free. "Show me."

TWENTY-EIGHT

BETH

I couldn't believe I'd just said that. *Show me? What in the name of the heavens was I thinking?* Nox had tensed, the wolfish hunger in his eyes intensifying.

"No sex," I said quickly, my lips stumbling over the three-letter word and it coming out an awkward mumble. I closed my eyes and took a short breath. *Get it together, Beth. Get it together.* "I want a taster."

"You've tasted me in your dreams."

"I want proof. Proof that you can deliver what you say you can." It was partially true. But more than that, I wanted him. I wanted him so much that the ache between my thighs was painful. I couldn't handle another dream where I woke up unsatisfied and frustrated. In fact, I couldn't stand another minute on the couch with him without his touch. I felt like every damned cell in my body was charged, primed, ready for him.

"Oh Beth, I assure you that my word is good." He shifted on the couch, so that he was facing me.

"I want to know that I can trust you. You said lust bared your soul."

He raised an eyebrow. "It's true. And your suggestion is an excellent way to prove that you can trust me. Here is my offer. One hour, and I will remain clothed. My entire attention will be on you, and despite not feeling the wetness of a woman around my cock for eighty years, I will refrain from even touching myself."

His piercing gaze bore into mine, and heat rolled from him in waves that seemed to caress my already flushed skin.

My breath grew slightly ragged at his words, as an image of the beautiful man before me naked, his hand wrapped around himself, filled my head. "And our deal remains? You will still help clear my name of murder?"

"In return a full night in your company. Yes."

I paused for barely a beat. "I accept."

Nox's face changed as I spoke, and I swear my heart missed a beat. As though a switch had been flicked, his whole body came to life. His features seemed to sharpen, his eyes grew bluer, his skin glowed. He pushed a hand through his dark hair and just that movement was enough to make my thighs clench together.

He was beyond gorgeous. "Your desire is fueling my power," he said, his voice deep.

I didn't know if that was good or bad, so I just stared at him. Were all angels this beautiful?

Nox stood up, breaking the spell. I took a gulp of wine, my body practically vibrating with anticipation. As soon as I lowered the glass, Nox moved before me, taking it out of my hand and striding to the desk. He set it down, then turned back to me, leaning against the dark wood. He folded his arms. Dangerous swirls of desire gleamed in his eyes as he watched me.

I expected to feel self-conscious, or nervous, under his gaze. But to my surprise, I felt my chest pushing out, and my knees slowly parting as I faced him. A low rumble came from deep in his chest, and I bit down on my tongue as I clenched involuntarily.

"Is this your magic?"

"No. It is your own lust." His voice was slightly strained, and a flicker of doubt forced its way through the erotic thoughts filling my head. He spoke again and the strain was gone. My doubt vanished with his words. "Tell me, Miss Abbott. Is your pussy wet?"

My stomach muscles clenched as I bit my lip. This wasn't a dream. This was real. He may have put a few feet between us, but he was there before me, flesh and blood. If what he'd said was true, then there was no going back from this. Hell, even if he was exaggerating his prowess, which I suspected he wasn't, there was no going back. He was my boss. And the freaking devil.

"I'm not sure," I lied.

A muscle in his jaw ticked, and his arms tighten ed across his chest. "Stand up."

I did as he told me. "Beth. You said this was about

trust." I nodded. "Then tell me the truth. Is your pussy wet?"

I nodded again, unable to speak. My knees were unsteady, now that I was standing. I wanted him there, his strong grip around me, his hard chest pressed against me like in my dream.

"Show me."

"What?"

He took a step forward, pushing himself off the desk. "Take off your jeans."

His voice carried a sultry power, a command I was unable to disobey. I stepped out of my shoes. Nox took another step closer. I unbuttoned the top snap of my jeans. My heart raced faster in my chest, and Nox took a sharp breath as I hooked my thumbs into the waistband of my jeans. His eyelids were low, his hooded gaze fixed on my waist. The knowledge that he wanted me caused a surge of confidence, and I bent to the ground, taking my jeans with me. I stepped out of them as gracefully as I could, the cool air kissing my bare legs. Nox gave a hiss of approval as he took in my panties, visible under the hem of my shirt. Since meeting Nox, it wasn't just my make-up that I had taken more care over. The constant sexual awareness he caused in me had led to some slightly bolder choices of underwear, and I was wearing a black lace thong. Not expensive, but pretty.

"Turn around." I blinked at the command. I wanted to see him. I wanted to revel in the need in his gaze, the sight of his tense body under that suit. "Turn around, Beth."

Slowly, I turned. I heard another growl, presumably as he took in my bare ass. I closed my eyes, blocking out the wall before me and picturing him as he had been on the rooftop, shirtless and golden.

"Kneel on the couch." My initial instinct was to say no, but my knees were bending before I could speak. They sank into the leather, and I gripped the back of the chair. My shirt rode up over my ass as I bent, and a wave of heat flowed over my body.

"You're beautiful." His voice sounded closer, the words a heated caress. Everything felt hot, I realized. My skin was alive with anticipation, and I squeezed my legs together, both trying to stop myself from squirming and trying to apply some pressure where I needed it so badly.

"For this hour, Beth, you're mine. Do you understand?"

"Yes." I wanted nothing more than to be his.

"At my mercy. Utterly."

I should have felt fear or discomfort at the idea of being at the devil's mercy. But my voice was clear as I answered. "Yes." I needed to know if he was telling the truth, if he really could change my life in an hour, without even making love to me. I needed it more than I needed anything else, the ache between my legs forcing out all rational thought.

"Bend over. As low as you can."

I took a deep breath, then dropped my shoulders and bent, still gripping the back of the couch as I lowered my head between my arms. The thin fabric of my panties were all that stopped him seeing me totally bare, and aroused. This time, when he growled, it was animalistic. A thrill shuddered through me.

Touch me. Touch me. Touch me. The words rolled around my head until they were a shout. It was all I could think.

But he didn't. I stayed there, unable to see him, ass raised in the air, heat pooling hotter and hotter at my core.

"Please." The word left me in a rasp, and then heat engulfed me. A feather light touch behind my knee made me gasp. Warm fingers moved slowly, too slowly, up my thigh. I writhed, and they stopped.

"Don't move."

I drew in a breath and tried to stay still. The stroke resumed, hot and measured. His fingertips reached my ass, and with barely more pressure than a feather he moved, until he reached the small of my back. He ran his finger gently under the top of my underwear, and ever so slightly, pulled. The fabric of my panties tightened over my core, and a moan escaped my lips at the slight pressure. More. I needed more.

But he let go instead of pulling tighter, his light touch resuming. He brushed his fingers back down my ass, running them close to the line of my underwear. I was so wet that I was sure if he moved just a few millimeters he would feel it. I pushed my hips back, trying to force his fingers closer, but he paused again.

"I told you to stay still."

I ignored him, rolling my hips, parting my knees. I opened my mouth to speak, to beg even, but nothing but a breathy sigh came out. His fingers left my skin, and I froze. For a painfully long moment nothing happened. I started to lift my head, pulling my shoulders up, when I felt the touch of his lips. On my thigh. Barely an inch from the throbbing wetness between my legs.

He began to kiss me, up and down my thighs, over my ass, tantalizingly close. I did my very best to stay still, but the muscles in my legs were quivering, and my shoulders were straining. I would give everything I owned for him to touch me. Everything.

"Say it."

"What?" My question was a gasp.

"Say it. Out loud. Tell me what you want."

"Do you know what I'm thinking?" I lifted my head to turn, but he pushed his hand into my hair, holding me still. I felt the fabric of his shirt brush over me as he moved his arm, then his hips press into the side of my ass.

"I know what you want."

"Then why should I tell you?"

"I want to hear you say it." His voice was sex in sound, irresistible.

"I want you to touch me."

"Where?"

I swallowed, and dipped my head. His fist loosened in my hair, and his fingers ran down the back of my neck, then all the way down my spine. My nipples tightened under my shirt, pleasure firing through my whole body at his touch.

"My pussy," I whispered.

"Good girl."

His kisses resumed, but his fingers were moving under the line of my underwear again, this time rolling them down. Exposing me to him completely. I heard that low rumble he'd made earlier, and when he spoke, his voice was gravelly, laced with his own desire. "Press your legs together." I did as he said, shuffling until my knees were closed tight together. Need pulsed through me, and I knew he would be able to see my arousal. I couldn't help pushing my hips back, thrusting myself at him.

He ran a finger up my thigh, stopping just shy of my aching sex. A growl soundedand I realized that this time it had been me. Again, and again, he stroked me, landing soft, hot kisses on my skin that moved tortuously closer every time.

"Nox, please," I half-whimpered.

"I like it when you say my name, Beth. When I fuck you, I want you to say it."

"Yes." I'd say yes to freaking anything, bent over in front of him, desperate.

"And I will fuck you Beth. I will fuck you into oblivion. Into a place you've never been before and will never want to come back from." I could hear the desperation in his own voice, rough and lacking the cool control he usually had. "I'm not going to fuck you today. I've waited too long to rush this. But I am going to make you come. Will you come for me, Beth?"

Christ, I was half-ready to come just listening to him. "Yes."

His hot, wet lips closed over my swollen clitoris, and I cried out. My hips bucked, and his strong arms wrapped around my thighs, holding me still. His tongue flicked again, and pleasure rocketed through me, pulsing out from my most sensitive spot and not stopping. I arched my back as I felt his fingers glide over my skin, then moaned long and loud as he finally touched me. I heard him hiss a breath, and then his tongue was flicking fast as his finger slid exquisitely slowly into me.

"Oh god, oh god," I gasped.

"God has nothing to do with this." He withdrew his finger, just as slowly. "Imagine this is my cock, stretching you, filling you." His breath was hot against me, and when I felt him slide into me again, it was with two fingers. I ground my teeth together to stop myself crying out. My mind filled with the image of him naked and hard, pounding into me, and I pushed back onto his hand hard. He growled, and I felt his tongue on my clit again, hot and wet.

Days, possibly even years, of pent-up desire flooded through my system, the pleasure so intense it made my head spin. He moved his fingers slowly at first, in time with his tongue, letting me savor every movement. But as he began to build his pace, the pressure inside me grew, and the pleasure began to consume me. I felt my whole body tense and rock, and a low cry issued from me as I clenched hard around him. His tongue flicked faster, and an image of him, wings spread behind him, filled my head. *Come for me.* His voice was in my mind, and I let myself fall into the abyss he had led me to. Wracking waves of release washed through me, pulsing out from my core and rolling all the way to the ends of my fingers, my toes. I shuddered as I cried out, and I heard him saying my name through the haze of electrifying bliss.

"You're mine, Beth."

His arms tightened, and he flipped me over, setting me down on my butt on the couch. I gasped down air as I stared hazily at him. His eyes were blazing. Actually blazing. Blue light danced fiercely as he swept his eyes over my still shaking body.

"I've never come like that," I breathed, instantly feeling stupid for saying it out loud.

"You're fucking stunning." He stood up, and his body was hard as a rock, tension rippling from him. I closed my legs, suddenly very aware that I was a lot more naked than he was. "You should never cover up perfection," he said, and his sultry lilt was back. "Kiss me."

The waves of residual pleasure still washing through me sparked, and I stood up. He ran a finger down my cheek, and I laid both of my hands on his chest.

"I think I can trust you," I said. Passion exploded in his eyes, and he pulled my face up, closing his lips over mine. Every ounce of his own need was evident in that kiss, and hell, I almost came again. His other hand wrapped around my waist and pressed me into him, his hardness tantalizingly obvious against me.

He kissed me with a hunger I hadn't even known was possible, until I'd felt it myself on the couch. His desperation matched mine, there was no doubt.

With a visible effort, he pulled away from me, stepping back so that there was an arms distance between us. His whole body glowed faintly, his eyes bright and fierce.

He looked like the damn embodiment of sex, an Adonis with the promise of a world that I was desperate to explore oozing from every pore.

"Come with me." The effort in his words was clear as he took another step backward. I pulled on my underwear and jeans and followed him out of the room. I hardly noticed where we were going, my mind was so full of erotic thoughts. My body still pulsed with desire as he led me up a grand staircase. Pushing open a door, I saw a bedroom, decorated in soft grays, a dark black breadspread across an enormous bed. Abstract paintings in shades of red hung on the wall, and black drapes covered the window.

"Is this your room?" I breathed. He turned to me.

"No. This is a guest room. Your case is there." He nodded to the right, and I saw my case propped in front of a mirrored closet door. "I can't stay in the same room as you. Not like this."

"Why not?"

"My control is good, but not that good. I have waited nearly eighty years for you, Beth. I will wait a little longer."

TWENTY-NINE

BETH

I awoke on sheets that felt cool and crisp and nothing like my own. I stretched, luxuriating in them for a moment as the sleep cleared from my mind. Then last night whirled through my thoughts like a freaking hurricane. I throbbed with lust as the events played out in my head, and I rolled over, burying my face in the feather pillow.

"Oh god," I mumbled aloud into the fabric.

I'd succumbed to the charms of Nox. Lucifer. The devil.

"Ooh, god," I said again, and turned onto my back. The room was dark, the heavy black drapes drawn across the large windows, and I squinted up at the decorative plasterwork on the ceiling.

What the hell was I going to do? There was no way on this earth I was going to be able to say no to sleeping with him. No way. The way he'd kissed me filled my mind, making heat swirl through me. He wanted me, no question. But that was because he couldn't have me.

If we had sex, if he actually claimed me as he'd promised he would, he would lose interest in me, or realize I was shit at it. And then it would be over. I'd spend my whole life looking for someone like him and being perpetually disappointed.

A tendril of doubt worked its way through me. What if he already knew I was boring? I mean, I'd done nothing at all last night. He'd been completely in charge, so my skills were yet to be tested. But he might have worked it out? What if he was totally uninterested when I saw him?

An unnecessarily large stab of loss hit me when I imagined him dismissing me, and I groaned. I was doing exactly what I hadn't wanted to do. I was becoming desperate for him, giving him all the power.

"I've waited nearly eighty years for you, Beth." His words echoed through my mind, and I clung to them. All those things he'd said to me... He wasn't a playboy. The man hadn't had sex with anyone for, well, a lifetime. And he wanted me. He could *only* have me.

But my brain was struggling to accept the idea that he couldn't get hard for anyone but me as true. How could it be? Why would his body only respond to me? He could definitely be lying — it was a great line to use on women. There was something undeniably thrilling about the whole notion.

A new thought occurred to me. If it *was* true, did I want a man who was only with me because he had no other choice? That felt weird, too. Blowing out a sigh, I sat up and swung my legs over the bed.

Right now, I knew that Nox made me feel like a freaking goddess. He'd made me come harder than I knew was possible, and if I was being honest, I felt great. A sense of satisfaction nestled in my gut for the first time in as long as I could remember. *Take each day at a time, Beth,* I told myself. I could worry about the rest of my shit-show life later.

I showered in the en-suite washroom, wishing like hell that my own shower was as powerful and sleek. Bulgari toiletries were laid out neatly on the shelf and I couldn't help feeling like I was in a fancy hotel. Not that I'd ever been to one, but I had a TV. Well, I used to have a TV. Before Alex stole it.

"Asshole," I muttered, as I wrapped my hair in a towel. I dressed in jeans and a gingham shirt from my case. I put some mascara on but didn't want to spend too much time on my make-up. I was getting twitchy, wanting to see Nox. I needed to make sure he was still interested, now that he'd had a taste.

"Good morning." He was in suit slacks and a white shirt, standing over a frying pan, when I entered the kitchen. My steps faltered, and my skin tingled as he turned, shooting me a smile. Blue eyes, dark hair, rough stubble and... A promise. There was that same promise in his face that made my knees feel weak and every muscle in my body tighten.

"Hi." Beelzebub skittered across the hard floors towards me, crashing into my shins. I laughed and crouched down. "And hello to you too," I told the dog, petting him as he tried to lick my hands.

"Are you hungry?"

"Yes."

"So am I." I knew he wasn't talking about food. I could hear it in his voice, feel it in the charged atmosphere. My god, I wanted him. Needed him.

I cleared my throat. "I'd love a coffee."

"Of course."

I stood up as he moved to a complicated looking chrome machine on the side. "Show me how to do it, and I'll make them," I said as something sizzled in the pan.

Making breakfast in the sunlight-filled kitchen would have felt normal, if it weren't for the fact that we kept finding reasons to brush against each other, kept throwing glances over our shoulders that were filled with desire.

He was not done with me. That much was clear.

When we were sitting where we had the night before, rich coffee and bacon omelets before us, he spoke.

"Madaleine left me a message. She wants to meet with me."

The mention of the angry angel caused the charged excitement in my core to dip. "Oh?"

"She says she has a proposition."

"Do you trust her?"

"I think I need to talk with her. Do you want to come?"

An awkwardness filled the air, the undercurrent of his question clear. We hadn't done too well last time we'd been around the power of Wrath.

"Yes. But can we meet her someplace that isn't that weird white office?"

I thought I saw a flash of relief in his eyes before he answered. "She keeps her home and office all white to help her relax. Bright colors exacerbate the anger. But yes, I agree that we should meet on neutral ground."

"I want to ask Max some more questions about Gordon, and he's more likely to answer them if you're with me. Why don't we meet her at the club? We already know she goes there."

Nox nodded. "The Aphrodite Club it is."

"Okay. What time?"

"An hour."

"What? What kind of strip club is open at," I paused and pulled my cellphone out of my back pocket to check the time. "10am?"

"The time doesn't govern lust," Nox answered, his head dipping and his eyes darkening as he looked at me. "People give in to it more at night, but it is always there."

I watched his face as he took a long sip of his coffee, unable to stop the memories of last night playing in my head. *More.* I wanted more.

I wanted everything.

～

The stale beer and bleach smell of the Aphrodite club was starting to become unnervingly familiar. There was nobody behind the little counter when we arrived, and the beat of the loud music was oddly absent.

When we emerged through the red curtains, I saw that the club was as gloomy in the daytime as it was at night. Any windows the place had were hidden by the deep red fabric that lined the walls, and the colored spotlights that lit up the stage provided the main light source. Music was playing, but much more quietly than usual, and there was a girl on stage, dancing half-heartedly for one man at a table close to her. He turned as we walked in, muttered something, then stood up and headed for the men's restrooms. The girl on stage threw us an annoyed look, until her eyes focused on Nox. They widened, then she hurried down the steps at the side of the stage, disappearing behind it.

Nox strode to over to the small, empty bar like he owned the place.

"No sign of Madaleine," I said, unable to keep my apprehension from my voice.

"She's not prone to being on time."

"I'm going to use the bathroom," I said, and headed toward the ladies. I glanced at the door behind the stage as I passed it, where the girl had gone. I paused when I heard raised voices from behind it.

"For fuck's sake, why are they here again?"

"I don't know Max. It's nothing to do with me. You deal with it."

"Don't fucking tell me what to do."

There was a pause, then the female voice said, "They're probably here about Gordon. The guy's a fucking creep. I bet he did Sarah in."

"I told you not to talk about Sarah. It's bad for business. Get back on the bloody stage and use those tits to make us some money. Now."

I hurried away as I heard footsteps, yanking open the door to the washroom and slipping inside before the dancer saw me hanging around. So, she thought Gordon was capable of killing Sarah? That was interesting.

When I came out of the washroom, the atmosphere in the quiet club was tangibly different. I saw why immediately. Madaleine was seated at a table opposite Nox, her pet demon sitting next to her. I was relieved to see that he was clothed this time. Madaleine was wearing a white jumpsuit, her long legs crossed elegantly, and she had her hair in a braid that started high on her head. She turned to look at me as I walked over, giving me a slow smile. My palms began to sweat instantly as her unsettling magic washed over me. Self-doubt and vengeful anger began to pull at me as I got closer.

"Hello," I said as I reached the table. I was not going to sit and be silent this time. I was as much a part of this as they were.

"So glad you could join us," she said. I sat down.

"Nox tells me this was your choice of venue. You have gone up in my esteem." Her eyes gleamed with a mocking savagery.

"Yes, I just can't get enough of these naked women. Now, shall we start?"

Madaleine raised an eyebrow at me, and nodded. "Fine." She turned to Nox. A small smile was pulling at his lips as his eyes flicked to me, then back to her. "I have heard about a certain book hitting the market."

Nox's expression hardened instantly. "Who has it?"

"So it's true? Your stolen property is the Book of Sins?"

Heat rolled from him as he glared at her. "Yes."

"Then, I need to reconsider my stance on this matter. You and I both know that if someone else were to get the book and all of the pages, it would not end well. For either of us."

"Who?" The question popped from my lips before I could stop it. Both fallen angels turned their gazes to me. "Who don't you want to get the book?"

"Michael," said Nox, quietly. "Or Gabriel. Both hate me enough."

"Are they fallen angels too?"

"Just angels," said Madaleine. "They don't know the fun of falling."

"What could they do if they had the book and pages?"

"I don't know, and I don't want to find out. I am quite happy with our arrangement as it is, thank you very much," she answered. "But nobody is going to risk stealing from the devil without a good reason. They must have a plan."

Nox glared at her, shadows swirling in his eyes, but the volatile energy that had poured from him in her presence the previous day was absent. There was just a dangerous, simmering power emanating from him. "What did you want to talk about, Madaleine?"

"I want to offer my help. I have many contacts. I will help you find the book. And my page."

"In return for what?"

"You destroy the page for Wrath when you get it back."

Nox moved his head ever so slightly. "Destroy it?"

"So that Wrath can't be passed to anyone else. The page is not needed for the power to exist. Only to move it on."

"Madaleine, I alone can move the power of the sins between hosts. The page does not need to be destroyed if you have my word that you may keep Wrath."

She gave him a long look. "Your word?"

"You know that my word is binding."

"I want you to destroy the page." Red flickered in her eyes, and Nox smiled.

"You tried to destroy it yourself, didn't you?"

She dropped his gaze for a split second. "Will you destroy it or not?"

"No. You can take my word that you may keep Wrath, or we have no deal."

Her eyes were consumed by red, and she stood up abruptly. "I will sleep on it," she barked, then whirled around. "Cornu!" The demon leapt to his feet and hurried after her as she marched from the club.

I looked at Nox. "If you let her keep Wrath, then you can't break your curse. You said you needed all the sins back to get your full power again."

"I know. I'll make sure that the deal will work to my advantage. Not everybody reads the fine print." Mischief danced in his eyes.

"Hmmm. I guess you're a pro at making deals that work to your advantage."

"You should know."

"Was there any fine print to my deal that I should have read?"

"No. No tricks for you Beth. Just pure, pure lust."

The ravenous look in his eyes sent shivers across my skin, his heat pulsing out and caressing my body, working its way through me like liquid fire.

"Can I get you two anything?" Max's burly voice cut through the moment.

"No. We're leaving now."

The bar owner looked relieved. "Right. Have a good day."

"Before we go, though, a few questions about Gordon. The man who loans money to the dancers. Tell me what you know about him."

Max shrugged. "I don't like him loaning money to the girls, but they're all stupid. What can I do? They burn through cash like idiots, and it's not like I don't pay them enough."

Nox's face was impassive. "Tell me about Gordon."

"Oh, right, yeah. Erm, the girls don't really like him."

"He's a shifter?"

"Yeah. Fox."

"Do you allow shifting in here, Max?" A dangerous tone had entered Nox's voice, and the bar owner shifted, wringing his hands together.

"No, course not, only on designated Veil nights, and I always get a permit for that."

Designated Veil nights? I made a mental note to ask Nox what that was. A party night for supernaturals perhaps?

"I have a report from this young woman of Gordon threatening her and bordering on shifting. In your bar."

"I dealt with that," he answered quickly.

"Did you report him?"

"No, no, I didn't want any trouble. And besides, he didn't actually shift. He's a good customer."

"The fight he had with Sarah's boyfriend. Did he shift then?"

Max swallowed and dropped Nox's gaze. He didn't have to speak; it was obvious that the answer was yes. "I threw him out that night."

"But you didn't report him?"

"No. Dave hit him hard. Any shifter would've done the same, it's instinct." Sweat was beading on Max's forehead.

"Would you shift, if you were punched right now?" Nox's calm voice was laced with threat.

"Me? No, I erm, I..." Max let out a breath, a defeated look crossing his features. "I have control of my animal."

"And Gordon does not." It wasn't a question.

Max nodded in reluctant agreement. "I guess, when you put it like that…"

Nox stood up. "Thank you for being honest with me."

"Are you going to report me?" Fear filled Max's voice.

"No. But I want you to bar Gordon. If he can't control his fox in your establishment, you should not be letting him in."

Max heaved another sigh, this one I thought of relief. "Okay. Thank you, Mr. Nox."

"I want you to call me when he comes in."

"Sure thing. Rather you tell him he can't come to the club any more than me."

As soon as Max turned and loped back to the bar I jumped to my feet. "I have questions. Many questions," I said.

"You always have questions."

"More than you know."

THIRTY

BETH

"Who are Michael and Gabriel?" The first question flew from my lips once we were in the car.

"Angels."

"Like you? But not fallen?"

"Yes. They work for the gods."

"Are they the enforcers you talked about before?"

"They don't do the dirty work, but yes. They ensure supernaturals behave themselves."

"Why don't they like you?"

Nox gave me a look. "I'm the devil. I represent sin. They don't need much more reason than that."

"Oh. Do you think Madaleine will take your deal? Do you think she knows where the book is?"

Nox ran his hand through his hair and everything south of my ribs clenched. I forced myself to concentrate. "She has contacts I don't, and she is powerful. I have few allies. I think it would be beneficial to have her on our side, at least for now."

Our side. I liked that. Since when was I excited to be referred to as on the same side as the devil? The mad lady from Lavender Oaks popped into my head, and I let out a tiny chuckle. Nox raised an eyebrow at me.

"Sorry, I just remembered something. The day I met you, I saw Francis in the evening and an old lady at the home started screaming about me being in league with the devil."

"She must be a seer."

"What's one of those?"

"They see auras."

"Can they see the future? With crystal balls and stuff?"

Nox smiled. "No. Some djinn can do that, but it's extremely rare."

"Djinn?"

"Genies. Live in lamps in human popular culture."

My mouth dropped open. "Seriously?" Excitement was buzzing about my body. "I can't believe there's so much I didn't know about the world. Actual genies in lamps? I can't wait to find out what else there is." *And start looking for my parents again.*

A real smile took Nox's beautiful mouth, setting off my stomach flutters again. "I'm glad you're looking forward to it."

"How many types of supernatural are there? How did you know Max was a shifter, can you tell what people are just by looking at them?"

"Too many to count. And yes, I can tell what a super-natural's power is immediately, but that's a gift few have. Many supernaturals can tell if someone is not human, but that's all. I, on the other hand, can see everything, right down to what his animal is."

"What's his animal?"

"An eagle."

"Are there lots of types of animal shifters?"

"Yes, though most are canine in some form. Wolves dominate."

"What's a designated Veil night?"

"It's a night where the whole club will appear closed to humans, and all the supernaturals can let their magic go free. They happen all over the city, but they have to be cleared first, so that the venues can be properly hidden."

"That's so cool." The thought of secret magic parties all over London thrilled me.

"There are a few places that are permanently hidden from humans. They're filled with magic, all the time."

"I want to see them."

"You will. They'll be where we start to look for the book. But we need to find this killer and clear you name of murder first. I'm becoming quite keen to fulfill this bargain of ours."

So was I, for all the wrong reasons.

"Do you still think it was Madaleine?"

His blue eyes bore into mine. "Do you?"

"No." I shook my head. "I don't think she would be offering to help you get the book back if she had killed somebody in your office."

"Wrath works in strange ways. And can be incredibly impulsive."

"Hmmm."

"She might have stolen the book, purely in order to offer it back to me in return for having eternal control of Wrath."

I hadn't thought of that. I chewed on my bottom lip as I considered it. It did make sense. She was utterly untrustworthy. And there was the gleaming white feather... "What about Gordon though?" I said. "You haven't met him, he's creepy as hell. And that dancer thinks he's a creep too."

"I think he might be responsible for the note on your door."

"You don't think that was the killer?"

"I think the murder is connected to the book. I think the note was to do with whatever your ex has got himself involved in." He half-growled the words *your ex*.

I swallowed. "Oh."

"And let's not discount the angry mechanic."

"He was in love with Sarah, for sure," I mused.

Nox's cell rang, and he slid it from his pocket to answer it. His conversation was short and clipped, and he look annoyed when he hung up. "Beth, I have to go to the office. Do you want to go back to my house and wait for me?"

"How long will you be?"

"A couple hours."

"That's enough time to catch up with Francis. I feel guilty leaving her so soon the other day." And she was the only person I could talk to about the moral dilemma of having sex with the devil.

"No problem. Claude will take you there."

By the time the town car pulled up in front of the retirement home, I had made up my mind. I was going to tell Francis everything. About supernaturals, Nox being the devil, everything. She was my only true confidant, and I couldn't handle the amount of information and the decisions I was having to deal with without talking to someone about it.

Plus, I really thought she would believe me. And even if she didn't, she would probably play along, rather than call the lunatic asylum. I trusted her implicitly.

"Honey, you are a sight for sore eyes," she said as I found her in her La-Z-Boy. "They ain't arrested you yet?"

"Nope. Not yet. And I found them a new suspect."

"Tell me." She patted the arm of the lounger next to her and I slumped into it.

"Francis, do you believe in magic?" I fixed my eyes on hers, and they widened, then narrowed in thought.

"I believe in something. Dunno that I would call it magic."

"I... I found magic. Real supernatural magic."

"Is this like a finding God thing?" she asked, a note of worry in her voice.

"It's more like a finding the devil thing. Although there are gods too. And angels."

She raised her eyebrows in slow motion. "The devil?"

"Yes. The man who came here, Mr. Nox. He's Lucifer. The devil."

"You mean, the actual devil? Not like, a devil in the bedroom or the like, but the actual devil?"

I nodded. "Yup. And I made a deal with him."

"Ooh." She let out a long breath, her eyebrows still high on her forehead and her eyes wide. "You made a sex deal with the devil," she hissed.

"There was no guarantee of sex," I corrected her quickly. "But yeah. I made a deal with the devil, and now I can see the supernatural world. And it's all around us, everywhere. I met a woman who is a fallen angel, and she has wings. So does Nox."

Once I started, I couldn't stop. Everything I had experienced over the last few days poured from me, right up to the note on my door and Nox insisting I stayed at his.

"Then what?" Francis was hanging on my every word, and no part of her expression suggested that she was mocking or questioning my story.

"And then... He told me he was cursed because he gave up power of the sins he didn't want. The gods cursed him so that he couldn't enjoy the ones that he kept."

"Which ones did he keep?"

"Greed, gluttony and lust. He can't taste food, he can't keep money for more than a day, and... and he can't have sex."

Francis' face turned ashen. "Now that is a damn

crime against humanity, that is. That man is far, far too pretty not to be able to have sex."

"Well... It looks like now he can, for the first time in nearly eighty years. But only with me."

A huge smile plastered itself across her face, making her eyes crinkle. She clapped her hands together. "Honey, if he's lying to you to get you into bed, he's doing a damn fine job of it! What a way to woo a girl!"

I screwed my face up. "But Francis, why would he be able to with me, but not anybody else? I'm super-normal, just like Alex said. What have I got to do with a curse on the devil?"

"Who knows, and who cares? You get to have sex with him! And even better, he can't have sex with anyone else!"

Her eyes were gleaming with excitement and her voice was getting louder. The recreation room was empty, but I hushed her all the same. "He's going to try to break his curse. So he'll be able to... use his machinery again," I said awkwardly.

"Oh." Her face fell. "How long will that take?"

"I don't know."

"Then you should move quickly. Take advantage."

I shook my head. "But what if I like it too much? And he doesn't? He'll get bored of me, and I'll never be able to get back what I had with him."

Francis looked at me seriously. "Honey, I'm in my seventies. All I got now are memories of things I don't have any more. If I hadn't done them 'cos I was scared I wouldn't do them again, I'd have nothing."

Her words sank through my doubts, their weight enough for me to hear them properly. Was she right? Was a memory better than a regret?

"Your big night of passion doesn't happen until you find the killer, right?" she said.

"I don't have to fulfill my end of the deal until he clears my name of murder," I answered carefully.

"And who do you think it is?"

"Gordon. There was something so off about him. He's a shifter."

"A shifter? Does that mean he can turn into an animal?"

"Yeah. You're taking this surprisingly well."

Francis shrugged. "I've no reason to take it otherwise."

My phone buzzed in my pocket and I fished it out, expecting to see Nox's number. It was an unregistered London number. I answered.

"Miss Abbott?" I recognized Inspector Singh's voice. My heart skipped a beat.

"Yes?"

"Just an update. There were no prints on the note on your door. Cell phone triangulation has confirmed that there was a call made from the LMS building to the Aphrodite Club around the time of the murder though, so we are looking for Gordon Jackson. Please let me know if you run into him again."

Her meaning was clear. *Don't go looking for him yourself.*

My heart beat faster in my chest as I processed what

she'd said. For the first time, it didn't sound like she thought I'd done it. The suspect I'd found them could actually be the killer, and the police were looking for him. Relief rushed through me. "I believe Mr. Nox was hoping to be informed when he next visits the club. You should probably call him," I said.

"Thanks," she answered, then hung up.

"Who was it?" Francis had hauled her huge frame upright to lean forward eagerly.

"The police. Somebody called the strip club from the LMS building the day of the murder."

"So, who do they think it is?"

"Gordon. I knew I was right and Nox was wrong!"

"Does Mr. Nox not think it's him?"

"No. He thinks it's the fallen angel I told you about because she has white wings and the police found a white feather at the scene of the crime."

"A white feather? Didn't you say Gordon turns into an animal?"

"Yes, but not one with feathers, he turns into a fox." Something clicked in my mind as I spoke, and I gave a small gasp as the cogs turned slowly. "Francis, there is a bird shifter at the club."

"Really?"

"Yes! Max, the bar owner. Nox said he turns into an eagle."

"Are his feathers white?"

"I don't know." The cogs turned faster. "Sarah worked for him, and he's always crazy nervous around Nox. Plus, he's connected to the supernatural world, he would know about the devil's book!" I was on my feet without even realizing I'd stood up. "Francis, I think the killer is Max! I think he and Sarah must have been trying to steal the book, and something went wrong!"

Excitement surged through me. If I was right and I could tell Nox and the Inspector who really did it, they'd all stop treating me like a weak damsel-in-distress. And my deal would be broken. I would be in control. "I just have to find out if Max's feathers are white. Then I'll know for sure. Francis, I'm going to the club."

Francis's eyes were sparkling. "Not without me, you're not," she said, pulling herself to her feet.

THIRTY-ONE

BETH

"Y ou know, you really didn't need to come with me," I said for the hundredth time. Claude was looking at us in his rearview mirror so often I was starting to worry he would crash the car.

"I think you'll find I did need to come with you," she said, pulling at the seat belt across her round frame. "I can't have you visiting a killer alone!"

"This must be the fifth time I've been to this bar, it's not dangerous," I said. "I'm just going to talk him into shifting so that I can see the color of his wings. Nothing dangerous."

"If the mighty fine devil can't be here to help, then you'll have to make do with me," she said.

I glanced down at the phone I was still clutching in my hand. I'd called Nox twice, but neither call had got through. "Francis, you'd decided to come with me before I'd even tried to call Nox."

"Well, it's been a long time since I went to a strip club. I'd like to refresh my memory."

I sighed.

"Are you quite sure you and your friend want to go to the Aphrodite Club?" asked Claude nervously from the front.

"Yes, I'm sorry to keep doing this to you," I said. "I'm trying to call your boss, I promise." He gave me a small nod, flicked his eyes to Francis in the mirror, then refocused on the slow traffic.

"He's kinda cute," Francis whispered loudly.

"Who, Claude?" I whispered back.

"Sure."

"I'll do my best to find out if he's single," I promised her.

"You do that."

It was 2pm when we eventually pulled up outside the little door to Max's club. A healthy trickle of adrenaline had started to pump through my body, and I felt hotter than I should, even for an unusually warm spring day.

"Are you sure you won't stay in the car?" I tried one more time.

"Nope," Francis said.

It took longer to get up the narrow stairs than it would have taken me on my own, but when we got there, the bored-looking guy was in the booth.

"Three quid each," he said as we reached him. His gaze lingered a second on Francis, then moved quickly back to his phone. I picked six pounds out of my purse and took the small bits of cardboard from him.

"Is Max here?"

"Max's always here," he shrugged without looking at me.

The dancer from earlier was behind the bar when we got through the curtain, and a different girl was on stage. She was the one in cowboy boots and a big Stetson that I'd seen before. Three or four guys were sitting alone at tables, and there was a rowdier group of three near the stage.

Who knew there was so much trade for early afternoon stripping?

"It's loud," Francis shouted at me.

"Yeah. Sit down while I find Max. He's not going to do anything magic in front of you." She nodded, and I guided her to one of the booth seats against the wall. "Now, stay here."

"I ain't going nowhere. Can I have some money for a drink?"

I sighed, and gave her a five-pound note. "I can't believe I'm taking a pensioner for a trip out to a strip bar," I muttered.

"My boobs looked like that once," she said wistfully, staring at the girl shaking her chest to the music on stage. My boobs looked nothing like that, I thought as I stared. They were huge.

The guys in a group cheered loudly as the other girl brought over a tray of beers.

"Behave yourself," I said to Francis, and headed

toward the door behind the stage. It was closed when I got there, and I knocked.

No answer.

Carefully, I tried the handle. The door swung open.

"Hello?" I called, but I knew I wouldn't be heard over the sound of Tom Jones' Sex Bomb. I stepped through, the music becoming muffled as I shut the door behind me. I was in a kitchenette type room, —a small sink set in a counter with a microwave and kettle on one side, and mops and buckets and piles of paper towels and other supplies stacked against the other. There was another door at the far end, and I squinted at it, trying to work out of it exited on the other side of the stage.

It opened, and I took a step back in surprise.

"What are you doing?" Max stepped through, frowning at me as he shut it quickly behind him.

"Oh, erm, I'm looking for you," I beamed at him.

"Why?" He marched toward me, and I straightened.

"I'm trying to learn about the Veil, and you've been so helpful so far. I wondered if I could ask you some more about shifters."

He stopped a couple feet from me. Could he hear my heart beating slightly too fast? Was that one of his powers? "What do you want to know?"

"Well, the truth is... I've never seen anyone shift." I tried the pouting thing again. "I don't suppose you would show me?"

"You heard your high and mighty friend," he scowled. "No shifting on the premises."

"But nobody can see us back here. Please?" He said nothing, but I could see the indecision on his face. "I'd love to see your wings," I said.

His features sharpened as his expression changed. "My wings?"

"Y-yes," I stammered.

"How do you know what I shift into?"

"Mr. Nox told me." I took a step backward, closer to the door. The muffled beat of the music got a little louder.

"Why have you got so many questions?" I opened my mouth but couldn't think of an answer before he spoke again. "This isn't about the Veil. It's about Sarah." His eyes darkened, and a faint glow appeared around him.

"No, it's about shifting. I just want to see how it happens." Even I could hear the lie in my voice as I inched further backward.

"Is Nox working with the police?" Panic flitted through Max's beady eyes, then hard resolve settled there instead. "The police found the feather I dropped there, didn't they. That's why you want to see me shift." His voice was soft, and unmistakably menacing. My blood seemed to turn to ice in my veins.

It was him. I'd been right.

"If Sarah hadn't fought me, I wouldn't have dropped the fucking feather." He snarled, and I turned, throwing myself at the door.

His hand fisted around my hair just as I reached it, yanking me back hard enough to make me cry out. Both my hands went instinctively to my head as he kept pulling, dragging me father away from the door.

"I meant what I said. Your skull will crack slower than Sarah's." His voice was a hiss, and I felt sick with fear as he tugged me against his body. I kicked backward, as hard as I could, but his big arm wrapped around my waist and pulled me off my feet before I could make contact.

I screamed. As loudly as I possibly could. Somebody in the club had to hear me over the music. But then there was a blinding pain in my temple, and everything went dark.

I blinked, a throbbing pain in my head filtering through the haze. I blinked some more, trying to clear my vision.

Where was I?

I moved, and realized I was lying face down on something soft. I tried to push myself to my hands and knees, and discovered that I couldn't separate my wrists or ankles. Fear bolted through me, and I sucked in air as I rolled, trying desperately to see where I was.

A bed. I was on a bed with a disgusting blanket on it covered in stains. I lifted my arms, seeing that they were bound with black tape. So were my ankles. I struggled to sit up, a wave of pain crashing through my head so hard that bile rose in my throat. I closed my eyes as dizziness threatened to overtake me, taking deep breathes through my mouth — to avoid the putrid smell in the room.

"Don't fucking throw up on my bed."

The voice startled me into opening my eyes. My head snapped up. Max was sitting in a wicker chair, in front of a small portable TV on a stool.

I scanned the rest of the room fast. There was a window with cardboard taped across it, just a few cracks of light entering around it. *It was still daytime then.* Scuffed wooden planks lined the floor, and clothes and DVDs and magazines were strewn around everywhere. Empty takeout containers with bits of unidentifiable furry remnants were the likely cause of the horrendous smell.

I swallowed down my rising fear, adrenaline coursing through me so hard my skin felt like it was on fire. My chest was tight as I spoke, my voice a rasp.

"Let me go, now."

"Nah. I'm not going to kill you yet, though."

I took a shuddering breath. "Nox will find me." *Please, please say he was already looking for me. Please.*

But Nox, and the police, had the wrong suspects. Neither thought Max was involved.

"Nox is a giant fucking asshole," Max barked, and stood up from his chair. He moved toward me, stamping across the floorboards. "Sarah was all caught up by him too. *Oh Max, I can't do it, I can't steal from him.*" He parroted a woman's voice, high and mocking. "She called me. She called me from his office, dumb bitch. Told me she liked him, and refused to steal the book, like I had paid her to do. So I had to fly down there and fucking do it myself."

"Why did you kill her?"

"Because she was a pain in my ass. She was a fucking liability. She even tried to get the Veil lifted for your useless ex." Anger sparked in his eyes, and I knew right then why he had killed her. It was the same look that had taken over Gordon's face.

"You were jealous. She wouldn't sleep with you, would she?"

Max glowed and then suddenly his body began to melt into light, reforming as I watched. Cracking sounds echoed through the room, and my heart pounded in my chest as a massive white eagle flapped its grey-edged wings before me.

The bird darted forward, black beady eyes fixed on me. I threw my taped arms over my head just in time, and the pointed beak raked through the skin on my forearms. I cried out in pain and flattened myself to the gross sheets as the beak tore through more skin, moving down over my shoulder.

"Stop!"

I didn't feel the beak again, and my arms shook as I lowered them.

Max was panting slightly, fury in his face, and the glowing light around him fading. "You shouldn't provoke me, little girl. You shouldn't fucking provoke me. I've got plans for you."

Blood ran hot from the wounds on my arms, and I swallowed again. A lump was hard in my throat and my eyes burned. "What plans?" My voice trembled, and I wished I hadn't spoken. I didn't want him to know I was afraid. I blinked back tears. I would not cry in front of this maniac.

"I run a strip bar," he said, eyes dancing with malice. "I have a thing for pretty girls. And now, the devil's new pet will dance just for me."

THIRTY-TWO

BETH

I stared at Max, my insides knotting. "Dance for you?"

"I hit you pretty hard, and now you've got blood on you, so I'll give you an hour or so to clean up. But yeah, then you're gonna dance for me."

I shook my head, lancing pain accompanying the movement and making me fall still. "No. No, I'm not-" Max stepped forward, his hand raised, and I clamped my mouth shut.

"You'll do as you're fucking told." He reached out and grabbed the top of my arm, dragging me to the edge of the bed. Pulling me to my feet, I was forced to hop after him on my bound feet as he guided me to a battered door. When he yanked it open, I saw a small washroom. "Clean yourself up." He pushed me inside.

"Untie my wrists."

"No. And leave the door open."

He turned and strode back to his chair, moving it so that it faced the open washroom door.

I sucked in air and immediately regretted it. The toilet smelled even worse than the bedroom. I glanced down at the porcelain bowl and had to stop myself from heaving. It was beyond disgusting.

Instead, I turned to the sink. A filthy mirror showed a bruise starting to spread across my forehead, and blood trickling down my left shoulder and dribbling down my forearms. My hair was tangled, and there was a wild look in my eyes. I fixed my gaze on my own reflection, trying to slow my racing heart.

I had to stay calm. I had to stay focused. Max had killed a woman, and he had magic. This was as serious a situation as I could possibly be in, and if I lost my shit, I could very well lose my life, too.

I lifted my tied arms and awkwardly turned on the faucet. Water gurgled from the rusted metal. I put my hands under it, concentrating on the coolness. I realized as the water ran over my skin that I was thirsty. Really thirsty.

"May I have some water to drink?" I asked, turning to Max.

His beady eyes watched me a moment, then he stood up. After wandering around the room he came into the washroom with a dirty pint glass. He held it under the faucet a minute, then put it down on the side of the sink.

"There."

I said nothing, and he returned to his chair.

There was no way I was drinking from a glass that gross. I dropped my head and held my mouth under the faucet instead, trying not to let any of me touch the dirty porcelain. Cool water filled my mouth, and I closed my eyes.

I could survive this. Nox would be looking for me. Francis knew where I was. She would get in touch with Nox or the police.

"Keep bending over like that, and we'll cut the dancing and get straight on with it," called Max. A sick feeling made my stomach twist again, threatening to break the calm I was trying to fortify myself with.

Sarah hadn't been molested or touched in any way.

She just had her head caved in. Much better.

I forced away the image of the girl's dead body. As much as I hated her for sleeping with my boyfriend, it sounded like Sarah had gotten the raw end of every deal. Men believed that they had a right to have sex with her, and when she said no, they treated her like shit.

Max said she'd called him and told him that she liked Nox too much to steal from him, and he'd lost his temper and killed her. I tried to work through my churning thoughts logically. Why was he holding me captive instead of killing me? Was I only alive because he hadn't lost his temper yet? Because the blow to my head hadn't been hard enough to do more damage? I thought about what he'd said to Nox about shifter instincts and control.

I needed to keep him calm, I decided. I needed to prevent him from losing his temper and cracking my skull, either intentionally or accidentally.

I straightened and started trying to clean off the blood on my arms.

"So, why were you stealing Nox's book?" I asked the

question as casually as I could, and was relieved to find my voice steady. The water, and the vague plan of not pissing off my murderous kidnapper, was working to keep the panic at bay.

"None of your fucking business," he answered from behind me.

I nodded. "No. I guess not. I'm new to all this."

"Yeah, you are new. Why has a fallen as powerful as Nox chosen a human pet?"

I shrugged, the movement pulling at the deep scratch in my shoulder and making me wince. "I don't know," I lied.

"Is it something to do with why Sarah was interested in that druggie twat you were banging?"

I bit down on my tongue to stop myself retorting. I heard Max move and turned in time to see him right behind me. He snarled and pulled me away from the sink. "Clean-up time is over." He shoved me back toward the bed and turned off the faucet.

"I heard eagle shifters are a big deal," I said. I'd heard no such thing, but this man clearly had an ego.

He seemed to straighten a little, then moved back to his chair. I edged backward myself, sitting down on the bed.

"So, why are you and that Alex moron so interesting to everyone?" he barked.

"I don't know. I've never talked to Alex about the Veil. I found out about it after we broke up."

Max looked at me skeptically. "And now you've

moved onto Nox. The big, powerful devil. Bet he's an improvement."

I said nothing.

"Does it not bother you that he was fucking the same girl that your ex was?"

"He wasn't sleeping with Sarah," I said quietly. "Nox, I mean. Alex was."

Max scoffed, his face tingeing red. Alarm bells started to ring in my head. *Don't piss him off, don't piss him off.*

"Of *course* he was screwing her. You really think she'd turn down a job worth five grand for a guy she wasn't even screwing?"

"Maybe you're right," I said quickly. "Five thousand is a lot of money." From what Nox had said about the book, it was probably worth a lot more than that to the right person. Or the wrong person. "Where's the book now?"

"As if I'd tell you."

I glanced behind me at the unmade, stained bed. "My head hurts. Would it be okay if I had a sleep?"

Max scowled. "You can have the half hour it will take me to go to the shop."

He was going out? Hope ignited in my chest, spreading fast. Half an hour was enough time for me to bust out of the tape, I was positive.

He stood up, scooping something up off the floor as he did.

Rope.

My heart stuttered, along with the flare of hope.

"Come here."

"Can't I stay on the bed?"

"No. There's nothing solid to tie you to there."

He stamped over to me, pulling me roughly to my feet. I tried to resist him, but being unable to separate my legs caused me to fall hard to my knees immediately. I let out an *oof* of pain as my kneecaps smacked into the solid floor, then another as he hauled me back to my feet by my wounded shoulder. I hopped after him as he dragged me, until he threw me to the floor under the window. I tried to break my stumbling fall and failed, landing on my hip and banging my elbow. I saw a radiator on the wall in front of me, pipes running from the back of it under the floorboards.

It took him only a few minutes to secure my wrists to the pipes.

"How am I supposed to sleep like this?"

He walked to the bed, picked up a pillow and threw it at me. I turned as it hit my head, a vile stale-sweat smell puffing from it when it fell to my lap. "Sweet dreams," he said with a sarcastic smile. "Oh, and don't bother screaming, the building is empty."

THIRTY-THREE

NOX

"Is it true that you have lost possession of the Book of Sins?"

I ground my teeth together, eyes flicking over the brutal visage behind Exanimus. "It was stolen."

My gaze settled on the god. He was sitting in what could only be described as a throne, in a room that could only be described as the center of hell. It was hot enough that even I was uncomfortable. Rivulets of molten lava ran past my feet, from where they snaked down the mural on the back wall of the room. The carving depicted the Judgement Day painting in the Sistine chapel, demons and monsters dragging humans from their clouds in the sky into burning pits below.

I didn't know who had shown Michelangelo the mural, but he sure as hell hadn't come up with it on his own.

The rest of the room looked much like a chapel too, with a high domed ceiling, and stained-glass windows that burned with the orange flames that raged beyond them. I was in a chapel, in a pit of fire, in the very heart of hell.

"Lucifer, you astound me."

"I'm pleased to hear I haven't lost my touch."

"Do not mock me, child." Exanimus' eyes were solid black, and that was all I could see of his features. The gods took many forms, and Exanimus only ever appeared to me in this one - a mass of sparking light with eyes like huge black gemstones. I took a breath.

"Why have you summoned me here? I need to find the book, on earth."

"This is your true home, Lucifer."

"I am needed on earth."

"No. You wish you were needed on earth."

My wings stretched out behind me as my control slipped ever so slightly. "Let me return."

"Are you going to put things right?"

"I am going to find the book and the pages," I hissed.

"Are you going to regain control of the seven sins? And therefore your rightful position as punisher of evil?"

"I am going to try." Saying the words caused a pain to simmer up inside me. I had only spent a relatively small part of my long life devoid of my responsibilities. And for most of that time, the price had been worth it. Until my unfulfilled desires had grown, making time stretch and need build to the point of unbearable. But now... Now there was Beth. Now there was a chance to fulfill my needs and stay clear of my duties.

"You are lying."

"I am not." I was. If I could have Beth without taking back all seven sins, then there was no fucking way I was retaking my old position. Guard dog to the gods. Punisher of evil. Overseer of scum.

"Lucifer, your brothers do not wish you to hold your power. There is a reason for that. You have the potential to be the most powerful angel ever forged. You are bound to that potential."

The mass of sparking light grew as Exanimus spoke, and the great stone throne grew with it. The smell of sulphur washed over me, and a need to destroy exploded in my chest.

They must all die. Long, slow and agonizing deaths, fitting for the crimes they committed.

The thoughts filled my head and I shouted aloud. "Enough! I have told you that I am trying to find the book. Send me back, now."

"Your brothers are trying to find a weapon."

I froze. "What? Why?"

"There is a war coming, Lucifer. A war that you will force you to choose a side."

"Your side?"

"I will not want you on my side if your brothers succeed in destroying your soul. The only way to survive them is to regain your full power."

I snarled, feeling rage tear through my chest again. "You could have started with that information."

"I should not be telling you at all."

"Wars between the gods no longer concern me. Send me back and let me get on with recovering the book."

Exanimus loomed forward, and pain crept over me, searing my skin. I rarely felt pain. Anger coursed through me in response, and I felt my wings spread wide behind me, my body swelling with power.

"You are a shell of the angel you used to be. If, next time I summon you, you have made no progress there will be consequences."

"Send me back." The voice that issued from me was hissing, snarling, animalistic. It was a voice I rarely had need for on earth. One I saved for hell.

I hated it.

"I mean it. Grave consequences, Lucifer."

A wave of heat engulfed me. Everything flashed searing orange, and all of the air left my lungs. The next second, I was standing in my office.

"Asshole fucking deity!" I yelled, my wings knocking everything off the table as I whirled, smashing my fist into the solid wall behind me. Sparks flew from my knuckles as my fist caught fire briefly, the flames dousing as my damaged skin instantly repaired itself.

A small, feminine cough sounded and I spun back.

"Boss," Rory said with a nod. She was standing in the corner of the room, holding an iPad.

"That prick is toying with me. Do I look like a fucking toy to you?"

"No, but you are on fire a little bit." Rory pointed to my feet and I saw that my shoes were melting into the carpet.

"These are fucking Italian," I hissed, then pulled them off. "Get me some new shoes."

"Sure thing."

I paused as she turned. "Thank you." She threw me a smile over her shoulder, then left the room. I sat down hard in my chair, simmering anger still bubbling through me. Was he telling the truth? Were my brothers behind the theft of the book?

Michael and Gabriel had never liked me, but I hadn't thought that they would ever try to destroy me.

If a war was coming, then perhaps there was some validity to the almighty asshole's demands. Perhaps I did need to regain my full power.

The thought of spending endless hours having the worst of human nature paraded before me made my anger swell back up, and I slammed my fist down on my desk.

One thing at a time, Nox. Something was afoot in the Veil, that much was for sure. After decades of nothing, my book was stolen, and Beth showed up in my life.

Beth first. Then the book. I would tackle whatever this fucking war was, and whatever my brothers were up to, as and when it came up.

I pulled my phone from my pocket, opening it to call Beth and let her know I was ready to find Gordon. Fuck, was I ready. The second her name was cleared, my end of the bargain was fulfilled. Then it would be her turn. Need burned through me at the thought.

3 missed calls.

The notification flashed up on the screen. Phones didn't work in hell. Supernaturals and tech didn't mix well. I pressed the notification. Two calls from Beth, and one from an unknown number. My heart rate picked up. Why had Beth called me that many times?

I lifted my phone to my ear as I dialed the answer-phone. "Mr. Nox, this is Inspector Singh. I would like you to let me know as soon as you are aware of Gordon Jackson's whereabouts. We understand from Miss Abbott that you are in conversation with the club owner about this man, and I would like you to let us handle it. We traced a call from your building to the Aphrodite Club around the time of the murder, and we believe that Mr. Jackson could be dangerous. Please call me back."

I hung up, and pressed Beth's name. The ring tone sounded, but there was no answer.

Rory pushed her way into the room, holding a shirt on a hanger and some black shoes. "I noticed your cuff was singed from where you punched the wall, so I brought you a shirt, and someone will be in to repair the damage in ten minutes," she said.

"Rory, tell Claude to meet me here as soon as possible."

"Right away, Boss." She paused and looked at me. "How was your meeting? Was it about the book?"

I squeezed my jaw shut as I considered what to tell her, grinding my teeth until they hurt. There was very, very little Rory didn't know about me, and I trusted her with my life. "Exanimus says I'll need my full power back to defend myself against an imminent attack. He seems to think the theft of the book is part of something bigger."

She cocked her head at me. "All those reports of supernaturals acting out recently that you've had me working on, is that connected?"

"I think so. My priority right now is to find out who murdered Sarah and get a lead on the book. My research team is making some progress tracking down the lost pages, but it's not going to be easy to find at least two of them."

"Do we need to rekindle some of our more distasteful contacts in Solum?"

"Yes."

"I'll get on it. And, Boss?"

"Yes?"

"Why the interest in the human girl?"

I fixed my eyes on the pixie. Much as I trusted her, I wasn't going to tell her that it appeared that Beth was the only woman who could break through my curse. I opted for a part-truth. "She's connected to this."

"Really? How?"

"I don't know. But I intend to find out."

"Sir, I'm very glad to see you." Claude looked nervous as I strode to the car.

"Lavender Oaks, please Claude," I said as he pulled the door open for me.

"Miss Abbott isn't there anymore."

I froze and turned slowly to the ancient driver. "What?"

"She said she worked out who the killer was but needed proof. She swore to me that she called you."

"I was in the Veil, her calls didn't go through," I snapped. I already knew where she'd gone, without having to ask the old man. The Inspector said they traced a call to the Aphrodite Club, and that they'd spoken to her. "Is she still at the club?"

Claude nodded. "Yes, sir."

"Let's go."

My mind whirred, trying to follow the line of thought Beth would have taken. Why would she say she'd worked out who the killer was if she thought it was Gordon? She'd suspected him since she met him, so suddenly heading to the club to look for proof didn't add up. Every tortuous second we spent crawling through the London traffic made me more agitated and I cursed the human need for motorized vehicles. I could have flown there in an instant.

I was just riled up from my meeting with Exanimus, I told myself. It was infuriating enough to be summoned, to have to drop everything at his whim, but if he thought he could bully me back into the life I'd despised...

"I'm sure Miss Abbott is fine," Claude said nervously from the front of the car. "She had a lady with her."

I frowned. "Who?"

"A large, older, American lady."

Francis? Beth had taken a pensioner to the Aphrodite Club? I couldn't help the smile that ghosted over my lips. From the brief moments I'd spent with her, I could imagine that Francis was probably having the time of her life.

THIRTY-FOUR

BETH

Ten minutes after Max had left the gloomy cesspit he had trapped me in, my wrists were rubbed raw. I'd had no luck at all trying to escape the rope bindings, and I'd burned the skin on my hands repeatedly coming into contact with the hot pipes. I held a faint glimmer of hope that the pipes were hot enough to eventually erode the rope, but I deep down I suspected that the coarse substance was too sturdy.

Frustration was turning into panic, and I knew that panicking was the worst thing I could do. People who panicked made mistakes. Dad had always told me that.

I tried to relax my throbbing head, leaning it back tentatively against the window ledge, careful to keep my back away from the hot radiator. I closed my eyes and counted, letting my mind play through what I knew, praying something useful would come to light.

Max had loved Sarah. Or at least, he wanted more from her. I was sure of that. The way he spoke about her, and the jealousy that filled his face whenever Alex had been mentioned gave the strength of his feelings away.

Where did Nox and his book fit in, though? Somebody had paid Max and Sarah to steal it, and with Sarah having a job in the building delivering sandwiches, they had the perfect opportunity. Did somebody approach her because she was already working in the building? Or did she get the job purely in preparation for the theft?

Either way, somebody more wealthy than Max or Sarah was behind the plan. Could it be Wrath? Or the angels Nox had mentioned? At the thought of Nox, my eyes flicked open. Shirtless and fierce, gold wings behind him in the sunlight, standing over the city...

I couldn't die without touching those wings. Hard resolve coursed through me, and it was with some relief that I felt a spark of anger flaring to life in my chest.

Who the hell did Max think he was? This was real life. Men didn't go around kidnapping women and tying them to damn radiators! *He may be stronger than I am, and he may be able to turn into a vicious bird, but I'm not completely pathetic,* I told myself assertively. I was smart, and quick. *And a woman,* I thought, sitting up straight, ignoring the pain in my aching shoulders. The man had as good as admitted that his weakness was pretty girls. Could I play my sex to my advantage?

The thought of trying to seduce him made my stomach turn. The man had a screw loose, how could I come on to him? But if anything would convince him to untie me, it would be the lure of sex.

I looked around the room, searching for anything

that I could use if I were able to get out of the ropes. Max was bigger and stronger than me, and he had magic. I didn't know if I could outrun him, nor did I know where I was. There couldn't be that many empty buildings in London though. Were we further out of the city?

The sound of a key in the lock made my head snap to the door. Max pushed his way into the room, a carrier bag swinging from one hand, a four-pack of beer visible through the thin plastic.

"That wasn't half an hour," I said as he locked the door behind him and dropped the key into his pocket.

"There was no line," he shrugged. So we were very near a store. That was good. There were people and phones in stores. I just had to get out of the room.

"Right. I have my refreshments, it's time for you to put on the show." Max put the beers down on the floor next to his chair and came over to me. He untied the ropes from the radiator, and I was sorely tempted to seize my chance. But my ankles and wrists were still bound with the tape. I couldn't run, or open the door, or even get the key from his pocket.

"You know, I could do with five thousand pounds," I said. He snorted from behind me.

"Your boyfriend's a fucking millionaire."

"He's not my boyfriend. And he wasn't Sarah's either."

There was a hard shove between my shoulder blades,

and I went sprawling. My shoulder hit the wood first, then my chin. My headache exploded back into life.

"Don't fucking say her name!"

"Okay, okay," I spluttered. I'd bitten my tongue and could taste the irony tang of blood.

"You didn't know her. She was a tease. She told me that if I helped her get rich that we would be together. So I did. And she'd been fucking lying." Max grabbed a handful of my hair and pulled me back up. My scalp screamed in protest, but I managed to keep my lips clamped closed.

"I found us the perfect opportunity to get out of this shit-hole. And what does she do? Decides that the devil is a better fucking option for her. Then I find out she's screwing that waster that lived with you as well." His head came low over my shoulder, his stench making my head swim even more. "It seems to me, little Beth, that everybody Sarah was into, also likes you. So maybe, I can get what I need from you instead."

Fear coiled through my gut, my heart hammering so hard against my ribs that there was no way he couldn't hear it. "I have nothing to do with this," I gasped, as he pulled my head back further, pressing his knee into the small of my back.

"Bullshit."

"It's true. I'm only even involved with Nox because the police suspected me of Sarah's murder."

He shoved me to the floor again. I was able to let my elbows take the brunt of the impact this time, tensing my neck to keep my head from hitting the floor. "Are you fucking deaf? I told you not to say her name!" I heard his foot stamp hard on the planks and then felt it come down on my back, pinning me on the filthy floor. "You know what? They were supposed to think Nox killed her. But nooooo, of course that rich wanker wouldn't even be a suspect. Well, I reckon I can give the police another murder for him to be a suspect in. They know how much time you've been spending with him." He rolled me over with his foot, and I could see the glow of magic around him. His eyes had turned black and beady, and a weird tension spread across his features as he loomed over me. "Can you swim, Beth?"

"I hadn't planned to do this just yet, but you know what? You're not as much fun to have around as I'd hoped." Max's voice was a rasp as he pulled me to my feet and turned me away from him. Adrenaline charged around my body, making my limbs shake but the pain vanish from my shoulder and head. He gripped my neck with his rough fist and forced me forward, hopping awkwardly. When we reached the door, he paused, and I tried to turn my head. He held me fast, though, and then I saw his arm reach past me to put the key in the door.

We were leaving the room. This was it. This was how I would get away. There had to people nearby.

"Killing me isn't going to bring Sarah back," I said, as Max dragged me down the flight of stairs. Since I'd done the worst job possible of not pissing him off, I figured the next best plan was to piss him off so much that *he* made a mistake.

"Stop saying her name," he snarled, and slammed me against the wall. I slipped, my ankle scraping down the stair as I fell. His strong grip tightened around my neck and pain shot down my spine as he steadied me.

"Did you love her?"

He let out an angry bark, but he didn't answer. He said nothing the rest of the way down the stairs. We passed two other doors, but from the derelict appearance of them, it looked like he'd been telling the truth about the building being empty. When we reached a fire door at the bottom of the stairwell, hope surged through me. Daylight, and people, were beyond that door. Surely a woman with her feet and arms bound would be noticed pretty quickly.

Max stepped past me and kicked the door open, so he didn't have to let go of my neck. Light flooded my vision a moment, then a large van came into focus, parked across the doorway.

Anger began to replace the hope as he reached forward and slid open the side door on the vehicle. "In you go," he said, and wrapped his other arm around my middle, lifting me off the floor and into the van.

"Where are we going?" I yelled. It was dark in the back of the van, and it smelled of fish. I'd rolled around, shifting myself like a damn worm, trying to find anything that might be useful to me as he drove. But there was nothing. Just a damp sheet and a large metal box.

"The docks." His muffled voice came through the plastic interior.

I hadn't expected him to answer.

"Which docks?" The river Thames ran through the whole of London, there were docks and wharfs and piers throughout the city.

"Doesn't matter to you. You'll be dead."

THIRTY-FIVE

BETH

The van stopped about five minutes later, and when the side door slid open, I was ready. I'd gotten myself into a sitting position in front of the door, and the second I saw light, I kicked as hard as I could with my strapped-together legs. I felt a slight contact, then heard a laugh.

I'd missed. More anger raged through me. Tinged with panic. I was running out of time.

Max stepped up into the back of the van beside me and dragged the box toward him. I rolled, trying to get out of the van. I made it, my feet pulsing with pain as they hit the floor a few feet below. I stumbled but managed to steady myself.

We were parked on a ramp running down to the river, flush against the concrete wharf above. A crane loomed over us, and I could see piles of bricks and machinery littering the dock. I was on a building site on the riverside, I realized. But I couldn't see a single person. No high-vis jackets, or hard-hats, and not a single tourist.

I started to move up the ramp, one tiny jump at a time. I got about three feet before Max closed his fist around my neck. Icy fear gurgled up through me, making my chest tighten.

I couldn't run. I'd already known I couldn't run, but at least I'd had the hope of trying.

Max turned me around, marching me back to the van. The big metal box was open, and a length of chain ran from it, tied around the hinges of the lid. Bricks were piled up inside it.

Real terror gripped me as I realized what Max had planned. That box would sink straight to the bottom of the Thames. Along with whatever was attached to the chain. Or *whoever* was attached to the chain.

For a moment I was unable to catch my breath, my body numb with fear as Max reached down and pushed the free end of the chain through the small gap in the tape around my legs. The cold metal pressed against my ankles as it passed through, sparking my body back to life.

I thrashed, as hard as I could, and knocked him off balance. He straightened, bringing his hand up and smacking the back of it across my face. My head snapped back with the impact, and I gasped for air as stars exploded into my vision. He roughly gripped my waist as he finished wrapping the chain around the ankle tape, and I let my weight go, making him grunt as he was forced to hold me up.

"I'll make sure it ain't the police who blame Nox for

your death," he growled, dropping me to the concrete. "It'll be the gods. And they'll punish him worse than the shitty human justice system."

At the mention of Nox, I cast my eyes skyward. Was he out there, searching for me? *Please, please, let him be searching for me.* In a last-ditch hope that he was indeed out there somewhere, I screamed. I screamed with every bit of energy I had in my body, and I didn't stop until Max hit me again.

"Fucking shut up!"

He bent and closed the lid of the box, then started to shove it toward the edge of the ramp. Ice surged through my veins. I was out of time.

"You killed the woman you loved. This won't bring her back." My voice was shrill and desperate, but I didn't care. I was out of options. All I could do was try to distract him from sending me to a watery grave.

He glowed with magic and heaved the box again. It slid closer to the edge.

"She might have loved you, if you'd given her the time. But you took her life and now she's gone forever."

With one last shove, the box teetered on the edge, and the glow engulfed Max completely. Cracking sounds echoed around us, and as the box began to tip toward the water, the huge eagle dove at me. I threw myself forward, flinging my bound wrists over the bird, letting the talons tear into the flesh they met. He wasn't expecting it, and an unearthly squawk erupted from him at the same time there was a loud splash, and the chain tightened around my ankles. My skin scraped across the concrete and the eagle flapped the wing that wasn't trapped between my arms as we both skidded to the edge of the ramp and then went over.

The freezing water bit into my skin as the bird flailed. I managed to get in one big breath of air before I was engulfed. With a wrenching power, the eagle slashed at my wrists, trying desperately to get out of my grasp. I felt the tape tear as his talons met it.

The second I could move my hands I shoved the bird away through the water, doubling over to get to my ankles. I tore at the tape as the murky water around me thrashed and bubbled as the eagle tried to get to the surface. The light dimmed as we sank further, and my lungs were beginning to burn. Finally, my fingernails found the start of the tape, and I yanked, pulling desperately, unwinding the bindings that were dragging me to the bottom of the river. By the time the tape was free, my vision was almost completely black, the water around me was so dark. I didn't think I was sinking any more, and a tiny bubble escaped my lips as every impulse in my body tried to make me take a breath. I was out of air. I kicked my legs, and mercifully felt the chain fall away. I kicked again, my body moving upward. *I could do this. I could get to the surface.*

It probably only took ten seconds to reach blessed, life-saving air, but it felt like an hour. The less oxygen my body had, the harder it was to move my wounded limbs. It was like swimming through mud.

But I couldn't let that bastard win. I couldn't. A whole new world had been opened up before me, and I couldn't leave this life without exploring it. I wasn't ready to die.

When my head broke the surface I gasped down air, not even seeing the world around me. My eyes were burning from the dirty water, hot tears streamed down my face, and I could hear a screeching sound. Forcing myself to tread water, I blinked and blinked, until I could see.

Nox.

Nox was hovering over the river, his massive gold wings stretched either side of him. With a flurry of heat, I was lifted from the water and then I was whizzing through the air. I came to a gentle stop on the wharf, the black town car screeching to a halt beside me. The back door flew open before it had even stopped, and Rory leapt from the car, rushing over to me.

But I barely saw her.

In front of Nox was the white eagle. There was a flash of light, then Max's human form was hanging in the air over the Thames. He was screaming, and wounds were streaking his body, as though somebody was pouring invisible lava over his skin. Deep, charred gashes were winding their way across his chest. And Nox...

Nox's wings were gleaming gold, but his core was black. Shadows, flickering with deep red flames, engulfed his torso, and power beat from him in waves that smashed against the river, the concrete, *against me.*

"You will be punished for your crimes."

His voice was terrible. The most terrible thing I had ever heard. Every fear I had ever harbored, every doubt I had ever had, every memory that had ever kept me awake at night, crashed through my mind. I wanted to shrink into a ball and die. I didn't want to live in a world where such terror could exist.

A warm, pink light appeared abruptly in front of me, and suddenly I could breathe again. My muscles loosened just a little, but my horrified gaze was still fixed on Nox and Max. It was like a car crash - too brutal to watch, and too brutal to look away.

"Look at me." Rory's forceful voice cut through the awful terror.

"My magic can block some of the fear, but trust me, you don't want to watch this."

I dragged my eyes to her. She crouched beside me, holding a thermos flask and a blanket. I could vaguely make out Claude behind her.

A scream, shrill and terrible lanced through the air, and I thought I was going to be sick. I started to turn to the sound, but Rory's hand snapped out, gently catching my cheek.

"Look at me. And drink this. Before you go into shock."

Too late. I felt a blast of *something* wash over me, and a terrifyingly endless darkness filled my mind. For a brief moment, I was trapped. I was forever trapped in an endless void, darkness my only companion for the rest of time. Then my consciousness faded completely.

THIRTY-SIX

BETH

My head didn't hurt when I opened my eyes. I knew vaguely that it should, but I couldn't remember why. The haze of what must have been a very long, very deep sleep lifted slowly, and I squinted around myself.

I was in a hospital bed. A nice hospital bed, and there were flowers next to me. The pink roses lost some of my attention when I saw the tubes stuck in my arm, hooked up to the trolley next to me.

"What..."

"Beth."

I turned my head to see Nox sitting on a chair beside the bed. The memory of him, fierce and lethal and terrible filled my mind. I couldn't help the flinch that took my face. Shadows blazed through his eyes and his jaw tightened.

"Did you kill him?" My voice was barely a whisper.

"No."

Relief flooded me. Not because Max deserved to live, but because after spending all this time trying to clear my name of murder, the notion of being involved in one was too awful to consider.

"You had some pretty deep wounds on your chest from where you took Max down with you. And a suspected dislocated shoulder. But it turned out to be a sprain. The drip is just pain relief, nothing more serious." He pointed to the tubes in my arm. That was why I didn't have a headache then. In fact, I realized, nothing hurt too much at all.

"What did you do with Max?"

"I gave him to the authorities."

"But... You said you were going to punish him."

Danger danced through his blue eyes. "He will be punished. But not by me. I needed him in order to clear your name."

I swallowed and realized how dry my mouth was. "Is there water?" Nox stood up, and I noticed that his shirt wasn't as crisp as usual, and his tie wasn't quite straight. He poured water from a jug into a small glass and handed it to me. "The Veil authorities have sorted everything out with the Inspector. She'll be in shortly to speak with you, but she'll have no memory of you being a suspect. She'll just need to take the details of your kidnap and attack. Which she believes was carried out with a knife."

"Do I have to make something up?" I was too tired, and confused, to invent stories.

"Just tell her that Max pulled a knife on you at the Aphrodite club, put you in the van, and then..." His eyes darkened again, and heat rolled from him. I shuddered, and he blinked. "Beth, I'm sorry."

"For what?"

"For what he did to you. If you hadn't been courageous enough to drag him in with you…"

"You got there in time," I said, with a sigh. I leaned back on the pillow. "How'd you find me?"

"Francis. She'd just about convinced a group of men to storm backstage at the club to look for you when I arrived. Rory found Max's home address, and when we found it empty, I flew. When I heard you scream…" Something akin to pain flashed in his eyes, his expression strained as he stared at me. "I didn't get there in time. You saved yourself, Beth." He moved to me, gripping my hand. Sparks zipped from the contact, and something internal and conflicted fired in me. This man was terrifying. Truly terrifying.

"You looked so different," I whispered, staring into his face. "Over the river, made from fire and shadows."

"That is a fraction of my power, Beth. It is the punisher in me. The part of me I tried to abandon."

I felt my eyebrows rise. "That's why you gave up the sins?"

"Yes. Amplify what you saw by ten, and you will feel the true power of the devil's punishment."

"Then maybe you shouldn't get the book back," I said quietly. He said nothing, but his gaze burned into mine, more intense than ever. "I tried to ask Max what he did with it, but he wouldn't tell me. He killed Sarah because she refused to steal it from you."

Nox let out a slow breath. "He will suffer for what he has done. Just not at my hand."

The memory of his scorched skin, the deep gouges and bloodcurdling scream filtered through my mind. I tensed, and Nox must have noticed.

"He already suffered at your hand."

Nox nodded slowly. "A little. My control is not what it was." He let go of my hand. Mixed emotions boiled up inside me, instinct mourning the loss of his touch, sense knowing I needed the space. "Francis is here. She refused to leave until you woke up."

"Where am I?"

"A private hospital in Mayfair."

"Oh."

"I'll go and get Francis."

I watched him leave the bright little room, lacking the energy or clarity to do or say anything.

Francis made a massive fuss over me when she waddled into the room. She told me at length, and with many unnecessary swear words, about how she'd corralled the group of guys on a cheap bachelor night to help her rescue me, before Nox had showed up. "Honey, now that the police have their killer, you get to spend the night with that hunk."

I looked at her in alarm. *Our deal.* How could I spend the night with him? He had a real-life monster inside him, and now I'd seen it, I couldn't unsee it.

. . .

The Inspector arrived an hour later and read from a list of witness statements that I just had to confirm. She acted as though she barely knew me, and I assumed the magical authorities had provided the false statements.

A doctor came in next and told me that they wanted to keep me over night as I had taken enough blows to the head that they wanted to clear me of concussion before allowing me to go home.

The sky outside had turned dark when a nurse dropped off a tray of food, and I was finally left on my own. I devoured every scrap of the surprisingly edible hospital dinner, whilst trying to straighten out my thoughts.

Whatever avenue they took, I found myself coming back to two things I knew for sure. Firstly, I needed to explore the Veil. It was a new lead to find my parents, and there was no way in hell I could walk away from that.

Secondly, I knew as surely as I knew that my heart was beating in my chest, that I was not done with Nox. There was more to our story. There was more to him. And he wasn't just my ticket to the Veil. He was something to me, and I to him.

The Beth who had wrapped her arms around that eagle as it tore into flesh and muscle, was braver than any version of myself I had ever known. And that was because of him. I was sure it was. He brought my confidence to life, he made the doubtful, fearful voices in my head quieten down enough that I could ignore them.

Sure, he also represented my worst freaking fears in a mass of shadow and fire, but he was trying to leave that behind him. He'd sacrificed sex to leave that behind him, for heaven's sake.

I didn't know what my connection to the devil was, or why we had found ourselves where we were, but I knew, deep down, that I was exactly where I was supposed to be.

And we had made a deal.

THIRTY-SEVEN

BETH

"So, how did Max get into the building?"

It was the Monday after the craziest week of my life, and I was sitting at the bar in Nox's beautiful kitchen, a glass of rich red wine in my hand. The alcohol was doing nothing at all to settle my fluttering stomach.

The hospital had discharged me the day before, and once I was off the drip, I felt like I'd been hit by a truck. I had slept for almost all of Sunday. But when I'd awoken that morning, it had been to a message on my phone. From Nox.

You owe me. Whenever you're ready.

Boy, was I ready.

The bruise on my head had mostly faded, and the cuts to my arms and shoulders had healed fast after the attention they'd received in the hospital. I'd sprained my right shoulder, but that was the only part of me that hadn't fully recovered from the ordeal. So, I'd texted him back.

Dinner at your place tonight?

I'll cook.

I'll bring an overnight bag.

I knew I should probably wait until I felt better, until my shoulder was fixed, and I was more alert. But I didn't want to wait. I had decided to embrace the crazy, and the confident. I wanted my night with Nox. And I wanted it now.

"Max flew," Nox said, as he stirred paella in a large pan. It smelled divine.

"How? There aren't any windows up there, surely?"

"There are three fire escapes, as well as the skygarden."

"Did you manage to get him to tell you who paid him to steal the book?"

Shadows flickered across Nox's face as he knocked back a swig of wine. *That he couldn't taste.* The thought floated through my head and a pang of something gripped me. Sorrow? Pity? I wasn't sure.

"It was somebody powerful. Whenever he tries to speak of them, his tongue..." Nox paused, flicking his eyes to my face, unsure.

"Tell me."

"His tongue turns to ash. Then it rebuilds itself over the next hour. It is a dark and painful enchantment, but there are many who would be capable of using it, so it gives us no clues."

I screwed my face up, pressing my own tongue against the roof of my mouth as though ensuring it was still safely there. "Gross."

Nox dipped a spoon into the paella, then moved toward me, holding it out. "Try this. Tell me if it needs anything."

I blew on it, then did as he said. "It's perfect," I told him, truthfully. "I can't believe you can't taste it."

"I have a good memory." His eyes bore into mine. "But some things are better experienced in real life than relegated to one's mind."

I swallowed.

Light glowed around him, and he reached across the marble and touched my hand. Sparks flew between us, and I inhaled sharply.

"You know, technically, I'm not sure our deal still stands," I said mildly. Nox raised one eyebrow. "I found the killer. Without you."

"I believe I had some input after that point. Dealing with Veil authorities and human police is a tiresome process."

"Hmmm," I said.

"If you really feel that the deal is void then we can discuss it further. But as far as I'm concerned, I'm collecting." His voice was low and intense. Heat swooped through my whole body, anticipation making my muscles clench. I felt a bold smile take my lips.

"I believe, Mr. Nox, that you made some fairly tall promises last time I was here. I would like to find out just how good your word is."

THIRTY-EIGHT

NOX

Following Beth up the stairs was a sweet kind of torture, her perfect body swaying in front of me. I was so close. So close to feeling her heat, her passion, her arousal.

It was a warm night, and when we stepped onto the roof deck cooling air washed over my skin. Beth stopped, turning to me in question. I took her hand, the spark between us running straight to my groin, and led her past the glass of the kitchen skylight and to edge of the pool.

"Will you do everything I ask you to, Beth?" I asked her. She looked up at me, eyes wide.

"Yes."

"Good. Do you remember what I told you before?"

"Yes."

"Tell me."

Her cheeks and neck flushed in the fairylights. She sucked on her bottom lip a second, then spoke. "You want me to say your name."

"Say it now."

"Nox."

"Tell me what you want."

Alarm flashed in her big eyes, and her chest heaved as she drew in a breath. Fuck, she was exquisite to watch. I could see her desires play out before me, the power of lust sparking to life between us. All her self-doubt, her barriers, and her shyness were there to be destroyed, corrupted, burned to fucking ash. And I would be there to help her rise from the ashes, hot and fierce and strong. Powerful and sexual and stunning.

"You," she said. "I want you."

"More." The word came out as a barked command, but she didn't flinch. She straightened.

"I want you to..." My own breathing got shallow as she stared up at me, steeling herself. More walls crumbled around her, her defenses dropping, images of hands gripping sheets, her head thrown back, my golden wings beating, rushing through me.

Say it.

Say it.

"I want you to fuck me, Nox."

I pulled her to me, pressing my mouth to hers, my hunger barely containable. She kissed me back just as hard, her tongue finding mine, her hand around my neck and pushing into my hair. A delicious throbbing pulsed through me, my erection painfully present. What power did this woman have over me, over a curse of the gods?

Nearly eighty years. I would not let this go by in a

flurry of lost control. I would make this the best damn night of her life.

I stepped back, running my hands down her sides, breathing hard. "Let me see you."

"Here?"

"Here." Her eyes moved around the walls, checking there were no faces at windows, no places we could be seen from. I lifted my hands and unbuttoned my shirt. Her eyes snapped to my chest, darkening with desire.

Need pulsed through me.

Slowly, she gripped the hem of her own shirt and lifted.

I let out a strained breath, and she unfastened her bra and then dropped it to the tiles. The hairs raised on her skin, her nipples tightening to peaks in the evening air. I bit down on my tongue, hard, and sent waves of warmth to wrap around her. She gasped, and her shoulders relaxed, her beautiful breasts lifting.

"You're more stunning in real life than on the lake," I told her. She blinked.

"Your turn." Her voice was a whisper. I tilted my head in acknowledgement, a smile playing on my lips. She was growing bolder.

I shrugged my shirt from my shoulders, reveling in the way her eyes devoured my body. Many women had lusted after me, but the desire in Beth's eyes was completely new to me. I needed it, like a drug. The more she wanted me, the more I strained to claim her.

"Back to you," I said. With barely a hesitation, she slid out of her jeans. "Keep your knickers on," I told her, as she hooked her fingertips into the sides of her scarlet red underwear. If she took those off, I would lose myself.

"Feel free to lose yours," she answered, removing her hands from the lace.

"Miss Abbott. I thought I was the one giving out instructions."

"I said I would do everything you tell me to do. And I will. You never said anything about me making my own demands."

"Few make demands of the devil."

"Then I'll enjoy being one of them. Take off your pants."

THIRTY-NINE

BETH

Mercifully, I sounded more in control of myself than I felt. *I just demanded that devil take off his pants.* I wasn't sure what had come over me. I was not the sort of girl who stood in nothing but their panties, next to a glowing pool on a roof deck, before the most outrageously hot man they'd ever met.

I was the sort of girl who dimmed the lights.

But I knew how much Nox wanted me, and the knowledge was like a shot of confidence to the veins, taking me to a thrillingly surreal place where it felt like I couldn't do anything wrong. I was sure that nothing I said or did would make this man want me less. I felt invincible.

But I also felt as though I might explode if I waited a minute longer for him. Need was crashing through me, fueled by the impatient hunger he was mirroring back at me. My nipples were tight and hard, and heat was pooling between my legs as Nox reached down to undo his belt.

Shit. Maybe I shouldn't have told him to take his pants off. I didn't actually know what I would do, presented with a fully naked Nox. Slowly, eyes locked on mine, he unzipped his slacks and let them drop.

I tried. I tried to keep holding his gaze. But I couldn't. As though my eyes were possessed, they drifted down his hard pecs, the cords of muscles wrapped around his ribs, the male-model six pack, and the trail of dark hair that led down into boxer-briefs that fitted like skin.

A noise that I wasn't sure had a name escaped my mouth, and I bit down on my lip. He was too big to stay in his underwear. The gleaming, hard tip of his erection pressed against his stomach, the elastic holding it in place.

Sweet Jesus.

"Want to see a trick?" Nox's voice was a liquid caress, the promise of mind-blowing sex in audio format. I gave a small squeak in response.

His underwear caught fire. I gave a louder squeak, and then it was ash, falling to his feet and leaving him, completely, gloriously naked.

My brain stuttered to a halt. I'd not been with many men, but I had always been a little intimidated by what was between their legs. Convinced that they would be better at handling it than I would be. But staring at Nox...

He was perfect. Large and hard and perfect. Whatever the opposite of intimidated was, it swallowed me whole, and I took a step toward him in a daze, like some sort of penis-obsessed zombie. Before I reached him, he moved, and with a small splash he slid into the water of the pool. I blinked, and my senses flooded back from wherever they had temporarily retreated to. Smells and sounds seemed to rush back to me, the quiet gurgle of the pool filter, the scent of the flowers that lined the deck, and the slight scent of chlorine.

"Get in."

"In my panties?"

Nox just growled as he stared at me. His bottom half was obscured by the moving water, just the color of his flesh visible in the softly lit pool. I sat on the tiled edge, easing my legs into the water. It was warm. I slid the rest of the way in, unable to not notice the liquid lapping at my over-sensitive skin as my body was submerged.

Nox lifted one arm, running his hand through his hair, wetting it. Water dripped from him, bicep bulging. Christ, he looked like something from a TV commercial, but better because I could *feel* him. Feel his heat, his presence, his promise.

"I want you." The words left my lips before I could stop them.

"And I want you. More than..." He trailed off, muscles tensing. "More than I knew was possible." Pleasure fired through me at his words.

How could I mean something to a man like this? "Tell me. Tell me what you're going to do to me."

Lust danced through his eyes. "I knew you liked it when I talk dirty."

"I do," I told him. I moved through the pool, letting

my nipples move in and out of the water, the feeling of the cool air kissing them when they were exposed making me clench. "If you're not going to touch me, then tell me what you wish you were doing."

"Fuck, Beth. I'm supposed to be in control here."

Seeing what my words were doing to him was addictive. "You are, Nox. I am yours, for one night. To do with as you wish."

A rumbling sounded from his chest. "What I wish is to hear you scream my name as I obliterate every idea you had of pleasure. What I wish is to take you to a place you never want to leave. I want to feel you come around my cock over and over, until the only thing you're even aware of is me. I want to take you apart one blissful moment at a time and rebuild you as the fucking goddess you deserve to be."

My mouth fell open, the almost frightening hunger in face as he spoke sending shivers through me. "I want that too."

Nox's golden wings burst from his back, sending water spraying up either side of him and taking my breath away. Shadows swirled across his bare chest, and swells of heated promise pulsed out from him, slamming into me and making my knees weak. "Fuck," he swore again, his voice ragged. "I wanted to wait. I wanted to sit you on the side of this pool and tease you until you begged me to take you."

"I'll beg," I breathed. He was a god. A god of light and heat, with *wings*. I'd do anything to be his.

He was at my side in an instant, scooping me up. Everywhere his skin touched mine fired to life, and then we were rising, leaving the water. I gasped as we rose, not just because we were freaking flying, but because I could feel his hardness pressing against my skin. My mind was a haze of desire, and I twisted in his arms, trying to move myself toward him. He tensed, and his wings beat harder as his grip on me tightened. A dimly lit window came into view, and it blasted open in a flurry. Surprisingly gently, he tipped me through the window before following me in. I blinked, struggling to take in the room around me.

It was a bigger, more luxurious version of the guestroom I had stayed in, I realized. A bigger bed, soft grays and deep blacks everywhere. Before I could take in any more, Nox was pulling me to him, wings still glowing behind him, erection pressed into my stomach as he buried his hands in my hair and kissed me.

Images exploded in my mind, and a painful throb of desire took me. I moaned into his mouth, and his arm wrapped around my waist, lifting me off my feet. He walked backward, still kissing me ferociously, until my calves hit the bed.

"You're mine," he breathed, lowering me onto the mattress and staring down at me.

"Yours," I said. He dropped into a crouch, head level with the bed as he hooked his hands into the sides of my panties. His wings extended wide as he slowly rolled them down my legs. Slowly, too slowly, he parted my legs, my knees spreading wide. A primal growl escaped him as he stared down at me, pulses of golden light coming from his beautiful wings.

"Perfection." He bent his head, planting a hot, soft kiss directly on my core. Pleasure shocked through me like electricity, making my back arch. His fingers brushed over me, all the way from my belly button down to my ass. A moan left me.

"Please."

"There's no going back, Beth. When I claim you, you will be mine."

"Yours," I repeated, pushing myself up on my elbows, staring at his otherworldly eyes. I was too far gone to work out if giving myself to the devil for eternity was a good idea or not.

All I knew was that Francis was right. I would rather experience whatever this man had to give me and spend the rest of my life unfulfilled, but with a memory to die for, than believe that the height of pleasure was whatever half-assed version I'd known all my life.

Nox stood and took his length in his hand. My heart hammered against my ribs, my breathing coming short.

"I want to hear you scream my name," he said as he pressed himself to my entrance. I clenched in anticipation, and his wings fluttered. He moved his hand, touching my wetness gently, around the head of his erection. "I'm going to start slowly, Beth. Let you get used to me. But make no mistake, I'm going to fuck you like you've never been fucked."

I let my head drop back onto the bed as he pushed slowly into me. Slowly, so slowly, he stretched me, and my body relaxed around him, allowing him in. Pressure built hard and fast, trying to make me tense, but his finger stroked around me as he slid further in, filling me. I knew soft moans were issuing from me, but I paid them no heed. There was nothing but his length, his hardness, his presence. Pleasure turned almost to pain as he pushed all the way into me, his hips pressed against my raised thighs.

"Look at me." I lifted my head, staring at him through a haze of wild desire.

A god. He was a god. The most gorgeous, intense man I'd ever known, and he was looking at me as though I were his goddess. "You were made for me, Beth."

My body convulsed around him as his fingers moved. "Yes," he growled, then began to slide out of me. I clenched, as though my body was trying to prevent the loss of him, and he hissed as he slid nearly all the way out. "Tell me you want me."

I was barely capable of speech, and my words came out a slur. "I need you." He pushed back into me, flicking his fingers across the whole of my hot, wet sex. "Fuck, I need you."

"I like it when you say fuck, Beth. Say it again." He slid out, and I moaned.

"Fuck. Fuck me, Nox." I gasped, my back arching right off the bed as he pushed into me hard. His other arm moved under me, holding me up, pressing me against him as he moved, filling me utterly with every thrust. His fingers never stopped moving, brushing, flicking, in time with his cock pounding in and out of me. My arms wrapped round his neck and I cried out as the pressure built to something on the edge of painful, the need for release gripping every part of me. He stood, lifting me with him, and then he was moving faster, harder, the sound of him slamming into me filling the room. Heat flooded me, and I realized that I could hold on no longer. I was vaguely aware of my fingernails digging into his skin as I let go. Pleasure exploded from my core, powering through my body, making every muscle in my body spasm. My mind blanked, nothing but bliss able to penetrate the waves of light and color blasting through my mind.

Nox roared, a sound that brought me crashing back to earth, and he jerked inside me, his shoulders tensing to stone as he shuddered. With a flash of light, his wings vanished, and he turned, falling backward onto the bed and wrapping both arms tight around me as we fell.

He rolled so that he was on top of me, planting kisses all up and down my jaw, my neck, my collarbone. I felt the aftershocks of his orgasm pulse through me and tightened my legs around his waist.

"Mine," he growled into my hair. His mouth found mine, and he pushed hard into me again.

I panted against his mouth, trying to draw in more air, pleasure tingling out from my center, making me dizzy. But before I could fully get my breath back, he rolled again, so that I was on top of him.

"Sit up," he said, and the command was so forceful I obeyed it immediately. I sat up and sank fully onto him.

"Oh my—"

His hand whipped up, covering my mouth. "Don't you dare say god" he said, giving me a filthy smile and then bucking his hips. I bounced against him, and he groaned with me. His hand moved round the back of my neck and fisted in my hair. He pulled gently, exposing my neck to him, making my back arch and my breasts thrust toward him.

I ground my hips, letting the fullness overtake me. Then, slowly, I lifted a little.

"Yes, Beth." I sank back down. "Again." I moved again, further this time before I sank back down. "You're so fucking wet." His words made me clench and his fist tightened in my hair. His other hand went to my hip, and together we rocked, my hips rising and falling in time with his. "Tell me how it feels to fuck the devil."

His hand loosened in my hair so that I could look at him, and his stomach muscles rippled as he sat up, mouth meeting mine. He ground hard into me with the movement, and I gasped against his lips.

"Incredible. It feels incredible," I breathed. He lay back down, drawing me with him, then planted both hands on my ass.

"Stay still. And I want to hear my name," he said, his face inches from mine as my hair fell around it.

Gripping me hard so that I couldn't move, he slid out of me, then pushed hard back in. His eyes glowed with blue light, desire pouring from him.

"Nox," I whispered. He thrust again, and again. I drew in the scent of wood smoke and sweat as I inhaled, trying to savor every single inch of movement. He filled me so perfectly, the balance of too much and just right shifting with every movement. His grip tightened on my ass, spreading me as he got harder. I felt the delicious build up start to pool, a knot of tight pleasure growing in my center, expanding with every thrust. "Nox," I gasped again, knowing it would make him react. It did, and he powered in and out of me, his body hard and hot under me. My thighs convulsed first, tightening around him as I bucked, my orgasm ripping through me. "Nox. Nox. Nox." I chanted his name as I rocked back on forth on him, letting wave after wave of pleasure take me away, nothing but him mattering. He bucked with me, his hand tightening in my hair, his breath leaving him in a long moan, that sounded a lot like my name.

FORTY

BETH

He was insatiable. And so was I. He had the excuse of not being able to come for eighty years. I had none.

I just couldn't get enough of him.

Over and over, we delighted in each other's bodies, and at no point did I feel even a flicker of self-consciousness. Every time he brought me to the brink, whether it was with slow teasing strokes with his hands and tongue that left me writhing, or massive powerful thrusts that I knew I would feel the next day, he took me over the edge. I'd had no idea that sex like that existed. I'd had no idea that it was possible for a mind to empty so completely, pleasure causing an almost delirious state of bliss. He'd been right. I never wanted to go back.

. . .

"My shoulder should be hurting," I said as we stood in the shower together, him sponging my body erotically attentively. "But it feels absolutely fine."

He paused and looked at me. My god, he looked good wet. "Sex can cure anything," he grinned.

I punched him lightly on the arm. "So it's not your power that's helped it?"

He shook his head slightly. "No. Not really a devil power, healing others."

"Huh. But godlike stamina is?" That earned me a second grin.

I looked into his eyes, and allowed the question now plaguing my mind to leave my lips. "So, what happens next?"

I was almost as nervous about his answer as I had been about spending the night with him.

Had he had his fill of me? Had he discovered how boring I was? Nothing about the last few hours had felt boring to me, but doubt gripped me anyway.

He might disguise his dismissal of me by telling me that the Veil was too dangerous, or that I had no reason to be a part of his life now that our deal was complete. But that would be a dismissal all the same.

"Finding the book is the number one priority. Rory is looking into some of our more unsavory contacts, and my research team has good leads on two of the pages."

I kept my voice casual. "Do you know where to start?"

"Solum. That's where all magic in London starts." His eyes danced with bright blue light as he stared at me.

He knew what I wanted to hear, I could see it in his face. His lips curled up slowly, his smile breathtaking. "I'd like to offer you a new job, Miss Abbott. On my special research team."

"You would?"

He nodded. "It is dangerous, but there are a few perks to counter that. The pay is significantly higher than your current salary. There are opportunities for travel. And you would have access to information that can be used to find lost things."

Excitement burned through me, relief and confidence making my body buzz.

"What would I do every day?"

He tilted his head, gaze boring into mine. "How about a new deal? Help me find the book and the pages. Then, we'll look for your parents."

"You'd really help me find them?" I breathed. My hands gripped his arms, my heart racing.

"I must safeguard the devil's power first. I... I have received a warning. There is a time pressure to this that I'm afraid I cannot avoid."

Sincerity shone in his eyes, and I knew he was telling the truth. There was nobody in the world of magic better positioned to help me find them; this was a lead and an opportunity I'd never thought I'd get. If I had to wait a little longer, then so be it. I nodded. "I accept your deal."

"I am pleased, Miss Abbott." A filthy look took over his face. "Now, may we get back to showering?"

He pressed me against the tiles, dipping his head and

running his tongue over my nipple. It hardened instantly, and I pushed my hands into his hair.

"Yes. Let's do that."

I wasn't sure I'd had more than an hour's sleep when I woke in a tangle of silk sheets the next day. I rolled over, blinking the sleep from my eyes. Nox wasn't next to me, and a bolt of panic gripped me, until I realized I could hear the shower running.

My sore body pulsed, and a happy feeling blossomed from my chest. He did want me. Last night hadn't been faked. He'd offered me a job. *He did want me.*

A little thrill rippled through me at the thought of seeing his face, and I swallowed. *I was hooked.* Addicted to the devil.

I rolled from the bed, looking for something to wear to get me from his room to the kitchen, where my overnight case was. I pulled open the mirrored closet door and saw rows of neatly hanging shirts and lifted one from its hanger.

I froze as I closed the closet door and caught sight of my reflection.

So faint that I could barely see it, but definitely there behind me, was the shimmering gold outline of wings.

"Nox!" He stepped into the room from the washroom quickly, naked and wet. He caught my eyes in the mirror and then paused, his face visibly paling as he saw the faint gold wings, fluttering gently. "Nox, why do I have wings?" I tried to keep my voice steady and failed.

I watched in the mirror as his own wings burst from him. My breath caught in my throat, the sight of them still utterly intoxicating. Nox closed his eyes for an overly long moment, then swore loudly.

"We haven't broken my curse. We've just started a new one," he hissed, shadows and light warring in his eyes as he opened them.

"What? What's happening?" He stepped up behind me, his gaze flicking between my face and the ghostly wings flowing from my back.

"Beth, I'm not entirely sure you're human anymore."

My heart stuttered in my chest, energy fizzing through me as my mind went numb. "What?"

"I think it's time for us to make another deal."

THANKS FOR READING!

Thank you so much for reading Lucifer's Curse, I hope you enjoyed it! If so I would be very grateful for a review! They help so much; just click here and leave a couple worlds, and you'll make my day :)

You can find the next book,

Fallen Feathers, here..

You can also get exclusive first looks at artwork and story ideas, plus free short stories and audiobooks if you sign up to my newsletter at elizaraine.com and you can hang out with me and get teasers and release updates (and pictures of my pets) by joining my Facebook reader group here!

Printed in Great Britain
by Amazon

60615941R00194